THE
WINDSOR SECRET

Rq

40p

THE WINDSOR SECRET

a novel by

Fanny Cradock

W.H. ALLEN · LONDON
1986

Copyright © by Fanny Cradock, 1986

Photoset in Candida by
Phoenix Photosetting, Chatham
Printed and bound in Great Britain by
Mackays of Chatham Ltd, Chatham, Kent
for the Publishers, W.H. Allen & Co. Plc
44 Hill Street, London W1X 8LB

ISBN 0 491 027354

Part I

CHAPTER I

'A pretty kettle of fish.'

– HM Queen Mary

11 am November 10th, 1936

Behind the heavy drapes at the windows of the King's private sitting-room, the uncrowned monarch sprawled in a great leather chair alternately sipping a whiskey sour and twitching at his tie, while his peoples at the gates of his Palace and throughout his far-flung Empire held their collective breath.

Facing him sat his friend and equerry, Sir Frederick Musgrave, Bart, CMG, CVO, DSO, MC and bar, known to his intimates as 'Fluff'. His long legs were stretched out as he gazed sombrely at the small, restless figure in the arm-chair. The King's mouth was set in the stubborn line all too familiar to Fluff. He sighed. 'It cannot be allowed to happen, sir, surely you see that?'

The fidgetting increased. 'But Wallis says . . . Wallis simply refuses . . . that is – er – she cannot even be expected to consider the inescapable slur . . . one which could never be eradicated,' the King replied, stammering badly. He jerked himself out of the chair and crossed to a sofa table to mix himself another drink. This he carried to the window where he stood looking down at the uneasy crowds below. When he next spoke his voice had shed its hard uncertainty and was wistful. 'I have always thought it would be the most marvellous experience . . . I have often dreamed of the day when it would happen to me . . . there must be some way . . . surely?'

Fluff felt himself weakening, then hardened and exerted privilege. 'Am I to understand, sir,' he asked with some irony, 'that this is a situation in which you are determined both to have your cake and eat it?'

'Yes,' this time the King spoke without any hesitation, 'that's right. I want just that if it can possibly be contrived. If so, I am convinced you are the one man who could pull it off for me.' He swung round to face his equerry. 'You do appreciate I hope, Fluff, that I am not only asking you to do the impossible but also to achieve it in such a way as to satisfy Wallis absolutely. That must always be the first consideration.'

'We have so very little time left, sir,' Fluff reminded him wearily.

'We have five months and possibly a few extra days,' the King retorted.

Fluff stared abstractedly at his left shoe. He murmured, as to himself, 'Absolute secrecy, a total obliteration of all tracks leaving not a vestige of a trail to be picked up now or in the future. A mere sinecure, eh?' He looked up, his eyes glinting in his lean patrician face. 'To sum up then, sir, your wish is that I encompass all this for you and Wallis in such a manner as to ensure no possible discovery while you and she stand centre stage with the spotlights of the world upon you.'

'Exactly so,' agreed the King. 'That's it in a nutshell. How do you fancy your chances? Meanwhile come and mix yourself a drink.'

3.30 pm November 10th
The black-gowned figure of the Queen Mother, the Dowager Queen Mary, stood with one white jewelled hand on her silver-topped stick, waiting in her drawing-room at Marlborough House to receive her son's Prime Minister whom she had summoned to a private audience.

He was shown in – a stout sack of a man in ill-fitting clothes which looked as if he had made them himself. The lady-in-waiting announced him, curtsied and at a slight gesture from the jewelled hand, curtsied again and withdrew, closing the door softly.

8

The great old gentlewoman spoke. 'Well, sir,' she observed tartly, 'here's a pretty kettle of fish.' She sat down abruptly, ramrod straight on a chair upholstered with her own *petit point* embroidery. She kept her caller standing. 'Can nothing be done in your opinion to persuade His Majesty to relinquish this woman?'

'Madam,' the unhappy man shuffled his feet, coughed and then asked, 'have I Your Majesty's permission to speak frankly?'

'Of course, of course,' she snapped, 'We require complete frankness and no hanky panky, if you please.'

He raised a worried face, his swinging jowl vibrating. 'Then, madam, the reply is – no. In my opinion there is nothing more that can be done. It has all been said. We – my Government and I – have explored and exhausted every possibility. I am sorry to say we have laboured in vain. The last time I spoke with the King he seemed a trifle – er – mad. He is besotted by her. He cannot envisage a day – not even an hour – without her by his side. I am absolutely convinced now that he will go to any lengths to achieve his declared intention.'

'Marriage?' The word fell between them like a stone.

He nodded sadly. 'Marriage. I fear he is bewitched, madam.'

The next words seemed to be dragged out of her by superhuman effort. 'What . . . is . . . she . . . like?'

The Prime Minister took time to reflect. The Dowager Queen waited. Then she said, as if in extenuation to herself for having asked an unbearable question, 'We only saw her once – when she was presented to us – and then only very briefly. Her curtsey was very neat. She seemed to have composure.'

The Prime Minister took up the theme. 'She is, as Your Majesty knows, both small and excessively neat,' he confirmed, 'but far indeed from a beauty. I think the French describe it best – a *jolie laide* – with trim little feet and large ungainly hands which she manages very discreetly. She dresses elegantly with great restraint. She is at all times completely composed; her poise is remarkable. She has a sharp wit and is very amusing company. She surrounds herself with people who are, I am given to understand, referred to as café society. These are the ones whom His Majesty enjoys and is at ease with – at his best in fact. I would sum her up as having a swift and unexpected intelligence, devastating charm and a bearing as impeccable as her dress. I would add that she has a will of iron, very carefully concealed.'

It was now his turn to wait in silence while his royal interrogator stared unseeingly across the room. At length, 'I see,' came from her shaking lips. Momentarily her shoulders drooped but her mouth was firm again as she gathered her courage together and asked, 'Would you not then say that it would be advisable for us to speak of our second son?'

The Prime Minister bent his head submissively, by no means unmoved by the pathos behind the pride. 'For my part, madam, I would say inevitably, since I am convinced His Majesty will abdicate.'

The hand which still rested on the silver-topped stick tightened visibly, but the voice was only chilly as she replied. 'We will not deny the horror, the regret, or the tragic waste of so much great potential. However, we accept your opinion. The Duke of York is possessed of an inestimable blessing in his Duchess. She is not only a most exceptional wife but also the one person who can steer him through the shoals of kingship when he had expected to live his life out as a private gentleman. Would you not say at this juncture – and if your premise is correct – that another ruthless woman spoke the *mot juste* for this calamitous affair?'

He took her point instantly, murmuring, 'Indeed, madam, "If it were done when 'tis done, then 'twere well it were done quickly," and that is the opinion of my Government.'

She rose at this, a movement of dismissal, which the man felt was because she was on the edge of breaking point and that, he knew, no one could ever be permitted to witness. She pressed the little bell at her feet, the

10

lady-in-waiting curtsied her way in again and in moments the King's mother was alone.

9 pm November 10th
The King dined alone with Mrs Simpson.

Since September the intimacy between them had been a *fait accompli* to those in their closest circle. At long weekends Mrs Simpson played hostess at the King's retreat Fort Belvedere where almost invariably Thelma Furness, the Duff Coopers and Emerald Cunard were among the guests. The twice-married, Baltimore-born American chose the menus, selected the guests and called the King 'David', dutifully tacking on the 'sir' and bobbing to him in the presence of others, for she was at all times determinedly correct. Her jewels were so magnificent that one famous beauty lamented at her lavish self-decoration with 'costume' jewellery.

She was thought poised, calm, correct; yet it seemed to those who watched her and discussed her endlessly that she was extraordinarily confident. Totally ignorant as she was of the implications of constitutional monarchy, she believed implicitly in her own dream destiny.

They told her that kings of England do not marry their mistresses. Sipping Lapsang Souchong in their Mayfair drawing-rooms, she countered, 'They have not done so in a long time,' secure in her conviction that 'the King's Grace' still persisted and that what the King wanted, he could have. She frequently put this to the test, as, for instance, the time at the Fort when she ordered American club sandwiches for an *al fresco* luncheon around the swimming pool with only two footmen present. The sandwiches failed to appear. She complained. The fiat went forth, 'There will be American club sandwiches if Mrs Simpson orders them.' She told the King she was dazzled but she held herself on such a tight rein that none of her intoxication showed.

Wallis Simpson's divorce suit had been heard at Ipswich on October 27th. It was disclosed that the quiet man she had married had spent a night at the Hotel de Paris in Bray with a woman rejoicing in the unfortunate name of Buttercup Kennedy. This was as alien to his character as it was deliberately contrived. Mrs Simpson had duly obtained her decree nisi, an event which one American newspaper saw fit to announce with the banner headline, 'King's Moll Reno'd in Wolsey's Home Town'.

Soon after her return to London Mrs Simpson had spoken with the King on his personal, scrambled line. They talked for nearly three hours. The King had then summoned Fluff Musgrave, for he knew no one else who had any hope of helping him resolve his new dilemma.

Now the King sat at the unique dining-table René Lalique had created for his American client – an illuminated glass tank in which a collection of tropical fish swam. Between the courses the light dimmed gradually to a faint, soft glow.

'I, too,' Mrs Simpson said firmly as the door closed behind the last of her servants, 'must descend into the twilight, David.'

'Six months,' his voice was slightly hoarse, 'not to see you for six months, it is unthinkable.'

'So is the possibility of intervention by the King's Proctor,' her voice was brisk. 'I must leave England, whatever else happens and I must go away as soon as it can be arranged.'

They were talking in riddles, this pair on whom, as Fluff had said, the eyes of the world were focussed.

He then told her he had spoken to Fluff.

'And what did he say?' Her hand slipped beneath the table casing, pressed a small button and the soft illumination increased again. The tropical fish resumed their swimming.

'I left him in my private office. He is surrounded by telephones. He knows the urgency and has no doubt whatever of your wishes. I stressed that above all *you* must be absolutely satisfied with the – er – arrangements.'

'When will we know?'

'As soon as he has devised a workable plan. It is difficult, my dear, even for a king.'

With a touch of petulance she said sharply, 'Everything seems difficult for *my* King.'

The soft light caught tiny slivers of brilliance as she moved and her jewels flashed. It reminded him of something. He slid one hand into the pocket of his dinner jacket, withdrew a long flat box and held it out to her. Her eyes sparkled as she pressed the catch. 'Oh, David, it's wonderful!' she exclaimed.

'Crown jewels,' he told her. 'Serves them right. They should let me marry you. It's ridiculous. Besides there *is* a precedent.'

She thanked him, held out her wrist for him to fasten the wide diamond cuff, and said to his bent fair head, 'Insist upon it. After all, David, you are the King.'

He smiled, crinkling up the corners of his eyes. 'I am also a Constitutional Monarch,' he reminded her regretfully.

'You mean you are willing to let them turn you off your throne?'

He shrugged, selected a fresh cigar and said almost sulkily as he pierced it, 'I never wanted to be King, you know.'

She led him back to speak of Fluff, wisely seeing she had reached a point of no return. 'I must go *soon*,' she urged. 'When you get back to the Palace will you telephone me and tell me exactly what Fluff plans.'

He agreed to do so. They then spoke of how they would communicate across the abyss so soon to separate them. He promised that all she asked for would be done; so mindful of many things, she set herself to amuse and entertain him. When he left her shortly before one o'clock, she went directly to her dressing room, took out a key, gave it to her drowsy maid and received from her hands a very large shagreen jewel case of many hinged tiers. She dismissed the maid. Looking over the tray-loads she said softly, 'Dammit, I shall have to leave them

13

... temporarily,' and so saying called her maid back again and let her prepare her for the night.

> 'When I died last, and, Dear, I die
> As often as from thee I go,
> Though it be but an hour ago,
> And lovers' hours be full eternity.'
>
> – John Donne, *The Legacy*

1 am November 11th

When the King strolled into his private office again Fluff was replacing the telephone receiver. At his elbow rested a tray of uneaten sandwiches and a tantalus of whisky which had been punished heavily. These kept company on the great tooled leather desk with a jade ashtray loaded with cigarette stubs. One glance at the King's face and 'He's all bright-eyed and bushy-tailed – God, what a bloody coil!' flashed through Fluff's exhausted brain.

'Well, Fluff,' the King asked, 'made any progress? Wallis has asked me to telephone her with whatever news you have. I see you have drunk quite a lot of whisky and smoked a great many cigarettes but eaten nothing!'

'I have spent lavishly on long distance calls, sir, to France and Switzerland. If I may now eat some of these excellent sandwiches,' Fluff took one and bit into it, 'I believe I can outline the bare bones of my plan.'

The King poured himself a brandy, lit a fresh cigar and settled in his favourite chair. 'I told Wallis,' he sounded complacent, ' "you can leave it to Fluff, he'll come up with something brilliant, I'll swear to it." But you must understand she is – er – somewhat anxious. She feels that the sooner she is out of the country the better pleased she will be, although the wrench will be terrible. I wonder what I shall do,' he added reflectively.

Fluff finished the sandwiches, obtained permission to order coffee and after the coffee tray was brought and the footman dismissed, he began to speak.

'I am leaving England at 6 am, sir. As you gave me *carte*

14

blanche, I have asked Tommy to fly me to France and thence to Switzerland. Until I return I cannot say for certain that anything will eventualise. You and Wallis will have to bear with me in as much patience as you can muster until I get back.'

'Don't come here then,' the King jumped up and began pacing up and down. 'I'm bayed by my ministers, telephoned incessantly by members of my family and now to cap it all, I am to be deprived of the company of the woman I love. I shall go to the Fort. You can report to me there. At least I'm better placed there to keep the wolves at bay . . .'

Fluff waited patiently until the King had exhausted himself and then, very quietly, he outlined what he hoped to do. When he had completed his report, the King jumped up again. 'Capital!' he exclaimed. 'Brilliant, always assuming you can persuade her. It must come off, Fluff. It *shall* come off. You see Wallis wants it and as I told you that must be the first – no,' he corrected himself, 'the only consideration.'

The King reached for the telephone. 'Darling, Fluff is still with me and we'll be working for hours. I'll ring you in the morning with all my news.'

There were indeed other matters to be handled tactfully – money, for one, always an irritant to the King. Certain letters Fluff had already prepared still required the royal signature. Dawn was breaking before he was free to return to his rooms in Albany. He bathed, changed, gave some packing instructions to his valet and eventually took a taxi to the Royal Mews where a car was drawn up waiting for him.

As he drove, he ran over the bare bones – the very bare bones – of his plan, wondering if he dared take Tommy into his confidence but dismissing the idea as impossible. By seven o'clock he was walking across the tarmac to where the captain of the newly formed King's Flight, Wing Commander 'Tommy' Sopworth, DSO, MC stood waiting for him beside the King's new aircraft. The two old friends shook hands and in moments they were

15

airborne on what only Fluff knew was a formidable quest.

November 27th

The King stepped into his car outside Buckingham Palace, the footman closed the door and slid in beside Ladbroke as the car moved slowly out of the courtyard, past the sentries up Constitution Hill to Hyde Park Corner heading for Fort Belvedere.

Fresh editions of the London evening papers were drawing a crowd to the news-stand outside St George's Hospital.

'Stop the car, Ladbroke,' the King demand. 'Get me the latest papers.'

Ladbroke moved off again as someone recognised the King, cried out and the crowd turned, surging forward.

The King unfolded a paper and the headlines screamed at him, 'Mrs Simpson's windows stoned – angry crowds outside No 16'. When the car pulled up at the Fort he jumped out before the footman could open the door. He strode into the library, snatched up the red telephone, gave a number and waited drumming his fingers impatiently. Finally, 'Mrs Simpson, please, this is the King . . . Well, when is she expected to return? . . . Is Mrs Merryman there?' and at last, 'Is that you, Aunt Bessie?'

A tearful voice answered him. 'Oh, sir,' Aunt Bessie sounded beside herself, 'I must speak with you. I am so startled and bewildered I scarcely know what I am doing. Last night our windows were stoned. The house is surrounded by Press and there are two policemen trying to control them.'

The King sought to calm her and presently succeeded. He told her, 'You must come back here. I shall send Ladbroke to collect you. You cannot stay another night in that house.'

'But, sir, Wallis refuses to leave,' she wailed. 'She has had the windows boarded up. We shall be all right now.'

She could not tell the King that Wallis had forced the

16

servants to say she was out as she had anticipated he would ring her, telling her aunt angrily, 'I will not leave here like a fugitive. I mean to stay at least until I have supervised the packing . . .'

'Where is she?' the King pressed.

'I don't know, sir. She said she would be back shortly.'

'Then I shall telephone again in half an hour. In the meantime please see if you can find her.'

He was distraught as he banged the receiver back. The very fact that he could not speak to Mrs Simpson was enough to unnerve him without all the other thoughts that crowded in on him. Half an hour later he telephoned again only to learn that Mrs Merryman had left immediately after his previous call and Mrs Simpson was still out.

A few minutes later a car's tyres crunched over the gravel and drew up outside the doors. The mountain had come to Mohammed. The King was watching from a window. He ran out, waving the servants away, and opened the car door himself. He bent to kiss Aunt Bessie, noticing that her face was tear-stained and her eyes swollen. He led her inside, persuaded her into a comfortable chair and rapped at the hovering footman, 'Bring coffee immediately.'

'Oh, sir!' she raised her blurred face to him and again her eyes filled. Out came a wisp of handkerchief with which she dabbed at her red eyes ineffectually. 'How frightening this is! I was pursued by the Press in cars.'

His eyes dark with pain, the King demanded, 'Forget about the Press. Tell me what Wallis said to you. I need her here, you know. My equerry, Sir Frederick, has a plan.'

'Wallis said,' Aunt Bessie choked on the words, 'she is pregnant with your child.' Her voice was muffled and uneven. 'She told me she would not even consider – er – getting rid of it. She said, "I cannot murder a King's son," for she seems convinced it will be a boy. She also told me she could not condemn herself to the criticism which would follow if this became known. She spoke of

17

some scatterbrained scheme to conceal it all. How can you?' Her voice rose to a wail. 'How can you hope to conceal such a thing?'

The door opened. In came two footmen with the coffee tray. One attempted to serve Aunt Bessie.

'Leave us,' the King snapped. As the door closed behind the footmen, he reiterated, 'Sir Frederick has the whole matter in hand. He will be back shortly to tell us what he has arranged. I undertake he will not fail to find a solution to what seems to you insoluble.' He spoke with the assurance of a lifetime in which his slightest wish had always been met, except where his father was concerned.

It was sufficient to stem her tears. She stared at him incredulously. 'But, sir . . .'

'It will be done,' he repeated stubbornly. 'Then when enough time has elapsed, I shall be able to see my son for Sir Frederick will become his official guardian, so please do not distress yourself unnecessarily, I beg of you . . .'

The King broke off as one of the footmen appeared again with a message on a salver. The King snatched it, read the few words and then passed the slip of paper across to the woman who was looking not unlike an Aylesbury duck which had just passed through a tornado. 'I told you so,' he remarked with extraordinary complacency. Aunt Bessie peered at the four words and a signature. She read, 'Mission accomplished. Returning instantly.' The signature which had already drawn a quirk to the King's lips was Sancho Panza.

'I am far more anxious,' he said, 'to ensure your safety now. You must move in here immediately. Then at least I shall know you can be adequately protected. It is unthinkable that Wallis should be exposed to such peril daily.' He paused, frowned and then added, 'More especially in her present condition.'

He began the familiar drumming of his fingers on the table top. He jumped up abruptly and started pacing the room. 'Take Ladbroke,' he said. 'Let him drive you. Your driver had better take your car too, so you can bring as much of your luggage as possible. The rest can be collected later. My mind is resolved that you must never spend another night in that house.'

It occurred to Mrs Merryman that the King's nervous excitement was not only due to the implicit danger of their present situation but also the prospect of having Wallis with him again if only for a short time and however unwise this was.

The King pressed a bell and ordered the cars to be sent round immediately. He gave Ladbroke instructions to wait outside No 16 and then bring Mrs Simpson and Mrs Merryman back as swiftly as possible. As the two cars swung onto the open road, a dark blue Ford sedan closed up behind and followed them. The Press were hanging onto their quarry doggedly.

The crowd outside No 16 had grown. The two policemen did what they could to hold them back as Mrs Merryman hurried into the house, but they could not prevent her hat being knocked askew so she presented a somewhat rakish appearance. Huge piles of luggage overflowed from the small hall spilling in through the opened doors of two rooms.

As Mrs Merryman climbed the stairs, panting, a footman with more luggage drew back for her and a voice called out from above, 'Is that you, Aunt Bessie?' She hurried into Wallis' dressing-room, closed the door behind her and gasped out, 'The King insists we leave this house tonight. He's beside himself with anxiety for your safety.' She stared at her niece incredulously. 'Wallis, what in the world are you doing, dear?'

All the usual impedimenta had been swept from her dressing-table on which bracelets, rings, necklaces, brooches and earclips were now tangled into a rainbow blaze of emeralds, diamonds, rubies and sapphires.

'Enjoying my treasure chest, dear Aunt,' she replied abstractedly picking up an earclip and trying it on. 'Or should I say David's loot? It's largely from the royal coffers,' she gave a harsh little laugh, 'for the woman the

King loves, but at whom his peoples fling stones, refusing to accept her as their Queen.'

'Oh, Wallis,' sighed Mrs Merryman helplessly, 'really, dear!'

Wallis stood up. 'We'll go,' she agreed, 'but whatever else we leave behind, these come with me.' She laid a possessive hand on the jewels as though she drew some comfort from so doing. Then she rang for her maid. They spent some time deciding what she would wear. The woman packed the clothes she chose for dinner that night and for the following morning, after which Wallis sat down again, studied her reflection critically and told her maid to re-do her hair.

8 pm November 27th
The King seemed in high spirits as he hurried out to meet them. As soon as they were alone, he told them that Fluff had telephoned. 'He will reach England tomorrow morning. Meanwhile, dear Aunt Bessie, I am afraid you are going to be rather rushed. There is a ship sailing from Southampton tomorrow at 8 pm. She puts in at Le Havre. We have booked a cabin for you on A deck. I'm bound to say that I think you should go. Otherwise you'll not be at your Castello in time to make all the necessary arrangements for Wallis. A car will meet you. There's no need for secrecy. If the Press elect to follow you, so much the better. It fits our plans admirably.'

'David,' Wallis stared at him, 'how did you find this out?'

He smiled. 'Fluff,' he said simply. 'He fixed it for us from Paris.'

Aunt Bessie then checked with him, 'So if they corner me at any of our stops and want to know where I'm going, I merely say the Castello. If they ask how long I intend staying, shall I just tell them as long as Wallis needs me?'

'That's capital,' the King said. 'Now come along, let us go into dinner.' Seemingly revitalised he insisted on playing them into dinner and marching round the two

20

women at the table with his bagpipes. Wallis, ever quick to respond to his moods, duly exerted herself to amuse him and thus the evening passed with some semblance of gaiety.

11 am November 28th
Fluff arrived soon after breakfast. While the nation and Commonwealth waited for the King's decision, the four people most closely concerned sat in the library at Fort Belvedere, listening to Fluff report on what he had done to make the impossible become possible.

He began, 'While you, sir, dined with Wallis I set the machinery in motion to trace someone I had known when she was a very young girl. She was born in Brussels. Her parents were prominent on the stage in America and throughout Europe. She first played with them when she was a small child. In fact her ability was such that she was regarded as a child prodigy. Since she learned her English from her parents and spent so much time in those formative years in the United States, she speaks with a markedly American accent.

'As she grew up so her talent increased. In 1914 when she was eighteen the whole family were acting in Brussels. When the city was overrun by the Germans, they were caught there. In the end the girl saw both her parents shot. That was when we met. I was able to help her escape to Paris and from then onwards she worked in my unit as a special agent. By the time she was twenty-two and the Great War was over, she had lost all desire to return to her acting profession. Instead she married a Swiss painter who had been badly crippled in a ski-ing accident. They moved into a remote chalet in the Swiss Alps and remained there together until he died.

'While I waited for her telephone number that night, it struck me again how much, as a young girl, she had resembled Wallis. When I telephoned her, I asked if she were still ripe for adventure. She admitted she was profoundly lonely since Pierre's death and was considering

21

a return to the stage. I asked if I could fly out to see her on a matter of very private and urgent business. I was of course resolved to say nothing if my memory had played me false; but when she opened the door to me, it was as if Wallis were standing there. I had naturally armed myself with as many photographs as I could obtain in such a short time. I showed them to her and then asked her if she could impersonate Wallis successfully for six months.

'She studied the photographs and left the room. When she came back she had copied Wallis' hair style. The resemblance was by now uncanny. Later when I took all her measurements and compared them, I found they were identical with Wallis' except that she takes a size smaller in gloves.

'We then made our plans. Before returning to report to you I gave her ciné films and a mass of details for her to absorb. We then worked out how she could learn the rest from Mrs Merryman at the Castello.'

All this time Mrs Simpson sat, perfectly composed, her hands in her lap and her eyes fixed on the King. Now she said, turning to Fluff, 'I am curious to learn how you plan to instal my double at the Castello and me at the clinic in Switzerland under the very noses of the Press and above all where this substitution will take place.'

Fluff told her. The expressions of anxiety changed to relief and, as the ingenuity of the plan sank in, to manifest amusement.

'Oh, well done, Fluff!' the King exclaimed, 'and then Wallis assumes the identity of the woman who will adopt our child?'

Fluff nodded.

'Can this be done in such a way that you retain control over the boy's welfare? I think you should be his guardian.'

'With respect, sir,' Fluff ventured, 'that would be a little difficult. However, I have already been asked to stand as principal godparent at the christening and Diana and Michael Kincale also want to appoint me as

22

guardian in the event of anything happening to them before the child comes of age.'

In the pause which followed Wallis asked, 'How long have you known the adoptive mother?'

'Diana Kincale and I grew up together,' he assured her. 'She is English and was in fact presented to the late King during her first season. I know both Diana and her husband very well. They are immensely wealthy. The only flaw in an otherwise extremely happy marriage is the fact they cannot have any children. That is why I contacted them. I told them that I knew of the forthcoming birth of a child whose parenthood was impeccable and who could be adopted immediately after birth.'

'Where do the Kincales live?' the King demanded abruptly.

'They have a huge homestead in the Australian outback where they even have a private aerodrome. They are obsessive about flying. Both pilot their own aircraft and they have already chalked up some amazing records.

'I have arranged for Diana to stay at the Dolder Hotel in Zurich with the English nanny whom she has undertaken to engage. She will arrive some time before the anticipated date of birth. She has also agreed to return to Australia immediately after the child has been christened.'

'While I,' said Wallis with a curious inflexion in her voice, 'am returning to my own personality in my aunt's Castello to prepare for my marriage to David.'

'Exactly so,' said Fluff quietly.

Mrs Merryman glanced at her little jewelled fob watch and murmured apologetically, 'If I am to catch the boat train, sir, I think I should ask your leave to withdraw to see to the packing of my immediate needs.' She rose as she spoke.

Fluff reminded her, 'Mrs Merryman, you will be met by a courier who will conduct you safely to your cabin and generally look after you until you sail. Another courier will meet you when the ship puts into Le Havre, attend to all your luggage and see you safely into your car. I have made quite sure that you have a dependable driver who, incidentally, has all your reservations through France and Italy.'

'I really must say, Sir Frederick, I am most grateful. There is so much to attend to at the Castello. I shall have to dismiss all the servants I have at present because you see dear Wallis stayed there last spring when she helped me redecorate and furnish. There will have to be a personal maid for her too. Dear me! come along, Wallis, we needn't bore the King and Sir Frederick with such details. We can talk in my rooms.'

The two women sketched their curtsies. As Fluff closed the door behind them, he would not have been in the least surprised had he heard Mrs Merryman say, 'Oh, my paws and whiskers', she was by now so much like the white rabbit in Alice.

The moment they were alone, the King spoke of his great concern for Wallis' comfort in what he called her incarceration at the clinic. He insisted that by the time she arrived, all the necessary arrangements must be made for a private telephone line in her chalet so that at least he could talk to her daily in the guise of Mr Kincale. Fluff in his turn reported what he had told the clinic's director concerning the unusual length of stay prior to her confinement. Putting it as delicately as she could, he explained to the King that he had based this on the fact that she was no longer a young girl and that it was her first child; therefore her husband insisted she should have the most skilled medical care in the preceding months to ensure there would be no complications at the birth.

Then Fluff took his last hurdle. 'I also undertook, sir, on your behalf, that the sum of £25,000 will be transferred to a Swiss bank account when Lise, as I shall call her, returns to her chalet and the child has arrived in Australia with Diana Kincale.'

December 2nd, Windsor Castle
The Prime Minister delivered the ultimatum to the King.

He spoke quietly but with such resolution that the King sank deeper into despondency as he listened to what Mr Baldwin had to say.

'I have to tell you, sir,' he began, 'that the dangers of collusion over the divorce of Mr and Mrs Simpson and Miss Buttercup Kennedy are now such that in no circumstances should you see Mrs Simpson again until she has obtained her decree absolute. I have also to emphasise, distressing though it is to have to do so, that there are now only three courses left open to you, sir. You must either give up any idea of marrying Mrs Simpson, or you must marry her and abdicate or you could marry her against the wishes of your ministers. Here you are faced with the certainty that this would bring the Government down. Moreover, it is extremly improbable that anyone would come forward to form another government. Furthermore, you must make your choice with the utmost celerity. The matter is critical, for I am absolutely convinced the last thing you would ever wish to do is to create such a perilous situation that a complete schism could split your country in two. There are rumours already . . .'

'What rumours?' the King interrupted angrily.

'Rumours of the formation of a King's Party with all its concomitant dangers and distresses.'

'Bloody hell, no!' the King protested. 'That would be unthinkable.'

The expression on Mr Baldwin's face softened. He continued, 'In the matter of separation, sir, there is really no sense in minding whether the distance between you and Mrs Simpson is eight miles or eight hundred. I know, sir, that it is the separation which you bitterly resent.' He hesitated and then asked, 'Might I be permitted to enquire if Mrs Simpson is willing to visit her aunt, Mrs Merryman, at this time?'

The King nodded. 'Mrs Merryman has already left for Italy and I have no doubt that Mrs Simpson will agree to join her at the Castello and stay there until she and I can be reunited.'

The last word was potent. It seemed to echo in the air around them . . . reunited . . . reunited. It acted as a gauntlet with which the monarch had slapped his Prime Minister across his face. It effectively put an end to any further discussion. The old man rose, suddenly meta-morphasised into a figure of dignity. 'Then, sir, there is little more I have to report,' he said sadly. He sought refuge in formality and the King nodded, seeming not to notice it.

Instead he said, 'I have listened carefully to what you have said, Mr Prime Minister, which in free translation is "toe the line or get out". Doubtless my younger brother will be more compliant.'

'Is that your last word, sir?'

'It is and now I am driving to the Fort. I find this Castle untenable and can no longer sleep here. I must suppose,' he looked round him with a vague expression of surprise, 'I may have slept here for the last time.'

Thus was Baldwin dismissed.

The London the King had left behind was like a tropical forest in the last moments before the rains, when clammy heat palls the skin, no sun shines and the skies stretch a pewter canopy over the uneasy life below. Even the stray whisperings and conjectures were silenced now by the single thunder clap which had so shocked the people of England that tongues were mute while minds grasshop-pered as the reverberations of what they had heard sank in. They were silent as they thrust their pennies at the newsvendors, who struggled embedded in palisades of outstretched hands snatching at the latest editions. They moved away like zombies along the pavements obeying the sellers' hoarse exhortations to 'read all abart it'.

They read. Except for a privileged few who were famil-iar with the contents of American and Continental news-papers and those in high places who had long been aware that this storm was imminent, it came to the great mass of the people with all the sudden force of a hurri-cane. They were stricken.

26

They stood about, reading the banner headlines which proclaimed 'Abdication Imminent' and 'Will the King Go?' Some formed bus queues, still reading; as they climbed onto their buses. They stood clustered and unrebuked on the platforms while Cockney bus conductors aired their views.

At Speakers' Corner, Marble Arch, huge crowds gathered, listening to the soap-box rantings of a wispy little man in a ragged cloth cap who shouted rhetorically from his upturned beer crate.

'Why carn't 'e choose? I arsks yer, why not? And I'll tell yer too. It ain't the Yankee lady wots at the top and bottom of it – *it's the church*. Carst yer minds back. Didn't 'e go to see them pore sods of Welsh miners? Wot did 'e say to them? 'E said, "Summink must be done," didn't 'e? That's wot 'e said. When 'e come back 'e told 'is ministers, tax them "Ecclesiastical Commissioners" wot owns all the worst slums in the country but 'as more spondulicks than 'e 'as hisself. That put paid to 'im. The church won't 'ave nobody – not Prince nor King neither – gettin' their 'ooks on them 'oly Joes' money.

'Once they saw 'e was after their dirty loot the 'ole bang lot of them ganged up agin 'im. They decided 'e must go – and this is the peg wot they 'ung their 'ats on. Wake yer ideas up and do some remembering. Weren't it a saintly bishop wot spilled the beans? Yer mark my words – that's the trufe of wot's 'appening.'

Simultaneously an even greater concourse was moving down the Mall, working along Constitution Hill and Buckingham Palace Road, converging on 'Buck House', to be packed from the Palace railings to the plum pudding figure of Queen Victoria, while the motionless sentries stood at their boxes like painted wooden toys.

They could do nothing beyond prove once again that a British crowd never suffers from claustrophobia; but they drew some fragmentary comfort from being there, from the 'old lady' on her plinth and from those rigid, scarlet figures. As offices and stores closed, so the crowds multiplied until there were no more spaces – just people, *his* people – and still more came because they loved him. For them his charisma was magical.

The women loved him for his shyness, his fair hair, blue eyes and slender figure. It was centuries since the desire to be ravished by the monarch was the fulfilment of every woman's dream, but he had made it so again. He made young girls' hearts beat faster and brought back the sparkle to the faded eyes of raddled old women.

The men loved him too. They warmed to his appalling but fearless horsemanship, murmuring approvingly when he broke his collar-bone and calling him a 'ripe plucked 'un' when he took a toss on the hunting field. The older men never tired of telling how he had suddenly appeared among them across the mud of Flanders, a stripling boy evading his escort of brass hats to join them in the rat-infested, waterlogged trenches, crack a joke and smoke a cigarette before being hustled away.

When at last the people began drifting away, going reluctantly to their homes for their 'tea', they simply spread out the newspapers beside their tinned salmon or fish and chips, to read about the rules which govern Constitutional Monarchy and they hated them.

CHAPTER II

'. . . down the arches of the years
I fled Him, down the labyrinthine ways
Of my own mind; and in the mist of tears
I hid from Him.'

– Francis Thompson, *The Hound of Heaven*

THE HUNT WAS up. With Ladbroke at the wheel, the stolid detective beside him, and Fluff and Wallis settled in the back with the glass partition drawn across so that they could talk freely, the car moved out onto the main road. The Press cars were waiting. They pounced. They remained, strung out behind as the tally of towns grew . . . Sunningdale – Guildford – Horsham – Lewes . . . the signposts pointing ahead to Newhaven.

She wept silently at first. Presently she regained control and was able to ask Fluff, 'Where do you leave me and take *her* on to the Castello?'

'She is waiting for us now,' he assured her, 'as near to the French/Italian border as I could arrange so that you will be alone for the shortest possible time. I have arranged two communicating suites.'

'So that I slip into hers and she becomes me?'

'That is so. We shall be followed. We must seem to be doing our utmost to shake them off. In reality if they are not hot on my heels when Ladbroke heads for Tuscany, we shall be in a fine mess; but if all is successful, then immediately she is safely behind those high walls with your aunt, I shall return to you. By then I imagine the Press should be encamped beyond the Castello walls like a besieging army.'

'How will you get away?'

'By mule down the hillside to a small village where a car and a reliable driver will be waiting for me. He's an old *camarade*.'

29

Her sudden crack of laughter was not far from hysteria. 'In peasant clothes?'

'Oh yes, with mine concealed in one of the two mule panniers. I have taken great pains to select a *pissoire* in which to change back again. Then I shall stroll out, enter the car and be driven to Florence, where I dismiss the driver. I have the key to a lock-up garage in which is a suitable car for me to use for meeting you.'

She barely heard his last few words being shaken by another near-hysterical burst of laughter. 'It's no good, Fluff,' she choked, 'the mental picture of you on a mule with those long legs of yours . . . with a ridiculous straw hat pulled down . . . ha, ha!' Abruptly she regained her customary composure. 'I shall make myself think of it only while I take that last hurdle,' she said with firmer voice, stirring respect in him for her courage. 'I simply cannot imagine what I shall feel when I am bereft of myself, my personality, my clothes – I have never even acted in amateur theatricals.'

Although he could not like her or have sympathy for what she was about to do, he could only admire her courage, so reminded her with gentleness, 'At the end of that road the King waits for you – remember that.'

The instant they reached Newhaven docks, she hurried to a telephone to talk to the King. Fluff and the detective stood guard outside the box. They could see Ladbroke watching anxiously as the car was winched aboard the ferry and lowered into the hold. An officer approached them, said something which made Fluff and the detective glance at their wristwatches, then at Mrs Simpson who was still talking. Minutes passed. The officer spoke again, more urgently. With a shrug Fluff tapped on the glass and pulled open the door, saying, 'Please, Wallis, we must go aboard. There is no more time.'

Before she replaced the receiver he heard – as indeed all three men did – her saying almost shrilly, 'David I have to go. Now remember, you must be firm,' and a final almost valedictory 'after all you are the King.' She

was still aeons away from comprehension of his constitutional dilemma.

As she came out more uniformed men appeared to
escort her up the gangway, swathed in her light fawn
travelling coat lined and collared in mink from which
her sleek head rose in its little, slanting hat. They
vanished below into the captain's cabin. The detective
immediately stationed himself outside the door, large
and calm with his big hands placed firmly on his knees.
The ship began to move. Wallis stood at the porthole
staring out at what she knew was to be the last of England for a long time. Her lips were set tightly together,
her eyes were upon the widening watery gap between
her and the King for by now the land was symbolically
lost in darkness.

Behind her she heard a knock, then a reassuring voice
as the door swung open, 'It's all right, Sir Frederick,' and
she turned slowly to confront a steward with a tray of
sandwiches and champagne in an ice bucket, hastily
excavated, frantically polished. The man was dismissed.
As he rounded the corner pocketing a pound note, he
was crowded by pressmen.

'What did she say?'

'What was happening when you went in?'

The steward grinned. 'He said, "Thank you," and dismissed me. She never spoke. She was just standing
looking out of the porthole into the darkness. Nice pair
of ankles I must say!' He abstained from mentioning the
tip.

When they docked at Dieppe Ladbroke and a ship's
officer stood waiting on deck for the gangway to be run
up. The area behind them was roped off and further protected by a cordon of crew. As they let the chauffeur
through, the car was already up from the hold and dangling down onto the cobblestones. Immediately the
wheels settled, four men rushed forward to release the
clamps while Ladbroke opened the doors and slipped
into his seat. Mrs Simpson and Fluff stepped into the
back, the detective closed the door and ran round to

31

climb into the front seat. Ladbroke let out the clutch and they were away, their angry pursuers held back on the ferry, their cars still on board.

Fluff leaned forward, pushed back the glass partition and said, 'First stop Rouen, please, Ladbroke.'

'And from there, Sir Frederick?'

'I have made you a route,' he assured him. 'You will find the distances clearly marked from town to town; but now Mrs Simpson is exhausted as I expect you are too, so we will call a halt in Rouen at the Hôtel de la Poste. It's in the rue Jeanne d'Arc.'

It was already past two o'clock when Fluff ushered Wallis into the hotel's deserted foyer. Only a drowsy night concierge nodded at reception. He did not even glance up as Fluff asked for two rooms, signed the register as Mr and Mrs Harris. Fluff promised to call 'Mrs Harris' at first light.

She startled him again when she reappeared in the cold dawn as groomed as if fresh from the hands of her maid.

Ladbroke then took to the side roads, having narrowly avoided leading two pressmen to the garage where he had berthed the car overnight. Sir Frederick was forced to maintain the fiction of wishing to evade the Press; but his mind raced as he sat back, eyes closed, trying to devise a means of ensuring their attention before the all important rendezvous at the hotel on the further side of Chambéry. Wallis slept, only waking in Evreux where they again halted, this time for breakfast.

On the third stretch – destination Orléans – Ladbroke clocked up 123 miles with the detective map-reading, both still hell-bent on eluding their pursuers. The King had expressed his wish that this should be so in no uncertain terms. 'Get them there safely,' he had ordered, his face grim and lined with weariness, 'but above all do your best to shake off those confounded newshawks.' After this edict nothing either of his passengers could say would shake Ladbroke. As they came to the outskirts of Orléans even Fluff's control weakened. He began looking back over his shoulder.

At every stop Wallis asked Fluff to make a call to England, insisting that she be put through immediately to 'Mr James', the name they had agreed upon to confuse any possible eavesdroppers. These telephone calls were to become her lifeline to sanity when she was alone. She drew so much reassurance from them now that she relaxed and became quite talkative in the car.

After a while she began to speculate over what she would do with all those unwelcome hours which stretched ahead of her. Then she began inveighing against Mr Baldwin for whom she expressed great bitterness. To deflect such thoughts her escort began to question her concerning what she liked to read, what gramophone records she enjoyed and if she had ever found jigsaw puzzles amusing. 'This will help me,' Fluff explained, 'to ensure that Mrs Kincale has what she likes to help while away the time.'

These words evoked a sharp comment. 'The most important service you can do for me is to contact Mainbocher and obtain from him the sketches I need to see in order to choose my trousseau, my wedding dress and the clothes in which the King and I will go away together after our marriage. Mainbocher has a dress stand made to my measurements so we can do a great deal to avoid a rush at the end. David would hate anything to be rushed. I will give you other addresses so that hats, shoes and bags can be sent to me. I am supposed to be well off, am I not? I mean Mrs Kincale is, and these items will not be affected by what I believe is called "my condition".'

At every stop the telephone calls delayed them, although each time the line became more indistinct so that Fluff and either the detective or Ladbroke were compelled to stand outside and shout at each other to drown Wallis' near-screaming exhortations.

During the afternoon Fluff exerted authority and insisted on driving for a while to rest Ladbroke. It was then that a tremendous weight of isolation bore down on Mrs Simpson. There was no one now to whom she could turn for comfort. Aunt Bessie was at this very moment preparing for the arrival of 'the woman Fluff called Lise'. She, Wallis, was irrevocably separated from the man to whom her every wish was a command. She forced herself to acknowledge that it was her own choice.

It began to rain and twilight gave place to darkness as she faced one more thought. What would the outcome be if anything went wrong? If she died . . . she dug her nails into her linked hands as this final horror took hold and at that moment Fluff lifted one hand from the wheel to push the partition aside.

'If I am not very much mistaken,' he said, striving to keep the relief from his voice, 'we have the hordes with us once again.' They had halted in a traffic jam. The workers were going home huddled into raincoats, on bicycles, on foot and in cars. The traffic was completely snarled up. Then, with the rain intensifying, spinning coins in the puddles, glinting in the lights from shop windows, a way cleared on the offside. Immediately a car shot forward and Fluff glanced up at faces flattened against windows, peering . . .

They never shook them off again. As the tangle unravelled and they moved on, their pursuers formed up in procession behind them, often bumper to bumper . . . 'Doberman Pinchers,' Fluff thought, his relief so immense that he was hard put not to shout out his elation.

'We are expected,' he said reassuringly as he finally drew the car up outside a famous restaurant. The patron, two porters and a concierge rushed out to escort them in, to hurry them to the lift and finally to usher them into their suite. When the servants had left, the patron held out a key to Fluff and made a little, very Gallic bow.

'This is the key to connecting door which leads to the only other suite on this floor, Sir Frederick.'

Fluff pocketed it. 'And on the other side?' he enquired.

'De rien, m'sieu. Just your own bedroom and bathroom, next to Madame's, and then at the end of the corridor locked windows which overlook the garden.' He spoke with absolute confidence. 'Your dinner will be served to you in here whenever you are pleased to order it. I have reserved the services of a reliable maid for Madame if she wishes to avail herself.'

His eyes darted round to check all was in order. There were flowers everywhere – in the salon, in the tiny foyer with its huge armoire and more to be seen through the bedroom door. On a low table drawn up to the open fire of crackling logs stood the inevitable champagne in its bucket with a basket of crystallised fruits tied up with a satin bow. The menus and the wine list lay beside them. Wallis called from the bedroom belatedly, 'Madame will maid herself, thank you.'

She was already lifting the receiver from its hook, giving the number, repeating her litany, 'Mr James, please ... *Mr James, please, immediately*' ... the voice became louder and louder.

Fluff raised his voice too, thanked the proprietor, waited until he had closed the outer door behind him and then taking the key from his pocket, he inserted it in the lock of that connecting door and drew back the bolt.

> ... *'So like they were, no mortal*
> *Might one from other know.'*
>
> – T. B. Macaulay

Even the man who had organised it all was startled as he turned the handle of that door and walked into the adjoining suite.

She was standing at a replica window to the one at which he had left Mrs Simpson in an almost identical passive pose as she waited for her connection on the telephone.

He said quietly, 'Lise.' She turned to face him.

'No,' she replied equally quietly, 'my name is Wallis Simpson and I am going to marry a king.'

He stared at her ... at the sleek hair with the almost white line of centre parting ... at the replica suit, Mainbocher's ... on down to the slender legs and exquisitely shod feet . . . then up again to the enormous collar of pearls which were her only ornament.

Instinctively he looked away, waited a moment and then looked back. 'It is uncanny,' he told her. 'You make my spine tingle. How I wonder will you both feel when you confront each other?'

'That we shall soon know, my dear Marc,' she used the name by which he had been known to his comrades in the Ardennes.

As if she had not spoken, he resumed, 'You are a mirrored reflection of the woman I have just left standing on the other side of this door.'

'Then close it,' she spoke now in her own, slightly accented voice reminding him of her Belgian origins, 'so I can relax for a little longer. Besides there are still one or two questions to be answered.'

He smiled. 'I remind you, my dear, that at 2 am you will both meet and that by 3 am you and I will be sitting behind a glass partition being driven through the night by the King's chauffeur, Ladbroke. Then we can talk. It is over 300 miles to the Castello Gondolfo in the Tuscan hills. I will have ample time to answer all your questions; but now I can only give you your immediate briefing.'

'I think I know it,' she replied, moving with the other woman's composure, gesturing to him to sit down beside her on the Récamier couch. 'She comes through that door and hands me whatever jewels she is wearing. This,' she made a slight gesture to herself, 'is merely an example for you as you will appreciate. She removes her rings, hands them over and assumes "Mrs Kincale's". She remains here while I go through that door where her jewel case and travelling case become mine – temporarily. Meanwhile you will of course check the suite to ensure nothing has been overlooked.' She smiled reminiscently, remembering the past which they had shared. 'I have good reason for not concerning myself with that. We then go down together leaving the personality I have established here as "Mrs Kincale" in the hands of the other woman while I take hers to your Castello.'

36

'Whose Castello?' his voice had a sudden sharp edge.

'Why, dear, my Aunt Bessie's of course,' she slipped back easily into her role.

'Until then,' he said gravely, rising as he spoke, 'I need scarcely bother to emphasise the gravity of what we are attempting to do, except to repeat once again – at the end of what I most sincerely hope will be our last "mission" together – *merde alors, chère* Lise!'

He bent down, his kiss barely brushed her hand and then he was gone behind the other side of that door. She walked thoughtfully to the window and again looked out at the night, stippled with stars above, spangled with winking lights below; but these she scarcely saw. She was painstakingly striving to think herself into the mind of this woman whom she was to impersonate. She speculated, as she had done so often in the past three weeks, on the character of any woman who could even undertake to try and carry through this ruthless enterprise. What if the child she was to reject at birth were indeed a boy as she seemed convinced herself? Had she ever considered what he might become?

Her mouth twisted as she recalled Shaw's riposte when that dancer proposed they have a child together. Would the son of this union inherit the father's playboy love of luxurious trivia combined with the wilful acquisitiveness of his mother, or would the unquestioned seeds of greatness which had failed to come to fruition in his father sprout for the son and if so, for God's sake, to what end or purpose? Her thoughts squirrelled endlessly. Would he be just another frivolous lightweight, or would he develop the keen intelligence of his mother? If so and if this were to combine with the dazzling charisma of the King . . . why then anything could happen.

At last she sighed, turned away. There would be time enough for such speculations in the months ahead. Possibly the woman with whom she was to spend her time, this Mrs Merryman, would supply more clues to help her determine how it would all end.

There were other more urgent matters demanding her

attention now. She suddenly realised that she was hungry; at least, thought rebuked, 'Mrs Kincale' was hungry. She went to her bedroom and sat down at the dressing-table. She began obliterating Mrs Simpson and restoring 'Mrs Kincale' to her appearance. When she was satisfied, she tied the sash of her loose wrapper, lifted the telephone and gave her dinner order to 'Service'. Presently the waiter came with the trolley. He enquired if she felt more rested, was regretful that this was not so and agreed it was better not to go out in such terrible weather. He spoke in English since 'Mrs Kincale' could not understand French. Accepting her tip, he wished her 'Bonne nuit, madame' and went.

It was almost 2 am when Fluff had completed his inspection of the bedroom. His face gave no indication of his inward stresses as he said gently, 'Now, my dear Wallis, it is time.' Instantly, he saw a flicker of fear in her eyes just as there had been when he had suggested they might fly instead of travel by car.

'How long must I remain in there?' she gestured towards the dividing door.

'Unless anything drastic occurs, about four days. I do realise that this is a very stiff hurdle for you to negotiate – alone.'

The words were well chosen. They flicked her vanity. Up came her head, her resolution stiffened. 'It has to be done,' she replied coldly. 'Am I permitted to go out?'

'I want you to do so. Consider it as your opportunity for rehearsals. Gain confidence in being "Mrs Kincale" by your dealings with the chambermaid and the waiters. Then go downstairs. Take a walk – if you can do that, it will stiffen your confidence in your appearance. You will discover you are merely another guest in an hotel which is really only a restaurant with rooms on a very luxurious level, and justly famous for its cooking and its wine cellar. Accustom yourself in this way to being an unknown guest instead of a world-famous figure.'

She nodded, listening intently. 'Would you like me to tell you again whom I become?'

'Please do.'

'Here I am just an anonymous hotel guest who has come here from Paris to recuperate from an operation, which explains why I spend so much time in my suite. When I leave here, I am "Mrs Kincale" until my stay at the clinic ends.'

'Why the clinic and why so long before your child is expected?'

'I am an Englishwoman who spent many years in the States prior to my marriage. That explains my accent. I am the wife of a rich Australian who farms in the outback. We have been married for some time. We have tried unsuccessfully to have children. When I became pregnant this time my husband was determined I should be put in the care of the finest gynaecologist in Europe to ensure all would be well. Together we own aircraft which we fly, both separately and together. This is not surprising for wealthy people in the outback. My husband has made all the arrangements for me through you, his best friend.'

'How many months will you be in the clinic?'

'I figure the birth should be around May 10th, say five and a half months. For this period you have booked me a private chalet in the clinic's grounds and will instal a private telephone line so that my husband can telephone me every day.'

'That is done.'

'The telephone calls and your visits will constitute the only contacts I have with the outside world until it is all over.'

'Why me, Wallis? Give me some more details please.'

'Oh, because you and Michael were at school together which is why you will be the principal godfather at the christening the moment the child is handed over to the real Mrs Kincale. Because we fly, you will also be the child's legal guardian against the event of anything ever happening to us.'

'Beside which,' he supplemented, 'it will be sufficient to enable me to register the child's birth in Geneva and having done so either to obtain the addition of the child to her passport or to get a separate one.'

'I see.'

He looked down at her from his great height and was reminded, 'Smallness invites the protective instinct'; then he remembered her toughness and her unshakeable determination. He had an abrupt vision of her as she might have been as a pioneer like her ancestors, seeing her for a flash, standing against a covered wagon in button boots, the flounces of her cotton skirt blowing round her ankles. He dismissed it, hating what he was doing, so when he spoke next, his voice was harsh.

'Rest assured, you will not have to wait here longer than is absolutely necessary. When you receive a message from the worthy Patron that your car has arrived and enquiring if he may send up for your luggage, you will leave here and be taken to Lise's chalet. The keys are in your handbag. I shall collect you from the chalet without delay.'

She turned away to pick up her handbag, a coat and gloves. He took out a small pad and made a scribbled note. The door clicked and he looked up to find she had gone to the other side, so he sat down to wait.

The two women faced each other at last. They never spoke. Fluff had impressed this upon them both, since the hotel guest from Australia was supposed to be alone. For this reason he and Lise had barely whispered to each other.

Wallis stripped off her rings, held them out, received 'Mrs Kincale's' and then put up her hands to unfasten the safety catch on the pearls. Both worked swiftly, efficiently, knowing what had to be done. Brown saddle-stitched handbag with the initials DPK in gold on one corner was exchanged for black lizardskin.

Lise then steered Wallis to the bedroom where the clothes were laid out displaying labels from New York and Melbourne. When she showed herself in the open doorway, Lise gestured towards the dressing-table.

40

Obediently Wallis Simpson sat down and began unpinning her hair. A face tissue was proferred, taken to remove the bright lipstick and the mouth was repainted with a light pink one, while Lise deftly brushed out the hair, curling the ends after teasing them out until they curled above the shoulders – just. The long hair was then drawn back behind the left ear and fastened with a tortoiseshell and gold hair slide. The brown travelling coat banded down the front and collared in fox was held out. Finally a wristwatch was fastened to the left wrist and a gold charm bracelet to the right. Brown court shoes with bows completed the transformation which Lise stood back to appraise.

Lise held out a scrap of paper. On it was written, 'Practise the hair please. Remember your chambermaid is called Berthe. She has some lingerie which she took to be laundered. Tip her well. Money in handbag.'

Then she took the paper back, burned it in the salon's log fire, crushed the charred paper to powder . . . and was gone leaving behind her a drift of Wallis' own very special scent.

In the silence which followed, Wallis suddenly drove her knuckles into her mouth to suppress the scream which surged to her throat. She tore off the coat as if it stifled her and flung herself face downwards on the bed.

As the two figures came cat-footed round a bend in the staircase, the transformed foyer displayed itself in unlovely disarray. Men lying on the padded seating . . . in armchairs . . . even on the floor. The lights had been dimmed and they were all asleep. One man snored. Fluff led 'Mrs Simpson' between them. As they neared the doors Fluff could see, dimly, the dark outlines which confirmed that Ladbroke and the detective were waiting outside. Levelling with the last sleeper sprawling with his legs stuck out, his scuffed shoes kicked off, Fluff and 'Mrs Simpson' stepped over with infinite caution. Fluff opened the door, thrust her and the cases out to the waiting men. When she was safely in the car, the chauffeur at the wheel and the engine running, Fluff deliberately kicked the outstretched legs, leapt through the door, banging it shut, and the man woke, let out a shout and got to his feet. In moments the foyer was in uproar.

The one whom Fluff had kicked put on his shoes, tucked his jacket under one arm and wrenched open the door. Behind him the other reporters jostled each other as they stampeded to reach their cars. By the time Ladbroke approached the frontier, the two passengers were rayed by the headlights of their pursuers. As they passed into Italy, Fluff whispered, 'Eureka! Makes me feel young again.'

CHAPTER III

. . . Hoist with her own petard.

– after William Shakespeare

LADBROKE SLID THROUGH the great iron gates in the red walls of the Castello. The Press saw the gates being locked by a peasant wearing a blue blouse and old trousers. He came back to thread a padlock round the bars before slouching off round the curve of the brick tower out of sight.

The Press were left encamped outside the walls. They conferred and decided to roster their forays to the nearest village for food and drink. As the first car load edged down the hill, it passed the peasant with a straw hat pulled over his nose, his legs dangling down on either side of a rangy mule carrying two large wicker panniers, from one of which protruded a load of hay. Fluff was on his way again.

The next day a bulletin was issued stating that Mrs Simpson was suffering from acute exhaustion after the stresses of recent weeks and would be taking a long rest.

The driver of the hired car, who collected the convalescent Mrs Kincale, took no particular interest in her except that he, like most men, admired the excellence of her ankles. He drove across the frontier out of France into Switzerland to a simple chalet on the edge of a heavily wooded hillside. Acting on her instructions he transferred the luggage to the entrance hall, received her tip, touched his cap and drove away. Wallis found a note beside the telephone in the entrance hall. 'So far so

43

good. I shall join you in moments if the Gods are with us.'

Having read these words, she glanced out of the window just as Fluff emerged from between the trees – a singular figure, bowler-hatted and carrying a rolled umbrella and a brief case. She opened the door swiftly.

'Congratulations,' he said lifting his bowler. 'Was it very dreadful?'

'I imagine your journey was worse,' she answered surprisingly.

'Tiresome,' he agreed, adding, 'there is not much more. The woman I call "Lise" is safely installed. A bulletin has been issued to the effect that you are totally exhausted and will need prolonged rest and quiet. The Press are camped as I predicted outside the walls. Actually,' his eyes twinkled at the memory, 'I passed them on my mule yesterday morning. The first car load was on its way down to the nearest village for breakfast. They were not interested in me.'

Her mouth quivered. She gave him back, 'Congratulations,' then queried, 'what do we do now?'

'First let me bring the car round to the front of the chalet. Then when I have stowed your luggage in the boot, we can drive to the clinic where of course you are expected. I shall then return to England but I'll try to be with you again in a few days. In any event I will telephone. The items you asked for are already awaiting you.

'Now let me try to reassure you on one vital point. If anything bewilders you – let it. Remember this is as unique and unfamiliar an experience for Mrs Kincale as it is for you. If the circumstances were reversed, she would be equally lonely and isolated. Take heart from that. Your own exhaustion is insurance enough that your – er – husband's anxiety is justified. So cull every advantage you can from what has happened. Rest, try to relax but if you can't, then occupy your mind with making plans for the future. I undertake to keep in constant touch.'

She was silent for a moment. Then, 'David,' she said, 'is to go to Austria. Will you join him?'

44

'Of course,' Fluff answered. 'When he can spare me I will come to you.'

'Why?' she asked abruptly.

He prodded the pine floorboards with the ferrule of his umbrella. 'Because,' he said thoughtfully, 'the heart has its reasons.'

In her unfamiliar clothes, her curled hair still irritating her, she had spread a large scale map over her knees and thus was able to guide Fluff through the Swiss country-side following the route marked heavily in red.

The gates of the clinic bore the name in gold letters on the white flanking pillars. A trim little gate house stood inside the entrance to the long winding drive. A uni-formed man came out as Fluff braked. He waved them on after they had identified themselves.

Feeling faintly sick and gripped by sudden terror, the woman who was about to surrender her identity saw the figures of a small elderly man and two nurses waiting to receive her at the foot of a flight of white steps. In that moment of panic one hand reached for the car door, intent on escape. For an instant she was blinded by the situation she had brought upon herself, but in that moment her alter ego asserted herself and she stepped out calmly enough extending her hand to them.

That night she telephoned the King. This was her only consolation.

The following evening after Wallis Simpson had dined alone as Mrs Kincale from Australia in her private chalet in the grounds of the clinic, she sat beside the huge radio which Fluff had installed in her sitting-room and heard the abdication speech from the lips of the man she was to marry.

He had dined at Royal Lodge with his mother, his favourite uncle and aunt – the Earl and Countess of Ath-lone, and his brothers. Sir Walter Monckton then called and drove him to Windsor Castle where he was met by Lord Wigram as Deputy Constable and Lieutenant

Governor of the Castle. The King mounted the Gothic staircase to his old quarters in the Augusta Tower and was met by Sir John Reith. Shortly afterwards the listening world heard Sir John's voice saying, 'This is Windsor Castle. His Royal Highness Prince Edward,' then the voice of the man who had been King but was so no longer came over the wireless as he began, 'At long last I am able to say a few words of my own . . .'

She sat with her elbows on her knees supporting her head with those unattractive hands. She remained so throughout the broadcast, while the slow tears gathered, channelling down the unaccustomed rouge on her cheeks . . . falling unheeded. Her lips contracted into a tight hard line as the familiar voice came to the final vale. 'I now quit altogether public affairs and I lay down my burden.' They made her shake with anger and frustration.

In a few more moments it was all over. She knew what was to follow: the drive to Portsmouth, the *Fury* waiting alongside – the destroyer's complement on board at their stations – the waiting naval guard with rifles and fixed bayonets, the unescorted Channel crossing, the arrival in France and the final long journey to Baron Eugène de Rothschild's house Schloss Enzesfeld near Vienna. All this still had to happen before she could telephone and speak to him again. There was nothing left for her to do until then. She could only wait.

Presently a soft-footed, white-clad nurse brought in a thermos of fresh fruit juice and set this on the bedside table. She switched on the lamp to ensure it functioned properly. She then turned back the covers and methodically laid four hot water bottles on the sheet. 'I will bring fresh ones for you, Mrs Kincale, when you are ready to go to bed. You have only to ring for me,' indicating the bell, pinned with a large safety pin to the under sheet. Smiling pleasantly, she went out leaving Wallis alone until she rang that little white bell.

As she sat, the tears dry on her cheeks now, she at last acknowledged the truth of what had happened. Free to think, free to relax from the unbearable tensions which had mounted within her, she forced herself to face the fact that she had staked all upon a single throw . . . *and lost*! She knew this now, anger rising until its force almost choked her. 'In my hand,' she told herself, 'I hold a busted straight, so where do I go now from here?'

Thought churned on. She would marry David of course, but marriage to a de-throned king with herself wholly discredited was not what she had looked towards; yet now she must plan to create the best protection for herself in the years ahead. Even before that she must endure these terrible months of incarceration in a prison of her own making. Like many before her who were inveterate gamblers, she had construed her pregnancy as her final weapon – one which would force the King to assert himself, to exert the kingly authority which she still foolishly imagined had been his. Fate had decreed that she never would or could comprehend the narrow limits imposed by the rule of constitutional monarchy. She had always believed his imagined royal powers would raise her to that pinnacle of achievement, in which she saw herself as Queen Wallis.

Mental recriminations now gave her back her own words, 'It seemed unbelievable that I could be part of his enchanted world, share in such endless glamour. I felt myself under a shimmering star, saw the golden gates open to me and ran in. These things had made David irresistible, surrounded as he was with hitherto un-dreamed of privilege. For *me* trains were held up . . . yachts materialised! . . . the finest hotels put the best suites at *my* disposal!' And now just what remained? A reject by his own choosing, trained from birth to the privileges of princedom and of monarchy, who was now shorn of all that had attracted her – leaving just a little man whom she must keep amused – and even for that she could only sit and wait.

*   *   *

47

'Nay but you, who do not love her,
Is she not pure gold, my mistress?'

– Robert Browning

For Wallis the ends would always justify the means; in consequence she saw her present situation as the natural corollary to her own misjudgment. She neither reproached herself nor wasted time and energy regretting. The boulder had appeared on her intended path. Ergo, she set all in motion to achieve its removal and having done everything possible through the good offices of others, she merely set herself the task of 'finishing the job'. It was no more to her than this at any time. The clinic made all possible.

Such a famous – some said infamous – establishment was staffed by men and women for whom it was made infinitely worthwhile to turn a Nelsonian eye upon any discrepancies or anomalies in their immensely wealthy clientele. If any had been asked to give reasons for their attitudes, they would surely have replied, 'Satan finds mischief for idle hands; we merely provide the services to minimise or rectify such mischiefs. Beyond that point nothing surprises us, nothing raises queries which would imperil our interesting and highly lucrative employment in a setting which offers us both luxury and the opportunities for experimentation. Thus if a famous face is to become another face, it is no more to us than a duty to perform to the utmost of our considerable skills.'

In short, 'ours not to reason why,' so everyone who surrounded the so-called Mrs Kincale was predisposed towards thinking of her as that, even though at certain moments she gave glimpses of another famous person. In this sense she was protected by her deception. In another sense to the clinic staff she represented a variation on a very old theme, by coming to them for a delivery and not an abortion.

So at first this very tough little woman played herself into her reversal role by adopting as best she might the absolute antithesis of clothing and adornment to that which her own irreproachable taste subscribed.

Presently, when the obstetrical examinations were concluded, she found herself able to revert to her over-riding passion – shopping. This had begun in the days of youthful economies when 'Bessiewallis' had to go cap in hand for every cent to Uncle Sol. It was stimulated during her first marriage to Earl Winfield Spencer when she joined him in Canton. Her least fraught moments – when she was not at parties – were spent haunting the bazaars in quest of *objets d'art* available within her still limited arc of expenditure. It was this shopping mania, married as it was in her case to an immense, gradually awakening talent, which would have made her one of the world's greatest interior decorators had she chosen to rise another way.

As it was, her gimlet eyes assessed and squirrelled away for future reference, increasing her knowledge and stimulating a brilliance of ideas. When she was ulti-mately able to dip into the coffers of the Duke, she merely shopped on an infinitely more costly and fasti-dious level. *Au fond* her obsession was no more than a natural progression from that of every little working wife who drifts round 'Wooly's' and 'Marks and Sparks' in what is her only escape from the confines of the kitchen. That it was to culminate in such 'Bessiewallis' orgies of acquisition as would set the world talking, still lay in the future.

So, when she had perforce settled down, cocooned in luxury, she described her situation during one of those nightly telephone calls to Mr Kincale as 'my Calvary'. Responding in the only way he knew, he made innumer-able visits to Vienna in search of gifts to lessen her 'ordeal'. This was endured *entourée de jupes* as her allocated Swiss personal maid confided to her mother on one of her rare visits home, adding, 'There is one to mass-age her every day, another to give her a daily facial, a third to manicure, a fourth to pedicure, a fifth to dress her hair sometimes twice in one day if she has been blown by the wind on her daily promenade. She must be very, very rich to spend so much money on her appearance.'

In addition to these ministrations – all chargeable to Mr Kincale – there were the regular visits from Fluff who always came laden with parcels, while the postman brought a ceaseless flow of fat envelopes re-directed from the Castello in Aunt Bessie's flowing hand to Mrs Kincale and containing the sketches, photographs and patterns from the leading Paris houses to whom Mrs Simpson had entrusted her trousseau. She worked on these – altering, improving, eliminating absolutely 'anything fancy' and attaching copious notes before sending them back.

Ordering by post did not sufficiently assuage her shopping cravings. She was instructed to take daily walks, either in the spacious grounds or, if she preferred, down the drive and along the winding lane to the little village. Here, wandering aimlessly, she discovered a tiny atelier staffed by four middle-aged, convent-educated sisters who were renowned for their fine embroideries. On her first visit, swathed distastefully in 'hairy furs' as she designated the lynx, fox and fisher coats in which she was compelled to wrap herself as Mrs Kincale, she pushed open the little door which set the shop bell tinkling. The women rose from the big, scrubbed table at which they were sewing. All four bobbed, gave her *Grüss Gott*, then three sat down while one came forward. As soon as Mrs Kincale had explained her wishes, all four became exceedingly excited. Finally they began drawing their interpretations of her suggestions.

From the work she had seen in their window, she ordered dozens of table mats for luncheons in finest white organza hand-embroidered with wheat ears in pure gold thread. Timorously, the sisters conferred, quoted and with widening eyes at the be-furred lady's indifference to cost, heard her instant acceptance. They undertook to have a sample wheat ear, and patterns of

50

various fine linens, Swiss lawns and silk organza ready for her inspection within the next few days.

When she returned, she gave them work which would last until long after her accouchement, for fitted table-cloths and matching table napkins embroidered in a theme of butterflies and birds . . . all tied up with embroidered ribbons.

Thus she kept at bay for a while the boredom and claustrophobia which threatened to engulf her. When she returned to her chalet each afternoon, her special tea was ready, served in her own glass – Russian tea, pale golden with cherry jam, as it had been served to the Tsar and Tsarina of all the Russias. Then it was time for Mr Kincale's daily telephone call. This was the greatest thorn in the sides of all who attended her. No one was permitted to enter her chalet during these lengthy tele-phone conversations; the engaged sign was slotted across the door. Her dinner maid came and went off again with the tray until sometimes three hours had passed and the staff were all quite frantic.

From these telephone exchanges between the lovers came the somewhat biased, often hysterical reports on current events following the Abdication. He complained that Kitty Rothschild stayed on and on . . . she was get-ting on his nerves . . . he had thought Schloss Enzesfeld was only to be a temporary resting place, now it turned out to be a shipwreck. He found himself a man without a country, barred from Italy by the perils of the King's Proctor, with all friendly ports closed to him – and so on . . . and on.

The ex-monarch Duke wanted recognition for his future wife – he wanted storage space for his Fort Belve-dere possessions and also for Mrs Simpson's Lares and Penates. Some of his requirements were impossible as the royal ladies were adamant over refusing to lower any drawbridges in favour of she whom Queen Mary had scornfully dismissed as 'that adventuress'. Such matters and the incessant haggling over monetary affairs sup-plied more than ample material for their long telephone

51

calls. The Duke wanted his father's stamp collection, valued at millions, but it was impasse on that score too ... and so it went on while Wallis urged, cajoled, exhorted, commanded and pleaded. Three hours was little enough for such issues in all conscience, setting aside the plentiful ducal love transports.

Finally the clinic staff reached a compromise. Mr Kincale's telephone calls would be held back until 7.15 pm and Mrs Kincale would be served dinner at 6.30 pm. This meant by the time the receivers were replaced, the expectant mother was at least ready to embark upon the complicated rituals of being put to bed by her various attendants. The Duke merely reached for the brandy tantalus, lit another cigarette and re-attacked his tie.

CHAPTER IV

'My love is of a birth as rare
As 'tis for objects strange and high:
It was begotten by despair
Upon impossibility.'

– Andrew Marvell

FLUFF MUSGRAVE AND Diana Kincale sat side by side in the Bugatti he had bought. 'If,' he had apostrophised himself, 'I am to become a cross between a Lewis Carroll King's Messenger – without either portfolio or remuneration – and if at one and the same time I am to be a prototype for one of Ian Hay's "Sapper" characters, then I may as well give myself the pleasure of driving a suitably swashbuckling motor.'

Now he and his old friend, the Diana Kincale who was to adopt the unborn baby, sat beside the lake on the outskirts of Geneva under the dominating plume of water which spurted incessantly, a jet whose sole purpose was to spout as futilely as the leaning Tower of Pisa just leaned, looking like the sugar work of some demented pastrycook. Fluff turned his shoulder resentfully against the silly water jet.

Externally, the pair of them were just two people enjoying the spring sunshine. Internally, Fluff knew that by comparison with himself, Agag was a mere clodhopper. He, Fluff, sympathised with himself. He was faced with the most appalling delicacies of verbal manoeuvering, forced to pick his way between the Scylla of close friendship and the Charybdis of a short fall into some indiscretion which could thereby disclose his ex-King's secret.

After luncheon together at the Auberge de Lion d'Or, Fluff intended taking Diana to inspect the villa he had

53

hopefully bespoken for her as being a suitable transfer point for the baby when he collected it from the clinic. He also hoped she would be willing to move herself and the nanny, still to be engaged, from the hotel to the privacy of the villa and as soon as the christening was over, to take all three of them on the first available boat back to Australia. Only then, Fluff thought, could he begin to breathe again with any semblance of normality.

None of this of course showed in his demeanour. They exchanged news of mutual friends, spoke of her husband Michael and touched on old times until she, quite unable to control herself any longer, urged, 'Now come off it, Fluff. Let us finish with preliminaries. I'll tell you whatever you want to know later. *When* can I expect to have my baby? Surely you must know by now.'

He handed her his opened cigarette case, produced his lighter and answered lightly, 'Of course not, my dear, first babies have a way of being slightly unpredictable. If you asked me to hazard a guess,' he was checking every word now as he spoke, 'I'd say somewhere after the end of April which is three weeks from now.'

She sighed, then brightened. 'Well, anyway in a sense I am glad. It gives me time to prepare. You see I've brought nothing. I've been in Switzerland before and both Basle and Berne, as well as Zurich and Geneva, have the most marvellous baby shops, so I plan on getting everything here. First I must find my nanny and then we can go shopping together.'

He smiled. 'I have several women with suitable references lined up for you to interview. Then the future godfather will have to do his shopping too.'

She touched his sleeve. 'Dear Fluff, did you realise you said "first" baby just now?'

'Of course,' he replied, 'I should have said first, last and only. I realised it as soon as I had spoken.'

He leaned forward, switched on the engine and added, 'We can talk even more comfortably over luncheon and the view is infinitely better there than here. Let's go.' So saying, he let out the clutch and the engine snarled them away.

54

Over their coffees, looking out across the sweeping masses of jonquils and tulips overtopped by the budding lilacs and weigela, he asked her, more comfortably now, 'Do you mind which it is, Di?'

She shook her head. 'If I'd carried this baby myself, I should have had to wait until the birth to know. It really doesn't matter. Whichever elects to be born, I only know it will be the best loved baby ever. Michael could talk of nothing else before I left Australia and now all his letters are full of plans. These may be a trifle excessive but he is so totally immersed in the glorious prospect of being a father that I do not have the heart to damp him down.'

Fluff listened, his eyes on the lake which, scarcely ruffled by the spring breeze, lay below them like some giant silver salver. Then he said, 'If you like the villa I have found, I shall bring your baby to you there. Just beyond it down a winding lane is a tiny chapel where we can hold the christening. You do understand that the little creature must have some sort of local habitation and a name before embarking for its new home.'

'Of course,' she said dreamily. 'If it's a girl, I want to call her Chantal, but if it's a boy, Michael wants him called David after his own father whom he adored, as you remember. Then we shall give him a second name of Christian.'

Despite himself, Fluff started at the word 'David' and nearly dropped his cup, but her eyes were firmly focussed on the shimmering lake and she noticed nothing.

'Indeed yes,' thought poor Fluff, 'and both are among his illustrious father's string of names if only you knew it.' It had so startled him that by no means for the first time did the thought come to him unbidden, '*Is this to be an infant with a very significant destiny?*' Then he forced himself to act normally, pass Diana the *petits fours* and propose a small brandy. It all passed off well enough but he speculated as to what Papa David in his temporary Schloss would have to say about the names.

Presently he ventured to say aloud, 'David Christian Kincale, a trio of splendid names, my dear, quite heroic in fact.'

She made that little hand gesture again, laying it gently

on his sleeve. 'Dear Fluff,' she asked softly, 'how much *can* adoptive parents know?'

'Virtually nothing,' he answered, 'except that there is neither inherited disease on either side nor madness in the family; that both parents are sound themselves in wind and limb and in your case, my dear, and because it is I who has managed to pull this off for you, that the birth and background are beyond question. When he or she does arrive the finest of doctors will seek for a clean bill of health.'

'You know the parents?' she pressed, watching him keenly.

'I know the parents,' he agreed.

She sighed. 'It seems such a very long time since you first told me and still I know so little of my "foster child of silence and slow time",' she quoted.

'Keats,' he said absently. 'Well, you can add to your sum total of pre-knowledge "of English blood, if not wholly English," and, if I may look into your crystal for you, so shaped as to have high hopes of what Barrie called "charm", defining it as "a kind of bloom on a woman".'

'Did he say something too about charm in a man? I forget.'

'No, he did not,' said Fluff a trifle sharply. 'Now let's go and see the villa.'

He spent sufficient time with Diana Kincale afterwards to ensure the nanny was found, mutually approved and engaged; and to have a wave from Diana and 'Nanny Kincale', which the comfortable-looking Welsh woman informed her employer was what she would be called, as he left the pair setting off down the Bahnofstrasse in Zurich bent on a day's extravagance for the unborn child.

For his part it took him the rest of the afternoon to find the place where he would register the birth; to spend half an hour with the English clergyman who would conduct the christening and to find a florist who would

56

ensure that the chapel would be suitably flower-filled for the ceremony. In some curious way he felt it essential that he should arrange such matters himself. Finally he turned into a silversmith and there chose a small silver porringer of great age. Then with some thankfulness he returned to his hotel by the water's edge and from there put through a telephone call to the Schloss and talked with another David.

CHAPTER V

'. . . for, from this instant,
There's nothing serious in mortality:
All is but toys . . .'

– William Shakespeare, *Macbeth*

THE SEQUENCE OF events involved in bringing this matter to a successful conclusion had been so well rehearsed that the actual happenings seemed to Fluff to have no more significance than any of the almost daily re-runs which he had enacted in his own mind. The whole affair assumed the character of a particularly distasteful dream scenario, in which, with the illogicality of such experiences, he was able to achieve a duality born of the knowledge that he could escape by exerting the power he knew was his, in the sleep state, to awaken and by so doing, end it.

As each stage came to a successful completion, Fluff found himself again performing dual roles. Like a professional actor, he was able to speak his lines and move to his pre-determined positions with complete detachment, performing upon his technique and not upon his nerves which had been rack-stretched in their intensity. He was able to leave the other half of his divided self free to be an objective spectator.

He realised with some astonishment that he was all the time striving to analyse the feelings of the woman for whom the perilous enterprise had been attempted. He considered what toughness, what resolution, what absolute self-discipline had been required for her to endure that long waiting period in totally alien surroundings. Divested even – no, not even, thought amended, but far above all other considerations – of her own name, character and personality, she had been dependent on her own untutored instincts to maintain the deception upon which all rested. So far as he knew, there was nothing in her past life to prepare her for such an ordeal.

Lise, on the other hand, was not merely an experienced actress but had been a prisoner in German hands. Behind her, when she assumed the other's personality, lay a lifetime of training and the durability of spirit which had enabled her to survive many cruelties. With such a background her part had been comparatively easy. For her to act, dissemble and deceive was almost natural; but for Wallis, who had no such resources honed to near-perfection by life's training, what had gone on in her mind while she waited? Fluff knew he would never be told and could never be sure, just as he knew that he would never discover whether or not she cared for the ex-King she was to marry as he cared for her. This would always be his unresolved enigma.

With these thoughts paramount, he received the news that 'Mrs Kincale' had been safely delivered of a son. A week later Fluff drew up in front of the clinic. A young nurse emerged carrying a very young baby cocooned in fluffy white shawls. David Christian was on his way to his adoptive mama. Fluff installed the pair of them in the seat beside him. Purposely he was driving his Bugatti which was not large enough to accommodate the new mother, her baby and the incredible amount of luggage, so that it was totally acceptable for the nurse to leave first with David, who slept tranquilly throughout the journey. His new nanny was waiting on the doorstep of the chalet to receive him.

Fluff then took the nurse back to the clinic and collected 'Mrs Kincale', ostensibly to take her to the chalet too. Instead, with the accumulation of expensive possessions acquired during her stay, he drove her to Lise's chalet, outside which a big dark blue Daimler saloon was drawn up. He helped her into the front passenger seat and then eased his long legs into the driving seat. He carefully unwrapped the foil from the neck of the champagne bucket which protruded, just, from its ice bucket.

He pressed the little flap of a built-in cabinet and took out two flutes. She watched him silently as he turned the bottle to withdraw the cork. He poured out two brimming glasses and dredged up a reassuring smile for her.

'Your very good health,' he said quietly. 'I think we can safely claim now "mission accomplished".'

Her composure was impressive. She took the glass, murmured, 'I needed this,' and drank.

He sought for words which would seem acceptable to the occasion but what emerged was a trite, 'Now you can relax at long last.'

Her reply was matching in its triteness. 'That will take time, Fluff. It has been such an . . . unusual experience.' Her lips then closed in a taut, thin line.

Time in fact was to teach him that after today she would never again make any further reference to her experience. The subject was closed, the affair behind her and that, she did not fail to indicate, was to be the end of it – for her. It was to be a non-event – something which had never happened.

When all the luggage was stowed away in the big car and Fluff was sweating slightly, she asked, 'When can I telephone in safety?'

He replied as he switched on the ignition, 'When you are inside the Castello. I promise I'll get you there as fast as is compatible with your safety.' Moments later, he added, 'This really is the last lap,' and suppressed an inward desire to say, 'Courage, Puss, only ten miles to London,' which he felt would not amuse her.

Throughout the long drive they spoke only of the future. Although he had done so in some detail already, she let him recapitulate on what she called 'the final stages', meaning of course how and when her son would be taken to Australia. Mechanically, his eyes on the road, he repeated once more, 'They stay at the villa until after the christening, at which I am to stand chief godfather. I have already registered the birth, obtained the certificate, so there only remains the christening and that too is a mere matter of going through the movements. When David Christian Kincale has been baptised, there is nothing more to keep him in Europe. He, his adoptive mother and the nanny will sail home.'

. He paused to negotiate the big car through a particularly stupid herd of goats, agreed that the tinkling bells were excessively irritating and as the road cleared, resumed.

'More immediately, Lise will be waiting at the self-same door by which she entered the Castello. She will return your rings to you and the pearls which go with the suit you will both be wearing. Then she will come with me and thereafter you will never need to think of her again.'

Some time later she commented, 'An interesting exchange, Fluff . . . £25,000 for her and a King for me. If you make any play with a *jeu mot* on that, I think I shall scream.'

He crinkled his eyes in a smile of pure admiration at this, saying, 'That *would* be something to hear,' which lightened the exchange, but then she came back with '. . . a King moreover who despite his promises is extremely unlikely to present me with a crown . . . ever.'

He longed to ask her if that was what she had really wanted but decided the risk was too great and cognisant of what still lay ahead in terms of shoals, he deemed it wiser to remain *bouche fermée.*

As the great car began climbing the steep and twisting lane down which he had come by mule five months before, Fluff experienced the most peculiar sense of *déjà vu.* They saw no one and no one saw them, of that he was perfectly assured, since he had posted a warning look-out who would have signalled him had the way not been completely clear. Finally he braked, switched off the engine and stopped outside the self-same door through which he had seen Lise vanish at the onset of this lunatic enterprise.

He turned to Wallis. 'If I take all this luggage away with me to have it packed in some anonymous trunks, I can return with it sometime this afternoon. Then I can drive up through the main gates, Press or no Press, and seek hospitality from your aunt on my somewhat round-about route to Austria and the Duke. Will that be accept-able?'

She nodded. 'I shall expect you,' she answered crisply. Nothing more. She climbed out, shook down her straight little skirt, tugged at the close-fitting jacket, put one hand to her pearls, drew on her gloves and began pick-ing her way over the tussocks to the old studded door. For a moment she paused, then extended her hand to the ring handle and slipped inside so swiftly and through such a small aperture that Fluff was unable to see the confrontation when in the bright morning sun-light Lise and Wallis Simpson faced each other for the second and last time. Wallis again experienced the eerie sensation of looking at her own three-dimensional replica. The rings came off and were returned to her. She remembered her manners sufficiently to say a rather breathless 'thank you' and then Lise was gone, leaving in her wake a last waft of Wallis' special scent. Wallis leaned against the closed door for an instant, panting slightly.

To all appearances she was the same woman who had come down after breakfast and told Mrs Bessie Merry-man, 'I'm going out for a breath of fresh air, Aunt dear, it's such a wonderful morning.' Impulsively, Aunt Bes-sie, after glancing round her to ensure no one saw, had embraced her fondly and said a very grateful 'thank you for everything, my dear, you have been perfectly won-derful.' Now, equally carefully briefed, Wallis Simpson strolled into her aunt's drawing room murmuring, 'Come on out, Aunt Bessie, and let's walk together for a while — it is, as I said, a very beautiful morning,' so Mrs Merry-man obediently waddled in her niece's wake, making some quite innocuous small talk. Anyone observing her closely would have seen that her hands were trembling and the corners of her mouth twitching, while her eyes filled with tears.

The staff saw them walking together along the terrace. Everything was exactly the same as usual. When they returned and Mrs Merryman rang for coffee, Wallis picked up the telephone and gave a number to the operator. She waited impatiently until the connection was finally achieved.

Within ten days there was no need for any more telephone calls for they were together again.

The acceleration of time in the passing years is a factor of life which the mature inevitably resent. For a child, a summer holiday by the sea or a term at school represents near-infinity. Conversely to two people in middle years, the same periods mean enjoyment gone by in a flash or boredom dissipated in a few dreary days. Yet as proof that there is an exception to every man-made rule, age was to reverse the normal by dragging out the wearisome years for the Duke and Duchess of Windsor.

David Kincale went aboard the steamship in his nanny's arms, en route for the outback of a sub-continent and his adoptive father's extremely fine homestead where he would spend the next few years; while the ex-King Edward VIII of England pledged himself in holy matrimony – amid a welter of disillusioning slights. As Edward Albert Christian George Andrew Patrick David, he joined with Wallis Warfield – so made by deed poll beforehand – in the pathetically unhallowed château of an American millionaire. Here they, in company with the Reverend Jardine, rummaged among their host's treasures in a frenetic search for anything which might contribute a modicum of religious significance to the ceremony. Finally Wallis produced a fine lawn tablecloth exquisitely appliqued with lilies to be draped over the baroque unsuitability of the chest which served as an altar. Mrs Constance Spry wrought magic with her flowers.

When it was all over, the newly-weds embarked upon their honeymoon which was also the onset of their exile. This sadly left little scope throughout their shared life together for any of his finest qualities to be apparent,

63

those so memorably evinced during his previous years of service to his country. His charisma was dwindled by it; there were no counsellors left to handle his vacillations, compromises and foolish errors of judgment. Still above it all there rose his unswerving love and admiration for the woman for whom he had thrown away his birthright, becoming in the process an unwanted man, cold-shouldered by his old friends, courtiers and especially his own family.

Part II

CHAPTER VI

'O! that a man might know
The end of this day's business, ere it come . . .'

– William Shakespeare

THE MORNING OF David Christian Kincale's third birthday on April 30th 1940 began with a small domestic scene. Nanny, in stiffly starched white apron, her print dress her only concession to the great heat, launched her small charge from the top step of the homestead's verandah, watched raptly by 'Mummy', otherwise Mrs Michael Kincale, who leaned over the rail in white jodhpurs and silk shirt, wearing her heart in her eyes as the little boy handed himself down, behind uppermost, sturdy little legs reaching out for the next step, fat little paws pressed onto the preceding one to steady himself during the, to him, perilous descent.

Michael Kincale stood on the compound below, the Australian sun already hot on his bared fair head. He too watched the light of his life toddling towards him to receive his birthday present. He bent down, swung his adopted son into the air, kissed him and said, 'Happy birthday, old chap. Now you are going to have your first riding lesson.' He brought him down to the crook of his arm. The attending groom held out some sugar lumps on a gnarled palm. The pony stood waiting. David selected one lump and put it plus his own little hand into the pony's mouth, bent on exploration.

'What's his name, Daddy?' he asked as he fed the pony. 'Up, Daddy, I want to ride him.'

Settling him into the saddle, his father told him,

'We've called him Fluff after your godfather, Uncle Fluff.'

'Fluff,' repeated David, 'nice Fluff.' He leaned forward to stroke the pony's mane. 'Now let me ride, Daddy.'

Michael arranged the reins in the small hands and gave him his first instructions. 'You will have to learn this, David, if you are to ride properly, so listen carefully:

Your head and your heart held high,
Your hands and your heels held low,
Your knees pressed close to your horse's sides,
And your elbows pressed close to your own.'

David listened – solemn-faced. The women looked on in adoration, overhanging the verandah rail. Fair curls damp with excitement, David tried with great solemnity to copy his father's instructions, shouting, 'Say it again, Daddy,' until at length Michael led the pony off slowly. 'Mummy, Mummy, look I'm riding,' David shouted bouncing in the little saddle.

'Sit up very straight, my son,' exhorted the father.

'I am very straight,' retorted the son.

'Fair dinkum,' muttered the groom. 'Took to it like a duck to water. We'll have him over the jumps in a week or two.'

However it was May 28th before David was allowed to put his pony at a series of jumps which he cleared easily. Then he stood up in his stirrups, scarlet-cheeked and screaming, 'I did it, Mummy, Daddy, Nanny. David did it.' He went on 'doing it' until even the ranch hands acknowledged his precocious prowess.

Simultaneously, the fugitive Windsors had moved with their enormous accumulation of baggage from villa to house, from house to hotel and from hotel to apartment in a frantic quest for a compromise between their divergent tastes in the choice of a permanent home. Wallis disliked the country; the Duke disliked cities. On May 28th fate intervened.

Italy's imminent entrance into the war on the enemy's side and the build-up to the disaster of Dunkirk sent the

Duke dashing from his post in Paris with the British Military Mission in hot pursuit of his Duchess, whom he managed to convince should accompany him instantly to the Château de la Cröe. His prime objective was to secure her safety; hers was as much concerned with the safety of their possessions. By this time it was obvious that they were in danger of being hemmed in on all sided by their advancing enemies.

In a convoy of three cars – two of which were completely swamped with Windsor luggage – they took to the road again for a nightmare six-day journey to Madrid. Here they were urged both by the British Ambassador, Sir Samuel Hoare, and by telegrams from Winston Churchill to move on yet again to the greater security offered by neutral Portugal, Britain's oldest ally. To the immense relief of all concerned, the Duke and Duchess agreed and were eventually conducted aboard an American liner in Lisbon bound for New York. Ironically she was named *Excalibur*. She put in at Bermuda where the Windsors transhipped to Nassau. Thus they narrowly escaped the Germans' carefully laid trap to lure them back from Lisbon into Spain with the intention of taking them captive.

Arriving at Nassau on August 17th 1940 the Duke and Duchess were received as the incoming Governor of the Bahamas and his lady. Within a week the Duchess wrote to a friend on Government House writing paper, but first she scored out the heading and put in its place the single word 'Elba'.

Once again she sought consolation in her obsessional shopping habit: this time for 'doing this place over' at an expenditure of $21,000 of which the Assembly had authorised a mere $6,000. Dinner parties were then resumed. As had been the custom at both the Fort and la Cröe, the Duke marched around the table in his kilt playing the bagpipes. At this time she was described as 'a frail, tiny, exquisitely dressed woman, so tough she could have played tackle for the Green Bay Packers'. She worked increasingly hard during those years, hoping that by doing so they could gain a more advantageous posting thereafter; but despite her efforts she was not popular. The other women bitterly resented her fantastic wardrobe and her frequent trips to the American mainland for hairdressing, fittings and general amusement.

So, for the Windsors, the war years passed. By the August of 1944 they jointly decided they had had enough. The Duke sent in his resignation requesting it become effective on March 15th 1945, when they set off on a long trip beginning at Palm Beach, moving on to New York and then to Newport before sailing to France and a suite at the Ritz in Paris. Before this, quite unexpectedly, the Duke met his son.

Prior to leaving Nassau, the Duke had written to Fluff who promptly cabled back telling him that he would be in New York briefly 'while playing nanny to a friend's small boy to whom I am godfather'. This became the dominant thought in the Duke's mind. As Nassau sank below the skyline and they turned away from the taffrail to go below, he put a gentle hand on his wife's arm. 'Darling, would you care to see the boy? I shall, but you must do exactly as you wish of course.'

The question startled her. She played for time in which to work out exactly what reply she should make. She was never precipitate and in this matter instinct warned her it was essential to put herself in the most appealing light possible. 'So sudden ...,' she murmured. 'You must give me time, David ... I have to exhume my carefully buried heart's desire in order to answer you.'

In the event she did not raise the matter again until they were in sight of New York when she said abruptly, 'When you speak to Fluff, David, ask him to bring his godson to tea with us,' adding, as she took his arm, 'come now, we must prepare for the onslaughts of my country's unbridled Press.'

Fluff sounded alarmed when the Duke spoke with him

on the telephone from their suite at the Waldorf Towers. 'Are you sure that is wise, sir?' he ventured.

The Duke's voice came back slightly tinged as it was now by an American overtone, *'Qui s'excuse,* my dear Fluff. It's eight years now. What's the boy doing with you in New York anyway?'

'I'm taking him back to England to his prep school,' Fluff explained. 'I promised him visits to both the House of Representatives and the Senate. The child's obsession with anything to do with the body politic is amazing. Now please don't sidetrack me, sir. Are you sure this is wise?'

'No, but I think it is perfectly safe,' the Duke retorted. 'Shall we say 4.15 pm in our suite?'

Having replaced the receiver, he then rang for the American secretary and asked her, 'Where should I go for some toys for an eight-year-old boy?'

She replied with a smile, 'FAO Schwarz, sir.'

He nodded. 'Well, as the Duchess is otherwise engaged, would you be good enough to accompany me?'

She ordered a car and presently they spent a happy hour playing with trains, tanks and an array of toy soldiers including both the Confederates and the Unionists of the American Civil War.

At the appointed time the boy walked in beside Fluff and stood waiting as he greeted his old master. Then Fluff said a trifle stiffly, 'Sir, may I present my godson, David Kincale,' and the boy, clearly having been instructed, gave his father the formal bend of the head and then took the outstretched hand with complete assurance.

The two men's eyes met over the fair young head. In unspoken assent they acknowledged that David had the Duke's colouring but instead of inheriting the tip-tilted nose which women found irresistible in the father, the son's was almost Roman. The chin was very strong; the eyes much darker, a much deeper blue under thicker,

71

darker lashes. The Duke, watching the boy under those famous fair eyelashes of his, decided that no man had ever had nor could hope to have a more handsome son. That was when he looked up at Fluff. The Duke experienced a most extraordinary sensation, a compound of the desire for open ownership, for kinship and above all for declaration that this – for he who had dreamed of sons – was the epitome of all those dreams.

Young David seemed completely at ease with him – no vestige of shyness, just a young animal's natural curiosity, tempered by good manners for this encounter with a man who had been so very famous.

'Do you mind talking about when you were King, sir?' was one of his first questions. 'I've never talked before to anyone who has been a king and I forgot to ask Uncle Fluff if I might ask you, so please do not trouble to answer if it displeases you.'

The Duke's eyes creased at the corners with laughter. 'On the contrary,' he assured him, 'let us sit here, eat cinnamon toast and talk about kingship.' He nodded to the hovering secretary who promptly disappeared to instruct that tea could now be brought in.

'And that reminds me,' he waved a hand towards a very bulky parcel on a nearby coffee table, 'that is a present for you. I hope you will like it.'

'Oh, sir,' David exclaimed, 'how absolutely wizard! May I look now please?'

'Most certainly,' the Duke said, 'and then perhaps we can have a game . . .'

Thus it was that when the Duchess returned from her daily facial, she found all three of them playing with toy soldiers on the floor. As she entered, she heard a child's voice saying, 'Let's use this box for a fort, shall we?' Then her husband's voice floated out, 'I should have bought you one. I'll send it on to you if you remind me.' Then the boy's voice again, saying eagerly, 'Oh, yes, sir, I'd like that very much.'

Her face was completely unrevealing, however, as she sat down, poured the tea and chatted impersonally. Fluff watched avidly for some sign of emotion, but she had herself under her customary rigid control. She asked David how long he was staying in New York. When he told her, 'Just tonight and tomorrow, ma'am'; she smiled a little and said, 'Then you must ask your Uncle Fluff to bring you to see us in Paris in the holidays. You might like to look at the Duke's collection of porcelain soldiers – French ones. Some of them go back to the Battle of Agincourt.'

She hooked him. Watching her adoringly, the Duke was like a chameleon on a plaid pillow in his intensity of pride and pleasure in them both. 'That's a capital idea,' he said quickly. 'Fluff, see to it. We plan to be there for the winter. You might fly the boy over for a long week-end. If he's still politically minded we can take him to see the French Government in action.'

When the boy left, he thanked the Duke and Duchess charmingly, bent his head correctly and moved off with Fluff, followed by the Duke's man carrying the toys, only to run back and say, 'You asked me to remind you about the fort, sir.' The last they heard of him was his high boy's voice chattering to Fluff.

The Duke sat very quietly in the big chair after they had gone. Wallis went over to him and sat on the arm of the chair. Instinctively he told her all she needed to know by turning his shoulders and so resting his head against her. She put her arms round him and heard him say very softly, 'Wonderful Wallis, why must you excel in everything you do? Your son is all I hoped he might be.'

Looking over the top of the fair head she was cradling, Wallis thought, 'I do hope that David isn't going to get too attached to that boy.' But she said nothing.

By the time godfather and godson reached England, young David had come well within reach of exhaustion point for Fluff Musgrave. His questions concerning the Duke were unending, so much so that Fluff was constrained, partly through curiosity and partly to divert his young charge, to ask the question, 'What did you think of the Duke of Windsor, David?'

They were alone in a first class railway carriage, so David was able to while away the tedium of rail travel by trying to do sufficiently successful pull-ups on the luggage rack to haul himself inside. At this question he dropped down onto the seat, settled himself by sticking his hands into his pockets and kicking his heels against the padding, replied, 'Super, absolutely super. I say, he loves *her* very much, doesn't he?'

Off guard Fluff murmured, 'This side idolatry', which gained him a quick, 'What was that, sir? I didn't quite hear.'

'Oh, nothing really – just a quotation,' Fluff answered hastily. 'Yes, he does love her very much.'

'Have you noticed,' David then enquired, heels drumming fast now, 'how he watches the door when *she* isn't there and then sort of lights up when *she* comes in?'

Fluff nodded speculating as to whether or not the 'she' indicated dislike but he ventured no further. As if in vaguely unspoken affirmation David dropped her as a subject and went prattling on about the Duke to whose charm he had clearly succumbed immediately. He asked, 'When can we go to Paris? You heard him, didn't you? And *she* confirmed it. Do they live there? What is their house like? Would it be all right to go at half term? Would it be better to wait until my first hols? I say, you will take me, won't you?'

Instead of replying to this omnibus questioning, Fluff protested mildly, 'Rein in, David, first things first. I'll take you one day; but with people like that, you know they say things easily and forget equally easily, so you mustn't build too much on a chance invitation extended casually over a cup of China tea.'

David's face remained serenely unclouded. 'He won't forget,' he said with shattering confidence. 'You'll see. He likes boys. He'll remind you, I bet. Now can you please tell me what he likes doing most?'

'Playing golf and gardening, I think. Why?' Fluff stared, completely flummoxed.

'Just that I shall have to start learning to play golf so that when I write next time, I can tell him I'm interested too.'

74

Distinctly ruffled, Fluff took himself down the corridor to the lavatory, informing his reflection as he washed his hands, 'Oh, what a tangled web we weave when first we practise to deceive,' and adding to himself, 'that blasted boy has fallen in love with his own father! Here's a pretty coil I must say.'

When he returned to the carriage, he found David entertaining the ticket collector whom he had persuaded to sit down. 'My godfather is in the Gents but he'll be back in a minute. He's got the tickets, you see.' The amused man had instinctively obeyed him, which seemed to be happening more and more according to Fluff's observations.

When they reached London, David insisted Fluff took him to Lillywhite's to choose some golf clubs. Fluff had promised Diana Kincale that he would take David to a rising young photographer called Norman Parkinson who, after Fluff had prowled round the studio, admitted to also being the painter of several portraits which were turned face to the walls. These so impressed Fluff that he persuaded Norman to paint the boy. The result was so brilliant that Fluff took the painting to a miniaturist friend and thereafter sent both the photographs and the painting to Diana; but he kept back the miniature as a Christmas present for his Duke.

Its arrival, with a set of the photographs and an envelope stuffed with snapshots taken around his adoptive parents' homestead, caused the Duke to go shopping again – this time for an album into which he personally inserted David's photographs, writing the captions in his own handwriting and keeping the album locked in the safe which held certain other items of his personal memorabilia.

Presently a matching cutting book, also with lock and key, joined the album. For this Fluff made copies of David's school reports, which the Duke thereafter read and re-read during the Duchess' absences for facials and fittings. If David had fallen victim to his father's famous appeal, this was entirely reciprocated and the

Duke followed the boy's progress as the tally of years began to multiply, finding strange comfort in a prowess which owed absolutely nothing to his submerged rank or inherited distinctions. He was like a miser who gloated in secrecy over his hoard.

David and his Jonathan – a Welsh boy called Richard Llewellyn – roamed the 65 acres of Cheam School grounds in constant companionship. A great part of their conversation centred upon plans for the reorganisation of both the Lords and the Commons. When David became Head of School, no one rejoiced more than Richard, and the pair of them made careful plans for succeeding in the classic game of snakes and ladders which lay ahead and which was a natural corollary to their upbringing. Down they would go, inevitably to the bottom of the ladder, when they first arrived at Gordonstoun. Neither feared this; in consequence, it was only a short time before the pair once more began to make their special marks.

At the end of their last term at Cheam, David's report was sent to Fluff who as usual forwarded a copy to the Duke, who in turn made a copy which he carried about with him, pasting the original into the cutting book. Each morning, when he had ascertained from the Duchess what her plans were for the day, he settled to his chosen newspapers. Having glanced at the London *Times*, the *Daily Telegraph* and the *Daily Express*, he laid these aside and gave himself a 'refresher' by unfolding David's report and re-reading it. Then he turned back dutifully to his skimming of *Figaro* and closer attention to the Wall Street prices in the *International Herald Tribune*. Presently he knew the report by heart, from the first 'David' to the signatures of the joint headmasters, Wheeler and Back, which the Duke thought, his eyes twinkling, sounded like a music hall knockabout comedy act which is how he memorised their names.

'David,' wrote the headmasters, 'will be a loss to both

staff and boys. He is a natural leader with great charm of manner, and if he continues to develop as he has done here, he will undoubtedly become a first class all-rounder. His record is eloquent of this: Head of School, Captain of Cricket and of Rugby and consistently top of his class. He has a quick brain and a remarkably retentive memory. One aspect of the boy's mind interests us particularly. Since his earliest years with us he has shown an unusual interest for one so young in the body politic. We shall follow his further education with interest.'

With carefully suppressed eagerness the Duke awaited the first report to come from Gordonstoun, where David and Richard ardently fostered their already precocious interest in British politics.

CHAPTER VII

*'It is the nature of extreme self-lovers,
as they will set a house on fire,
and it were but to roast their eggs.'*

– Francis Bacon

WITH THE BENEFIT of hindsight it is easy to pass judgments upon events and people; yet it is difficult for any but a sage to discern in the way of life chosen by these two lovers – whose place in history was assured by his great lineage – any act or gesture which was not wholly selfish.

For his part the Duke remained his own man throughout, one deeply in love and finding no possible flaw in the perfection of the woman for whom he turned his back upon his family, friends, duty, heritage, country and destiny.

Of inexhaustible interest to the student of human nature – at least for those who have credence for heredity – is from where did the characteristics and talents of their natural son come? Charisma – oh! yes, that was simple – for in straight transmission the charisma of the father was flaringly evident in the son. Yet 'they' – whoever they may be – do say that children inherit the suppressed tendencies of their parents. If 'they' are correct in this presumption, then both great prince and adventuring woman were boon material to any psychiatrist who might well become astigmatised in searching for the original suppressed tendencies in the parents.

By this time the Windsors were setting the pace in international café society from their Paris house – No 4 rue du Champs d'Entraînement. This establishment was so staffed that when the Duchess was asked how many servants were employed, she replied tartly, 'Too many,' and promptly changed the subject. This too was a rented house. When Harold Nicolson asked the Duchess why they did not buy a house of their own somewhere, she told him, 'One never knows what will happen and I do not wish to spend all my life in exile.' The reasons why she subsequently hauled down this flag must have been considerably influenced by the generosity of the French Government, who offered No 4 at the peppercorn rent of $50 a year for their lifetimes. This certainly left more spending money for their next venture. No 4 resembled a small château set in two acres of grounds, well shielded from the curious by a bank of rhododendron bushes, enclosed by high, spiked iron railings.

Inside this enclave the Duchess set about creating the setting she had always envisaged as being commensurate with her royal husband's status – and, indeed, her own. The financial aspect had more appeal for him as, over the years, he had become markedly parsimonious until he automatically used the most blatant subterfuges to evade paying for anything from restaurant bills to staff wages, which always remained well below the average. It seemed as if stripped of monarchial power, he had become paranoic about money and lived in ever growing dread of becoming short of funds; in reality, he was many times a millionaire with a capital which was increasing steadily despite his wife's fantastic extravagances. These were such that when her assistant decorator witnessed the unpacking of some treasures, he described his feelings as being similar to those of a Baghdad merchant watching the unloading of a caravan from Samarkand.

Even so the results were as much eloquent of the Duchess' consummate taste and talent as of wealth . . . from the crown which topped the tall black lamp post in the curving drive, and the arched sprays of white cyprepidium orchids in the ground floor lavatory, to the birds, flowers, butterflies and hearts, which themes were the *leitmotifs* for the colour-matching embroideries on her

79

fitted tablecloths, executed in the colours of the dinner services of Meissen, Copenhagen and Lowestoft.

She also ensured that the royal theme was heavily emphasised. The great marble staircase provided a natural receiving point where the Duke could stand with his consort beside him to receive guests in a manner befitting his royal blood. Whether he wore the kilt or tartan trews at night, she saw to it that his slippers bore an embroidered crown on each velvet toe.

She transformed No 4 rue du Champs d'Entraînement from the austere residence of General de Gaulle to a baby palace for an ex-king. Despite the massive assortment of valuables they already possessed, Wallis quartered the ateliers of Paris in her Cadillac searching for more splendid antiques, rare tapestries and fabulous Chinese *objets d'art*, picking up along the way trivia which amused her, like Meissen-handled silver and cutlery and the 18th century musical instruments and their stands for the minstrels' gallery above the dining room.

Edouard from Alexandre came every evening to dress Wallis' hair. She had almost daily manicures, pedicures and massages. She spent never less than an estimated £36,000 a year on her clothes, achieving the, to her, enviable status of being among the ten best dressed women in the world. She established irrevocably that she and the Duke did not take luncheon together. When questioned about this, she retorted crisply, 'I married David for better or worse but not for luncheons.' Instead her Cadillac took her to L'Espadron, the Ritz or a friend's house where she often stayed on to play bridge, gin rummy or canasta, eternally bewailing the conservatism of the Parisiennes in refusing to play crap.

Whether or not David Kincale's years at Gordonstoun would have proved so successful if he had not had such exceptional adoptive parents is debatable. Both Michael and Diana were adamant the boy should have the advantage of going to Gordonstoun, even though this inevitably meant long separations. They rented an old

Cornish manor house so that they could spend some holidays together.

Both David and Richard were quick to perceive that Dr Hahn's precepts, evolved from his original policies and carried through after his retirement by Mr Chew, represented a determined effort to counter what both these men saw as a perilous deterioration in self-discipline. The school was no longer concerned with class distinctions but was dedicated to combatting the decay which was becoming so evident in modern society. David came under the guidance of a man who was committed to instilling in his pupils a renaissance of character through self-discipline. Service to the community, to the standards inculcated by this remarkable man, was paramount and this fitted exactly with what was already forming in embryo in the pupil from Australia.

Being physically very strong, David enjoyed the austerities, the physical demands of log cutting and of such initiative tests as canoeing from Hopeman Beach to Findhorn Bay and back for a 24-mile stint in rough seas. It acted on him like champagne.

The curriculum was as much concerned with service to the community and character building as it was with academic matters. To David and Richard, already precociously absorbed by their beliefs in the true ethos of 'politics' as a community involvement concerned with the welfare of all men, this was the catalyst. For it, they cheerfully shared chores instead of 'fagging', taking turns at table waiting, early morning weeding, emptying dustbins, cleaning their own shoes and making their own beds.

The boys underwent training in javelin- and discus-throwing, running and jumping; they also undertook manual work such as repairing fences and bricklaying. There were games periods three afternoons a week, for which both boys elected rugger in the winter, cricket and tennis in the summer. In addition they devoted a compulsory one day a week to such services as coastguard patrols, mountain rescue and surf life-saving. David and Richard both managed to win their 'greys' in their first term, which meant achieving sufficient status to exchange blue shorts for grey ones. David reached the top of his form, with Richard close behind him.

Among their 'requested' reading matter David asked for a number of leading works on political history which he shared with Richard who devoured regular copies of *Hansard*. He developed a dislike for the newspaper quotes which, very skilfully shorn of their context, enabled the reporters to present whichever aspect of the actual facts was most compatible with the political slant of their particular newspaper. With the black and white opinions of the very young, Richard became imbued with a detestation of what he called 'policy' journalism. He found it as unacceptable as the deliberate distortion of facts, widely practised by journalists of the 'yellow press', to obtain 'news-worthy' stories.

At least once every term Fluff took both boys out. He gave them substantial meals, replenished their pocket money, listened intently to all they had to say and made notes about David's particular reference book require-ments. Every visit culminated in a quiet talk with their mentors before Fluff made the long journey back to London and his rooms in Albany. Here he wrote detailed reports for David's adoptive parents and the Duke of Windsor.

When the Duke received these, he locked them away carefully, only bringing them out after his solitary luncheons. Then entries would be made in 'David's Book' and the documents carefully re-concealed before the Duchess' return. He would report to her whenever David excelled at anything, saying, 'By the way, darling, Fluff tells me young David has achieved Senior Training Plan . . .' or, '. . . is White Stripe and Colour Bearer Can-didate . . .' As the years went by, he was able to tell her, 'Fluff says David is now a Captain . . .' and later still an

Assistant and finally Guardian, which signified the highest honour attainable, translatable to the uninitiated as the school's head boy.

Once a year, usually around Easter, when he knew that Michael and Diana Kincale would not be coming to England, the Duke obtained Wallis' permission to 'invite the boy over for a day or two'. He would explain, 'Fluff can bring him over and there's no reason why he should disturb you in any way.' Thus the dog was given his bone, Fluff took care of David's golf clubs and St Cloud saw much of them both.

When the two boys were nearly seventeen an invitation was extended to include Richard. While Fluff was talking with the Duke on the telephone from Gstaad where he was ski-ing, the Duke said abruptly, with slightly over-done casualness, 'By the way, why not send those boys over to us for a week-end during their Easter holidays? I've heard so much about that chap Llewellyn I'd rather like to have a look at him.' To Fluff this was tantamount, as usual, to a command. They went on to speak of other things.

The Duke was in a particularly felicitous mood. By the time the Royal Arms had been positioned above the great console table in the hall of No 4, Lorjou's painting of peonies given its final placement, the Garter banner swung over the balcony and the last royal portrait settled on the walls of the blue and silver salon, where these intermingled with Boudin, Utrillo and Foujita, the Duke had found the compromise-replacement for his adored Fort Belvedere. This was colloquially referred to by them both as 'the Mill' and called properly Le Moulin de la Tuilerie. It lay south-west of Neuilly, near to the village of Gif-sur-Yvette. The 17th century millhouse still had its millstream; the property covered 26 acres.

The Duke ran on enthusiastically about all this to Fluff whom he had not seen for some time. 'Wallis and I have our bedrooms at the Mill but the guest rooms are being converted from the outhouses with an adjacent connecting wing for some too, which we already call *La*

Célibataire. Wallis of course takes care of all that. She has given me a very large room of my own on the ground floor. It is 40 feet long and will be my study cum library cum trophy room when she has finished it.' The Duke was also in transports of delight outlining his plans for the garden. He explained how Mr Russell Page would supply his impeccable expertise and how he would work with his five gardeners headed by a man from Alsace, so that everything could be discussed in German, the language he so much preferred to any other.

The months of separation from Wallis when he was in Austria had accustomed him to lengthy telephone conversations and he never lost the habit with those with whom he felt completely at his ease.

On arrival at the Mill a footman took the two boys directly to one of the guest cottages. When they were alone Richard whispered, 'I never dreamed of sleeping under the same roof as a one-time monarch.'

'Well, you won't now!' David told him. 'She said the Mill was so tiny that some of the outbuildings had to be converted into guest cottages. This one was once some cattle stalls, His Nibs said. She's a dab hand at interior decoration. Hang on just a minute . . .'

David jumped up, ran into their elegant little sitting-room and reappeared with a parcel.

'What's that?' Richard's dark eyes rested curiously on it.

'Don't know,' David said. 'That's why I'm unwrapping it,' his fingers worked impatiently on the elegant dark brown ribbon. As a very fine set of silver chessmen were revealed, he exclaimed, 'Oh, Rikki, just look.'

'Where the devil did you get those?' Richard demanded.

'Actually the Duke did write to tell me he had bought them for me. I told you he was a super person.'

'Maybe,' said Richard glumly. 'I wish to God you could stop larking about for long enough to brief me a

84

bit. I've been asking and asking what special protocol I ought to know.'

David grinned, his eyes on his chessmen. 'He has absolutely no side. You'll be perfectly all right so long as you remember to give 'em both the "nick-nack" at all times on entering and leaving. You address him as "sir" and her as "madam" – pronounced "mam" with a short "a" – and refer to 'em both always as Royal Highness. He insists upon it and gets hugely huffed if anyone fails to comply. It's his major beef and as of course he *is* absolutely in the right *legally*, I think it's a rotten shame.'

The hall of the Millhouse was paved with old tombstones covered by a *Flora Danica* rug, worked in *gros point* and depicting the thirty-nine flowers of Denmark. Richard confined himself to one soft 'Gosh!' as they were ushered into the 'rustic' salon.

'I wish I could have shown you the Paris house,' David regretted. 'You know I think she must be the most prodigious spender since Cleopatra.'

'Pearls and all?' Richard asked absently, his eyes on the two stripped elm saplings used as columns set athwart the windows and topped by two Louis XV *cachepots* from which a blaze of flowers erupted.

David flung himself into a deep yellow armchair. 'Not she,' he replied. 'She's far too practical a lady to chuck away a fifty thousand pound pearl.' Lapsing into French which he now spoke with effortless fluency, '*Elle est toujours pratique, Son Altesse Royale!*'

'But she isn't,' Richard objected.

He was reminded sharply, 'The Duke wishes that she is; ergo, she *is* within his boundaries and don't you forget it, my fine friend. Anyway you know what I think.'

Unwisely Richard added, 'He made a bit of a cock up all round over her, don't you think?'

Instantly David's blue eyes darkened with anger. He snapped back, 'No – at least not from where he stands. Pascal had the last word for it in my view . . .' and he quoted, '*Le coeur a ses raisons que la raison ne connait point.*'

85

'Sorry,' Richard apologised for what he always thought of as encroaching on Tom Tiddler's ground. He was also puzzling over what, many years later, he would come to consider David's only flaw, which was how he saw his 'irrational obsession with a man who had failed completely'. He stared reflectively at the long flame and yellow curtains, creaked a bit as he fidgetted in the Chinese bamboo chair he sprawled on and quickly leaped to his feet as the Duke appeared suddenly on the long verandah outside those wide windows. As usual a pug dog occupied its inevitable position – one foot from the royal heels.

The Duke greeted them warmly, shaking hands and saying, 'Delighted to see you both.' Turning that smiling, blue-eyed gaze directly on Richard, he then said, 'One supposes you must be Llewellyn – welcome to the Mill.' Sinking into an armchair, he continued, 'David, I am thinking of making a nine-hole golf course here. You must both come round with me and inspect the terrain in the morning. I think I can even get hold of some more land if you think I need it.'

'Delighted, sir,' David smiled, 'and now may I formally present this shockin' fellow.'

The kilted Duke settled himself deeper into the big chair and observed somewhat fatuously, 'You've grown tremendously, you know. You can't be far off six foot now.'

'Just that,' David agreed.

The Duke nodded, a curious expression in his eyes. Then he said, a little hurriedly, 'Well, just give me a moment and then I'll take you to Her Royal Highness. She's in the kitchen.'

Richard blinked. David repeated incredulously, 'In the kitchen, sir?'

'Yes, she's seeing to the installation of some special gadget that chef doesn't want and she is determined he shall use. Then we'll all have tea in my study with some of those splendid crumpets you brought with you as I heard a moment ago.'

86

He turned to Richard who already had begun to experience the pull of his incredible charm. 'It's superb,' his host amplified. 'Her Royal Highness undertook to bring the garden into the room and she's done it. My carpet simulates green grass . . . well, you will see for yourselves presently, no need for me to ramble on.' He jumped up abruptly, prey to his old restlessness, 'Come on through, I'll lead the way.'

All his life David Kincale would remember the little scene which followed. The Duke led them across the hall again, chatting companionably, until he reached the green baize door separating the servants' quarters from the rest of the house. Here he paused and put one hand on the baize. As he did so, he glanced down at Mr Disraeli, the pug dog, who was snuffling himself forward preparatory to making a dart into the kitchen as soon as the door opened sufficiently. Both boys heard very clearly the voice of Queen Victoria's great-grandson, once King of England and all her Dominions, saying in a voice of gentle reproof to a small pug dog, 'Mr Disraeli, *we* think you should not go into the kitchen!'

The Duchess was still engaged in conversation with her chef. Both boys duly made nice tidy 'nick-nacks' to her and thereafter shook hands with the chef, Monsieur Lucien Massy. The Duke had left them before the Duchess steered her visitors towards the baize door again.

Once this had closed behind them, she said complainingly, 'Do you know I spend *hours* in kitchen shops in America looking for clever gadgets which that wretch never deigns to use? Even that damned refrigerator is always empty and dripping. Whenever I see this, I have it turned up again of course; but it makes little difference. You saw for yourselves that huge freezer has nothing in it except for one poor little *cooked* grouse on a bread and butter plate. It's scandalous!'

Richard remained silent, unsure how to respond; but David risked reproof by telling her very gravely, 'But he simply adores working for you, madam. He even told me how good it is to work for someone to whom only perfection is acceptable.' In this David was manifesting his diplomatic talent, inherent in his partially royal blood, for what chef had murmured somewhat ruefully was, 'Son Altesse Royale est rudement exigeante,' which in more or less literal translation is, 'Her Royal Highness is bloody fussy,' accompanying this confidence with a huge Gallic shrug.

'Maybe,' she conceded, only partially mollified, 'but would you believe that stubby little Frenchman still criticises *me*! I happen to know he gets downright furious over my doing my favourite entertaining here nowadays – just because the facilities for him are inferior to those he enjoys in Paris!'

David managed to say, with a very serious countenance, 'Even so, madam, he is well aware of the honour you do him and, I am confident, is immensely appreciative.' This went down quite well although he was uncomfortably aware of the feet of Annanais sounding in his ears.

Over their tea and crumpets the Duchess talked most entertainingly. The Duke was content to sit back, watching her. The scarlet drum table had been drawn up for the tea equipage close to the chimney piece at one end of the big room. Logs crackled and burned companionably in the hearth. The Duchess spoke of her decor, waving an explanatory hand towards the long run of French doors which led onto the terrace, 'I promised I would bring the garden into the room so that the two would merge. That's why I based everything on this simulated green grass carpet.'

'It's brilliant!' exclaimed Richard, somewhat thickly as his mouth was full of crumpet. He apologised, crimsoning, but they only laughed.

Then the Duke said, 'You just wait until you see the transformation of the outside dining room.' He looked across at the Duchess adoringly. 'You have made both very special for me, darling . . .'

'Now, David, don't bore these boys with your eulogies,' she said, rising suddenly. 'I have to go. That nice Edouard comes all the way out here to do my hair so the least I can do is be ready for him.' She turned to go, the other two pugs, Davy Crockett and Trooper, at her heels, while Mr Disraeli settled again to slumber across the Duke's left foot.

'Come on, I'll be your guide,' the Duke eased his foot away and stood tamping down his pipe. Seeing the boys' eyes on his portrait, he told them, 'That picture is of me on Forest Witch; now that was a splendid mare.' He reminisced awhile before embarking on his conducted tour . . . the maps, the souvenirs, the various busts of himself on plinths, the loyal addresses and the horses' heads which completely surrounded the second mantel-shelf at the opposite end of the room. He showed them his fantastic collection of buttons containing an example of every one worn by the British army during the First World War. He took down some of his trophies from pig-sticking and steeplechasing contests, and handed them a curving Gurkha *kukri*, saying, 'Test that blade – it's razor sharp. It could cleave a man's head from his shoulders in one slash!'

When he reached his books, he dried up, whereas the two boys were rivetted. 'You two carry on and take out anything you like,' he told them and went back to his own special chair where he promptly fell asleep. David and Richard wandered on, examining the mugs struck for his coronation, and came to an abrupt stop beside a delicately carved Chippendale table. The top was covered with framed photographs of members of the royal family. Richard pointed to a small plaque and the boys bent down to read the words: *On this table King Edward VIII signed the instrument of abdication at 10.30 am December 11, 1936.*

David whispered, 'What a shattering reminder of a world well lost for love.' His eyes were sad as he looked across the room to the other fair head. The signatory just slept on, snoring almost imperceptibly.

Then Richard stood back, looked up and began

examining the Pipe Banners of the Grenadier Guards which hung from the walls above them. The Duke was woken by the rattle of his seven o'clock drinks tray heralding the whisky he always drank before going up to dress.

Walking back over the lamplit cobbles to their 'cottage', Richard ruffled his dark hair abstractedly. 'I dunno, but you and he seem to have struck up an extraordinary friendship; you seem to understand each other as if you'd been together all your lives.'

David replied dismissively, 'He's lonely, you know, that's all except he likes young 'uns. Did I ever tell you that he gave me a magnificent collection of American soldiers when I was eight? Uncle Fluff had taken me to tea with them. They were staying in New York at the time. We were on our way to England. His Nibs played with those soldiers on the floor just like any ordinary chap. We used a box for a fort, I remember, because he hadn't thought of buying one; but it came later. He actually remembered and, so I learned, he jolly well went out and bought it himself and had it sent to Uncle Fluff for me. Later he sent me English soldiers and French ones – a super collection. They just kept on coming at Christmas and my birthday. One day my sons will play with them. I know that even now.'

'You know some odd things about the future for a chap of your age, don't you?' Richard mused, his mind half on this and half on the extraordinary fact that he was about to dine with a one-time King of England. 'Your career, for instance.'

David gave him a curious look as they pushed open the door of the former cattle shed. 'I know where I'm going,' he agreed equably, 'but then so do you, so what are you drivelling on about? You're for political journalism and I'm for straight politics.'

'Ha! Those last two words make somewhat strange bedfellows,' retorted Richard.

'Maybe they do, but mine will be straight, I'll swear.

They may turn out to follow a circuitous route though, because there is no way I can see at present of achieving my objective without being a bit devious. Sometimes it makes me feel sick to think of it, but even so I *know* it's bound to happen.'

They found their dress clothes had been laid out with exquisite precision on their beds. They soon created a fair measure of chaos elsewhere. Once bathed and wrapped in the capacious towelling dressing gowns which Richard noticed from the labels had come from the Maison Blanche in Paris, they took up from where they had left off.

'Where will you start?' Richard asked.

'I don't know yet. I intend to ask His Nibs if I get the chance and then I'm going to tackle Uncle Fluff. *He* knows everyone. Anyway there's aeons of time yet; we've got to clear Gordonstoun and take Oxford in our stride first. Rikki, for God's sake, come here and let me tie that tie for you. It looks as if it had been chewed by one of those "tarnation" pugs!'

Gradually the dress clothes were assumed. Looking absurdly young, they inspected each other solemnly and eventually strolled back across the darkening gardens in companionable silence. The only sounds were the cheeping of drowsy, nesting birds and the faint drone of a small aircraft. As they neared the porch, a young moon rose shyly above the tree-tops like a debutante venturing upon some great scene and as diffident about it as they were themselves.

'A hell of an experience, isn't it?' Richard murmured doubtfully. 'I only hope I can remember it in detail afterwards.'

'I know you'll be more in your element sailing off Saltsjøbaden – three men in a boat is more in your line altogether – just hang on for a bit. We'll divert a bit of stream tomorrow morning with His Nibs, make suitable noises at their midday drinks party and go through the motions just until tomorrow night – with a couple of splendid meals to enjoy. Then Uncle Fluff will be here and we can leave.'

91

'Yes,' agreed Richard lamely, feeling that the ground had been cut off from under him and equally convinced that David had retired into his shell and would not be drawn further in the matter of the Windsors.

On their return to the cottage David flung himself down on his bed, laced his hands behind his head and let the impressions of the evening flow over him.

'Couple of smashing girls *Son Altesse Royale* got for us, don't you think?' he mused, staring reflectively at the painted ceiling.

'Very nice, very expensive, very sophisticated. Do you know mine was only fifteen?'

'Did you ask her?'

'No, she volunteered in a roundabout way. Said she didn't come out for another three years and later admitted that would be when she was eighteen.'

'Dishy, both of them,' David said appreciatively. 'I wonder what they'd be like in the Scottish heather.'

'On their backs or foot-slogging after grouse?'

'The latter, you dirty minded little beggar.'

That brought an unrepentant grin but it soon faded as Richard faced his Tertium Quid squarely. 'How long are we going to stay here?' he asked bluntly.

David answered his question with another. 'You don't like any part of it, do you?'

Richard chose to hedge. 'That's rot. It's been a most fascinating experience, one I shall never forget. Don't get it all out of proportion. I'm not out to criticise your idol. He's a basically likeable fellow quite apart from the aura which surrounds him – inevitably; but frankly I must confess I don't take to madam.'

He had never picked his words more carefully. David was his very special friend. Whether or not this contained a touch of schoolboy hero worship was a moot point. If so, he was unaware of it; but some atavistic instinct at work in his Welsh blood made him feel as he might on the hunting field, when from the van the ominous cry ''ware wire' floats back. Here they were in this wealthy, idle, witty but totally trivial set-up – 'trap' was the word he privately used – and it gave him little warning stabs of fear. He understood and appreciated the innate gentleness in the Duke which warmed him instinctively towards small animals and children; but this he felt was something else and knew he dare not probe too deeply, particularly as he disliked and despised almost everything the Duchess represented.

All this ran with the celerity of a bush fire through his mind. Eventually, he risked saying, 'Look here, it's just that I don't think either of us are cut out for sharing in their pattern; and I think *she* wants to draw you in. I caught her looking at you once or twice with a most curious expression. It may be nothing. So long as visiting them is just a bit of dabbling in the high life, why not? But do me a favour and include me out; it's simply not my scene.'

'Point taken and understood,' David conceded, evincing astonishing mildness. He was taking off his dressing-gown before climbing into bed. 'You must admit even so that you've never in your life eaten such a superb dinner nor drunk more marvellous wines. Nor, I think, are you ever likely to cap the experience at any other table,' but he spoke to himself for Richard was already sleep.

While Richard slept, David sat propped up against the down pillows, hands linked behind his head, his mind still active with the evening's events. Almost unconsciously he was comparing these to a dinner party given by his adopted mother the year before for the Prime Minister of Australia, Mr Robert Menzies. They were thirty too, and Diana Kincale was the only Englishwoman present, if, as David qualified, Nanny was excluded. She had kept an observant eye on the proceedings from a doorway, with a 'Psst!' here and a peremptory waggling finger there as the courses came and went.

As if with split vision this other dinner party superimposed on the dining room in which he had sat a few hours ago, so that he saw again the gleaming mahogany of his adoptive parents' D-ended Sheraton table, reflectting the candles in the Georgian candelabra. He could also re-envisage the water splashing into the supporting central bowl of ceramic birds with plumes of slender candles rising from their backs in the 'millionaire-rustic' setting in which he had dined that night.

Diana Kincale had worn her grandmother's pearls and a dress of finely pleated dark blue chiffon, both of which served to enhance the fairness of her throat and shoulders – her only concession to vanity. There were family portraits on the walls, her *gros point* on the seating of the mahogany-framed chairs, the sparkle of plain polished wine glasses and the winding trail of her precious red camellias.

The Duchess, David knew, had taken out her compact and powdered the walls of her 'rustic' dining room with her own face powder, so that when she sat, in the brilliant hand-painted Chinese silk which Balenciaga had moulded to her figure, the pastel background flattered her complexion. While on one wrist Diana Kincale had worn a four-strand pearl bracelet, the Duchess wore diamonds – hearts on one wrist, symbolic as she had explained to the boys of her husband's undying love, tiny crosses on the other, signifying the many she had been forced to bear . . .

The table talk on the Kincales' station was on myxamatosis, and the recurring invasion of rabbits, which one member of the cabinet had reminded them had been summed up by a hand as 'God rot the homesick Pommie who shipped the first rabbits here from England' . . . all said with ease of long friendship and so taken by the woman David called 'Mum'. They had talked too of the ten-year drought and their providential recovery, and of wool, notably Michael Kincale's fabulous Merino sheep whose long silky fibres were of peak quality and taken from the stock grazed on the plains of Queensland and New South Wales. The talk had finally turned to politics and David had learned much from what passed between them.

During the glittering evening just over David recalled the chatter carried on in French with smatterings of English and German from the Duke, whom the Duchess had pulled up short by reminding him, 'Some of our guests cannot understand you, darling'. They spoke of balls past and pending, of first nights in Paris, of the races at Auteuil and Longchamps, of the latest gossip concerning Bettina and the Aly Khan and, because she was not present, much time was frittered in debate about Elsa Maxwell's eccentricities. While David was perfectly able to understand the French spoken, some of the 'in' jokes were completely incomprehensible.

By the time he reached across and flicked off the light and stretched his long legs under the silk sheets, David decided sleepily, 'Rikki *does* have a point. When we finish at Gordonstoun he must come with me to Queensland. He'll find that so very much more to his taste.'

The Duchess too had been thinking about Richard while her yawning maid undressed her and put her to bed. She was perfectly aware as she lay waiting for the Duke to join her, that she must seek the opportunity of winning over 'that rather stiff young man', whom she had already learned was closer than anyone else to her son, save perhaps for his adoptive parents. She also knew, but preferred to keep the knowledge to herself, that the Duke already possessed a large cutting book in which he painstakingly filed all their son's school reports and the reams of photographs sent to him regularly by Fluff.

She acknowledged it was inevitable that both boys would talk of this visit and all it involved, especially to a very ordinary young man of no particular distinction, which was how she saw Richard. She determined that he would take with him not only the conviction that the one-time King of England still counted his world well lost for love but also that he too found her totally and devastatingly charming.

It was instinctive for her to recognise that at the moment there was a definite antagonism in Richard towards her; but she also knew that there is nothing so flattering to a young man as a manifest interest in his opinions and ambitions. So she planned to draw him out the next morning with consummate skill, first lightening the atmosphere between them with a little shared laughter until she perceived obvious signs of relaxation. She would then encourage him to talk about how he and David had first met, working with infinite caution towards Richard's own ambitions. When she had led him to the point of talking about his career, she would evince a tremendous interest. This always worked. Hadn't her own David declared, 'Wallis is the only woman who has ever shown any interest in my work.' Finally she too slept.

To what extent his Celtic blood was working on his mind, Richard never paused to consider, but he woke in the night and found himself again pursuing the thought he had been prudent enough to keep to himself when he and David talked. There was something about the Duchess which affected him so powerfully that he knew he would not be able to dismiss her, as he most ardently wished to do, until he had solved what caused him such disquiet. He lay there, trying – inside the limitations of his own inexperience – to resolve what was destined to become a puzzle upon which the world would speculate endlessly in the years ahead.

Why had she toppled such a monarchy to obtain possession of this rather sad and simple man? He had an aura of loneliness about him which seemed to this schoolboy to reveal itself in his anxious, seeking eyes which watched any door through which she passed, leaving him even momentarily alone and becoming instantly lost without the reassurance of her presence.

Even to this virgin schoolboy, a moment at dinner when she had turned the brilliance of those great blue eyes upon him gave him an intuitive recognition of her sexuality. Something disturbing and inexplicable had happened to him. It was as if she had slid experienced fingers across his loins. Grounds enough for a monarchial carry-on – his mind leapt to Lily Langtry and King Edward VII – but for jettisoning an Empire? Anyway Lily Langtry was a beauty; this one only had chic and charm and even her great wit had a waspishness which by rights should have been offputting to the ex-King. Richard decided the Duchess had no depth and pondered over the solution being that both were equally trivial.

With the intolerance of youth he thought this through until, not unnaturally confused by the whole experience, he concluded that although the ex-King of England was still obsessively in love after nearly twenty years of marriage, this was not love as he, Richard, envisaged it. Thus he arrived at some sort of solution: that fundamentally they both craved an international playground in which they could occupy themselves with their expensive toys if only to avoid thinking. It seemed curiously inadequate.

He decided, sleepily now, that *Son Altesse Royale*, as everyone called *her* to please *him*, was not in love. Otherwise how could she have said, 'My days are my own, my nights belong to David,' and gone off around noon to luncheons, poker games and beauty treatments. It left the Duke so lonely! During dinner Richard had learned that he liked to play golf between 12 and 2.30 – inside the sacred French luncheon hours – but found it difficult even among his close friends to find partners. He had little interest in luncheon himself, preferring, at the 19th hole, to produce his own little tea caddy and brew up his own tea. 'A fine ploy for a one-time King Emperor,' thought Richard as he slipped back into sleep.

In the morning David and Richard strolled over to the Mill and were immediately led to the breakfast room. The Duke was hovering over the chafing dishes, plate in hand, very much the country squire and wearing the kilt. Richard had become accustomed to what David called the 'nick-nack' and bent his dark head with as much ease as if he had been doing it for years. He became even more at his ease when he learned that the Duchess could not be expected to make her appearance until just before the arrival of her midday guests.

Eventually, the trio moved from the breakfast table across the grass carpet in the Duke's study and out into the garden through the French windows. The perils of sandpits and bunkers, the hazards of driving down a fairway past a spinney of trees were avidly discussed as they walked up over the rising ground to the planned concealed green. The Duke kept the boys absorbed in the details of the proposed 9-hole golf course for over an hour. Then he took them back to look at his partially completed rockery where to his surprise and delight the Duchess joined them.

She too wore the kilt and looked so exquisitely fresh and trim that Richard found himself admiring her albeit rather reluctantly. 'David,' she said gaily, 'I'm going to borrow your friend. It's high time we got to know each other better; but to begin with, Richard, I want to show you our *al fresco* garden dining-room which is just beginning to take shape.' As she moved off – Richard perforce following – she said over her shoulder, 'David, don't let His Royal Highness start damming little streams this morning or you'll be all muddy when our guests arrive.'

The Duke's eyes followed her as usual until her slight figure was out of sight and then much as had happened at the Fort twenty years before, he began deploying his son for shifting boulders to dam the little stream and form a pool, ordering and splashing about with the total absorption more usual in two small boys playing together. 'Good Lord!' exclaimed the Duke, straightening up and glancing at his wristwatch, 'It's almost twelve o'clock! Come on, David, we'll have to go and wash.' Still looking like schoolboys, they trotted towards the house together.

Driving back to Paris in Fluff's long, low Lagonda, David asked him if he would compile a list for him of the best biographies about the Duke of Windsor. 'It's the earlier parts of him I want to try to understand,' he told his god-father. 'You see neither Rikki nor I were born when he was young.'

They had barely left the village when he framed this request, yet as if his words had caused it, Fluff braked and turned off the road at a plain little building with a small parking area, where he berthed the car.

'Chez Ménessier,' he explained. 'I thought you might prefer somewhere very simple after all that. Actually this is one of their favourites. When the Duchess told someone I know that this and two Paris bistros were prime simple places for good food, the man was astonished. "But they're only bistros!" he exclaimed. "While I," she retorted, "am not at all a three star Duchess."'

On this line he pushed the door open and went into a plain room with a large iron stove at which an old man toasted his carpet-slippered feet. He started up when he saw them, greeted Fluff like an old friend and led them to a small corner table, to await their *Omelette du Curé*, a speciality of old M Ménessier, with which Fluff proposed they begin their dinner. He then reverted to the subject of the ex-King's biographies.

'No one,' he said, 'worked harder at his job than the Duke did from the time he was installed as Prince of Wales at Caernarvon Castle in 1911. He was a thorn in his seniors' sides every moment he was in France during the First World War. He actually managed to get up to the front line once to the consternation of all the top brass. He became the finest ambassador Britain ever had, spreading friendship and enhancing the Crown wherever he went and he went, as you shall read, to every corner of the British Empire. He was literally an idol. Women were crazy over him for he was extremely good looking in the boyish way that makes women feel protective as well as romantic.

'He had immense capacities for compassion too. Even

at the last when he was already besotted with Wallis Simpson, he flatly refused to cancel the arrangements to visit the worst areas of unemployment among the Welsh miners. He travelled down by train. He saw for himself their dire plight and there and then he pledged them that, *"Something must be done."* When he came back to London he made a personal, pretty healthy donation to the Miners' Fund. After that the tide of events swept over him and he was engulfed. Speaking personally I think that by this time he was a tired man and also a desperately lonely one. You know he said that the Duchess was the only woman who had ever shown any interest in his work.'

David listened, but not with his whole attention. The phrase of that pledge impacted upon him powerfully and he repeated it, as the old chef proprietor toddled in with his delicate creation of eggs, truffles, cream and salmon trout and opened a bottle of Wehlener Zeltinger Sonnenuhr 1949, saying under his breath, '"*Something must be done.*" Oh, Lord! what a waste it has all been!'

CHAPTER VIII

'Your children are not your children . . .
For their souls dwell in the house of tomorrow
Which you cannot visit, even in your dreams.'

– Kahlil Gibran, *The Prophet*

THE WORDS 'DAVE'S BACK' brought smiles to every face on the Kincales' vast homestead on the plains of Upper Queensland. News of his arrival with Richard the previous night had raced with the celerity of a bush fire throughout the station – from the unmarried hands' quarters and the married ones' homes to the great hangar where Michael Kincale's team, mostly English with a few Argentinians, sweated over the new aircraft in which the Kincales intended to fly round the world. People had come running out to greet them.

The two eighteen-year-olds, free from the rigours of education for some months, flew out from England after a brief stay with Fluff in London. They travelled BOAC in a Lockheed Constellation. Having seen the aircraft was full on take-off, Richard had to find out how many passengers were on board. When the 'No Smoking' light went off, he stood up and was asked what on earth he was doing by a stewardess. 'Counting,' he broke off to say, to which she replied sharply, 'We are seventy-eight excluding the crew, now please take your seat, sir.' Somewhat dampened, Richard complied.

When they touched down at the vast new airport in Rome which replaced the bombed-out old one, they used their waiting time to shop for absurdly cheap cameras. Then Richard spotted Johann Maria Farina cologne on the scent counter so bought a huge bottle, confiding in David, 'My Mum always uses it – it's my

101

most vivid nursery pong! Extraordinary, isn't it, the durability of trivial things in one's mind.'

Thereafter they re-boarded the plane and managed to sleep most of the way to Beirut. David scribbled in his ever-present diary, 'Resortish? Why should I feel as if I were walking on rotten corpses?' but found no answering response to enter later. Bombay came next which fascinated them, from the Gateway to India where they found a Sikh taxi driver whose English was excellent if a trifle eccentric. This worthy showed them the sights, adding, or so it seemed to his passengers, 'built by Sir Hedward Lutyens,' after declaiming the functions of every public building. Here David spent lavishly on saris for his mother and silk scarves for himself, after which they returned once more to eat and sleep via Colombo to Singapore. Here they made an overnight stay and found time for yet another shopping spree.

'Two to go,' David sighed, settling his long legs once again. 'I feel I've been on this aircraft all my life. Like that play we did, *Outward Bound* – do you remember?'

Richard did not because he was busy accepting yet another glass of champagne and announcing, 'If we go much further we shall end up alcoholics.'

They slept right through the Darwin stop and awoke again to find the aircraft taxi-ing along the runway at Sydney. 'Last haul coming up,' Richard grunted, reaching for his hand baggage. 'It's all change, isn't it?'

'You transfer now, sir,' the officiating stewardess confirmed, 'to the Trans Australian line for Brisbane which I understand is your final destination. And yes, your flight time with us has been sixty hours.'

They spent the rest of their journey peering out of the portholes of their forty-five seater Viscount because they could not think of anything else to do to cure their fidgets; but after what seemed an eternity Diana Kincale met them in Brisbane. Then, the huge station wagon was tightly packed not only with the boys' luggage but also the crated Christmas supplies which they had collected from freight, and finally, with the inevitable dust trail thrown up in their wake, they sped towards the homestead.

When David and Richard came down the verandah steps the following morning onto the green English lawn which was maintained at such fearful expense for the pleasure of Diana Kincale, they were both wearing the broad-brimmed hats affected by the hands. The sleeves of their open-necked white silk shirts were rolled up high exposing their arms to the already powerful sun.

Now, as Richard commented, 'stuffed, slept and stuffed again', they were off for the day together, intending to collect a couple of mares from the stables and ride off into the bush. For David this was 'Brideshead revisited'; for Richard it was to become an unending fascination of new sights and even smells. Later he inventoried them as combining the dry smell of grasses, sheep, kangaroo, emus, galahas and goannas.

As the two boys crossed the rose garden and struck out along the dust road towards the stables, Diana and Michael Kincale came out onto the verandah and leaning against the rail, watched them vanish between the fringing wattle and gum trees. Time had dealt lightly with them both. Aided by their way of life and the climate, neither seemed to have aged at all, save for the network of fine lines etched into the corners of their eyes by looking into the blazing sun when in flight or on horseback.

Wearing an expression of almost fatuous content, Diana murmured, 'Fluff did us proud, Michael, didn't he?'

'Too right,' he slipped an arm around her slender waist. 'He's a fine fellow. I like his buddy too. And they've both done very well at Gordonstoun, though I must confess I would have liked our boy to have done a turn at Geelong Grammar . . .'

'Only four more years,' she reminded him gently, bypassing this controversial observation, 'then he'll be home for good and we shall have fulfilled our promises to Fluff. In the meantime we have him here for Christmas. I thought we would have the Christmas tree by the swimming pool. We could set up a big table on the edge of the pool, in front of the barbecue area, so that we can keep all our hot dishes hot and as it's all illuminated now, you will have no trouble with the carving.'

Michael took her hand and together they went round the verandah to the steps which led to the large pool complex. Here luxury was evident . . . in the cabanas, the gaily-covered sun umbrellas, the padded *chaises longues* set on the pool edge, the giant canvas pillows and inflated palliasses on which they floated while pushing drinks trays across the blue water to each other. There was even a giant ball for their own exclusive game of push ball with its complicated rules.

Over all this hovered Billy-Boy, a crippled aboriginal youngster, with one leg much shorter than the other, which had dragged one shoulder down and given him a shambling crab-like gait. After greeting the boy, Michael sent him scurrying for a bottle of cold beer and two cokes before pulling a *chaise longue* towards his wife.

'No candles though,' Michael said inconsequentially.

Diana understood. 'Oh, yes,' she said triumphantly. 'I've got some of those large heat-resistant glass vases which have wide tops and sockets inside for tall candles. Then even if a breeze does get up while we're dining, the glass keeps the little flames burning steadily. The crackers and the food hampers have come from Fortnum's. The Army and Navy have sent us some marvellous new fairy lights. That super Mr Joy is Managing Director there now and he's done miracles with the merchandise. If it's new and exciting the Stores have it these days and for my money long may it last.'

Billy-Boy came scrambling back with the beer and cokes. Michael asked him if he had seen David yet and the aborigine nodded. 'Yessir, he come round with his cobber Rick. Ain't he grown something, eh?'

'Too right,' agreed Michael. 'And what do you think of his cobber?'

'Nice. Oh, thank you, sir,' Billy-Boy accepted the coke, drank and then volunteered shyly, 'the hands like him too. They call him Taffy.'

Michael laughed, 'Better than Pommy, eh?' He opened his throat and the beer went down, so Billy-Boy produced a replacement from behind his twisted back, saying, 'Ned told me it's silly taking one beer to the Bossman so I brought three.'

The boy moved off, laying the opener down on the table next to them, and resumed his gathering of fallen gum twigs into the improvised barrow – an oil keg over a stretcher affixed to two large wheels.

'Remind me to buy you a wheelbarrow of your own next time I'm in Brisbane,' Michael called after him. Then, turning to Diana, he asked seriously, 'What do you make of David's running mate now?'

She reflected a moment. 'How will this do? Of course first and foremost he's David's man, loyal to a fault but critical too. If David for instance went in for politics and backslid into any political chicanery, Richard would rend him tooth and nail both in newspapers and out of them. I think he's typical of the finest kind of Welshman: sturdy, clear-minded and omnivorous for knowledge. He should develop into a first-rate reporter. Not knowing his style I cannot comment on his potential as a writer; but I have a hunch he could pen a pretty speech if called upon. For that we must wait and see. I'd like to hear him sing too. It wouldn't surprise me one bit if we find he has a fine baritone. We must probe gently, my love.'

Michael frowned, sat bolt upright and clasped her hand. 'I think our son is turning into a political animal, don't you?' There was some anxiety in his voice.

She shook her fair head. 'The thought never crossed my mind, really, but perhaps he will be PM one day. I just think they make a rather special pair.'

'Fair dinkum,' relief made Michael incautious.

She rounded on him. 'Since when have you had recourse to Aussie slang?' she simulated anger.

105

'Sorry, darling, mustn't put my Pommy sheila off with outback expressions!' he ducked as she launched a mock blow at his head. 'But one does wonder sometimes, after such an education as he has had so far, back home in the Old Country, if all this will ever satisfy him,' Michael made a dejected movement intended to indicate his quarter of a million acres and all that was thereon. He was remembering one of David's early prep school reports: 'David shows a precocious interest in the political scene. He has a startlingly brilliant brain. Have you any intention he should pursue this bent? It would assist us to know.'

After receiving this, Michael Kincale had written back to the headmaster, saying most emphatically no such intention was theirs and explaining that one day David would inherit their considerable estate. Characteristically, he added, 'My wife and I are however determined his educative canvas should be as wide as possible. Please give him his head in whatever knowledge he seeks.'

David also managed to keep abreast of the Duke of Windsor's activities. Via the French papers he was able, without asking anyone questions which might lead to some form of interrogation, to add to his knowledge of his illustrious friend.

Since the war and their return to Paris, even during the acquisition and furnishing of the Mill and the Bois mansion, the Windsors' itinerary followed an almost unvarying pattern. In the spring they went by sea to New York because the Duchess was terrified of flying. They stayed in their suite at the Waldorf Towers where the Duke was constantly going AWOL to the suite of his great crony, Cole Porter. The two men walked their dogs together, gave parties for each other and had the same friends. Thus Noel Coward, Bea Lillie, Mary-Lee and her husband Douglas Fairbanks Jr and Elsa Maxwell were regular companions in the endless round of parties.

The Windsors moved on to luxuriate on the sands at

Palm Beach and came back to Europe for the summer, spending some time at Biarritz, then Venice and more recently in Marbella where the Duchess was toying with the idea of a third house.

Curious studies for a schoolboy; but ones which David pursued with the same singleness of purpose that he brought to everything he did. His sole confidant was Richard who listened with downturned mouth and manifest disapproval. David merely responded with the dismissive phrase, 'Well, I like them and they don't do *me* any harm.'

In the long gaps between his visits, David maintained a steady correspondence with the Duke. Fluff fulfilled his undertakings by sending him all cuttings which referred to his son. These the Duke carefully pasted into 'David's Book' with his school reports.

However, there were few thoughts concerning the Windsors in their son's mind as he rode out with Richard on a protracted tour of the station's buildings and their occupants. Everywhere David introduced Richard as his particular 'cobber' and ending up at the midday dinner hour at the cook-house, asked permission to join the hands for their meal. Richard was initiated into the dubious pleasures of hot roast meat, 'packet' gravy, wodges of potato and mounds of cabbage, followed by stodgy puddings washed down with great mugs of black, sweet tea.

Here the Welshman discovered just how deeply these people admired and liked the Kincales, and how highly they were thought of by this self-contained community. It was here too that he learned how the Christmas Barbecue was the highlight of their working year, when a whole ox was roasted in the traditional 'pit' and gifts were distributed to every man, boy and sheila on the station. His accolade was bestowed when an enormous bearded hand, whose bright black eyes peered through a positive jungle of black wiry hair, leaned across and said to him, 'Hi, Taffy, you comin' to the hop at Church Hall tonight?'

107

Forthright Richard replied with a grin, 'I haven't been asked.'

'Well, you're asked now,' said the hirsute one, 'ain't he, boys?' to which the table responded, 'Too right. Come along with Dave, he'll be there.' Then to David, 'And, my son, we'll be wanting you to hand out the presents same as always.' He reverted to Richard, 'First time Dave here did present-giving at our Christmas hop he was not much above four and very sleepy. So we give him a sip of ale which woke him up startling and he had a hiccup for everyone after that. Mrs Kincale come as near to bein' cross as ever we've seen her but it come out all right in the end, same as always.'

In the afternoon they went off again in companionable silence ending up, as David explained he had done since childhood, down by the creek where he had made dams and caught fish in a jellybag tied to a stick. They hitched their horses, slid down and sat on the bank, under the shade of an ancient willow. Presently a curious wallaby crept to the water's edge on the further bank where the creature examined them with great dark eyes and no vestige of fear. He then scooped up water for himself and tiring of their company, lolloped off into the undergrowth.

They leaned against the old willow and let the faint breeze ruffle their damp hair. They sat for some time without speaking, digesting yet another shared encounter – David with the adoptive parents whom he loved so deeply and for whom he had an equally profound respect; Richard with his first impressions of this vast continent to which they had flown from England.

'It's so bloody "gynormous",' Richard said suddenly. 'It makes me dizzy to think that if I shin up this willow and look out over the land in any direction, it's all to be yours one day. Your people must be fantastically rich.'

David nodded. 'I've grown accustomed to that. You see it's another kind of riches ... as far removed from the – er – Duke and Duchess as it is possible to be. It's muted wealth, not dazzling, flamboyant wealth. It spells sound folk about us, not chattering, gossiping ones, although some of them may seem brash to you at first. There are some flash spenders about of course, particularly the racing crowd, the horse-breeding wallahs and the absentee landlords who are always ill at ease with my parents. Of course the emancipated ones *have* got a chip on their shoulders. The English in particular give them an inferiority complex and this tends to make them scorn what they envy, but this is only a defensive measure. The trouble is while I understand 'em and respect 'em in many ways, Gordonstoun and Oxford next don't make me feel I could spend my life satisfactorily with them. Not that I'm worried on that score. It's Mum and Pop that worry me. Hurting them seems a most horrendous thing to do after what they've been to me.'

Richard bypassed all this with his customary forth-rightness. 'But you don't intend coming back to live and make the pattern of this huge ranch your life's career,' he pressed.

David ran an uneasy hand over his hair. 'I don't think I could,' he confessed. 'I suppose it's two things warring. My own blood links . . . well, you know as much as I do about *that* because being adopted I am groping in the dark,' he paused, then came back qualifying what he had just said, 'at least I'm groping in the half dark because I don't mind telling *you* I think I know who I am.'

Richard gave a start, stared at David incredulously and then managed to respond. 'I never knew you'd even thought about it,' he said rather lamely.

'Well, *you* have and I bet you've drawn the same conclusions anyway.'

'What conclusions?' Richard sounded strangely guarded.

'That Fluff's my real father. As I grow older I'm more and more convinced that is the truth. Knowing Fluff, it has to be someone English and distinguished who is my real mother. You can't imagine Fluff muckin' about with some barmaid, can you?'

109

On this their eyes linked and both burst out laughing, which eased the tension which had developed between them.

'Of course not, you idiot!' Richard said, but even so there was an odd note of relief in his voice. 'Fluff . . .' he mused, 'that would be the solution, wouldn't it?'

'Much more to the point, is it yours too?'

Richard was hamstrung. His was not the same choice; but he could not possibly name who was, nor could he lie to David. Eventually he managed, 'I'm not sure in my own mind,' – because that at least was the truth – 'but I think your choice is certainly the soundest.' He was hating this and sought to divert the discussion into less perilous channels. 'Does it really matter anyway?'

'No, except with relation to Mum, Pop and coming to spend my life here, don't you see?'

Somewhat desperately Richard reached back for schoolboy stuff. 'Of course I see, you ass, but it's fruitless viewing, isn't it?'

David's face fell. 'At least it explains why I feel the way I do about out here. You're the clot if you can't understand that. If you deliberately misunderstand me . . .' he broke off. Digging his fist into Richard's ribs, he resumed, 'Why don't you understand me suddenly? You always have done about things we've talked about together.'

'Oh, I dunno!' Richard was well and truly on the defensive now and determined that no way would he ever name his fancies for the roles of David's real parentage. 'We can both speculate but we will never find the answer, will we?'

David shrugged, staring out over the creek to where the wallaby was back scrutinising him with unblinking solemnity. Richard seized his chance, 'I expect your pa's a wallaby if we only knew.' Scrambling to his feet, he held out a hand to haul David up. 'Come and play tennis! I'm screaming for some exercise and those courts look in splendid fettle.'

The wallaby decided discretion was the better part of

valour and lolloped off once more, while the boys swung themselves into their saddles and rode off. Richard was determined to keep the vexed question at bay. Looking about him as they rode, he began, 'Your own petrol pumps, garage, repair shops, mechanics – what else have you got? It's like a town almost.'

'A bit,' David agreed. 'Our church is over there. These buildings are the shearing sheds and the animal sick bay. Those are the hands' quarters where we ate. Behind them are the married quarters and then – round that bend – there are the shops. Somewhere the women can buy their necessities and some fancies too, like lollies and toys for the kids. Then there's the school and the playground for the younger ones. There's a gym and playing fields for football; and of course there are buildings containing the machinery for the generators, the reserve tanks – with electric pumps nowadays, that's the most recent addition.

'Then there's what I suppose we'd call a village hall in England – it's a Meeting House out here. Behind that is another little group of shops where women can actually buy the cotton frocks they wear, stockings and things. Mum thought of that. She also brought out an English hairdresser. The Soda Fountain was another of her ideas. I'll take you there too. Oh, look! Mum and Pop are playing. Let's wait till they finish and then take them on.'

The following night, with the stars bejewelling a navy blue sky and the smell from wood fires burning dried eucalyptus, which he was trying to remember should be called gum, drifting in through the mosquito screens at the open drawing room windows, Richard stretched out in a huge chintz-covered armchair and looked around him with admiration. His hostess was pouring coffee from a George I coffee pot.

'We might be in some lovely Wiltshire manor house,' he said dreamily, 'instead of Queensland, Australia. This room is so beautiful. May I ask, Mrs Kincale, if that is a spinet?'

Diana passed him a Leeds cup. 'Yes,' she confirmed. 'I

brought it from England. It was my great-great-grandmother's.'

'How does it react to the climate here?'

Michael Kincale laughed. 'We fly a man out every month to keep it in tune and good trim, like the Bechstein. Then it works a treat. We do most of our shopping in the Old Country; but when it comes to books,' he glanced at the floor to ceiling shelves, 'we get American editions quite often. The spelling troubles us however, so we send every month to Hatchards. Now tell me something; what did you think of the wines at dinner? I'm not asking for a courteous and conventional answer. Because I'm almost an Aussie doesn't mean I think everything's perfect out here, but I do have the opinion that we are now beginning to produce some really fine wines. Our cooking is deplorable!'

'You don't mean those clarets were Australian, do you, sir?' Richard stammered.

'Do I gather you liked them?' Michael was smiling. 'David, what did you think?'

'Well, sir,' David considered his reply very carefully, 'Rikki and I are both wine buffs in embryo. I'd have put that first claret down as a fairly young growth St Emilion and the second one was perfectly splendid, a first growth, though I don't know enough yet to put a name to it.'

'Both Australian, my lad, which rather proves my point. But this cognac,' Michael Kincale lifted the decanter from its tantalus and began pouring some into small ballons, 'is very old and very definitely comes from the restricted Cognac area of France, a country by the way which charms and delights me.'

'For what, sir?' Richard asked.

'Women's clothes, the food, the wines and the way of life. The French have got a so much better slant on daily living, with their two-hour luncheons, even for factory workers or farm hands. Out here my lovely wife sees to it that we too eat French while I ensure we drink Australian, German and French wines, Continental spirits and eschew whisky, except for our guests. Thus we find the overall pattern eminently pleasing.'

Richard smiled back, 'It certainly is to me, sir.' He accepted his ballon and sniffed the contents rapturously. 'It seems as if you have drawn together the best of two worlds. In fact,' he hesitated, knowing he must add what was not the whole truth, 'in fact, David's a helluva lucky chap in my opinion for what that's worth.' He knew, within himself, even then that the bitterest disappointments lay ahead for these two nice people when David eventually told them that their homestead pattern was far removed from what he felt he must do with his life – in England, not in Australia.

CHAPTER IX

ὦ παι, γένοιο πατρὸς εὐ᾽τυχέστερος.
(Ah, boy, may'st thou prove happier than thy sire.)

— Sophocles, translated by Jebb

THE AUTUMN WIND was whipping fallen leaves down the High as David impatiently edged his old green Bentley sports car through the midday Oxford traffic. He and Richard – caps pulled low, muffled to their noses in scarves – were surrounded by motley impedimenta, proclaiming to both 'town' and 'gown' who spared them incurious glances that they were newcomers to these dreaming spires.

It was the Michaelmas term and thus the official beginning of the University year.

Richard brought with him a glowing reputation on the rugger field, where he played hooker, and as a javelin thrower, which skill he had dismissed as, 'Fat lot of use that'll be to me.' His past mentors had also been pleased to approve his academic achievements at Gordonstoun, an accolade he shared with David, who had also won approbation as a fast bowler and a boxer.

After he had enquired the way to New College, David settled back at the wheel, muttering with some inelegance, 'We're off at Bogside.' When he turned off the engine they sat for a moment looking up at their home for the next three years.

'Come on, let's present ourselves,' David unwound some scarves and jumped onto the ground without bothering to open the door.

Later that afternoon, formalities concluded, David and Richard flapped their way in their truncated gowns

114

across the quadrangle towards their studies. They had already clattered up the bare wooden stairs half a dozen times, so had begun to feel they had been members of their college for many years. As they thumped up yet again, they passed the notice board with Mr King and Mr Llewellyn writ upon it, so were in no way surprised when they heard a voice behind them, 'Gentlemen, will you kindly remove that car and be sure to see your little green light is affixed before you take it out again. It is an infringement of College rules for you to drive without it.'

David stretched out on his bed. 'So we're "gentlemen" now,' he mused contentedly. 'Do you suppose that fat bod knows where we get our little green light?'

'We'll ask him on the way down, you fool, and if he can't tell us, any garage will. We can't get rusticated for taking the car there.'

With the matter of the car settled, they returned to hang pictures and position their sundry possessions, Richard obligingly listing their numerous requirements. Having left a door open, heads began appearing, as various young men came to renew old friendships until the place more closely resembled a wine bar in the city than a setting for academic studies.

By nightfall they had been invited to dine at the Gridiron Club, been offered a day with the Heythrop by the Camstock twins who had been senior to them at Gordonstoun, and learned that New College also shared a beagle pack. David found himself promised to a University Labour Club to hear a cabinet minister speak one day and to attend a jazz session at the University Jazz Club on another. Strolling off with Richard, leaving a shambles behind them, David speculated, 'Wonder if there'll be any time to work here. That chap from Magdalen who was at Cheam with us said this was probably the hottest political corner of England today. Suits me but when are we going to learn anything? Hospitable lot, aren't they? I mean it's only our first day here.'

The end products of their welcoming committees were pink coats for two and after a lengthy wrangle David managed half to persuade, half to blackmail Richard into riding the second mount he intended buying 'pronto'. A few days later the pair raced up to London to Purdy's for guns in order to shoot in the surrounding countryside.

David began spending high, wide and handsome. They ended a night with the Gridiron brimming with port and brandy and weaving an uneven way to their beds. Waking with venomous hangovers, both boys were taken to the very experienced chemist 'round the corner' who persuaded them to set a limit on their drinking thereafter.

All things considered they settled down reasonably. They even found time to write to their own parents. David's letters to Fluff were duly copied and sent to the Duke, to whom David was writing anyway. In one letter he wrote, 'I wish now I had gone to Magdalen. I've seen your rooms there and heard that you drove a large open Daimler when you were up.' Some weeks later he was duly summoned to the porter's gate.

'Your car, sir,' said a uniformed man with a smart salute.

'My car?' David looked puzzled. 'My car's that old Bentley,' pointing over the man's shoulder.

The man produced a piece of paper and glanced at it. 'You are Mr David Kincale, sir, are you not?'

David nodded.

'Well, sir, this is your car – a 1918 Daimler, a replica of the one the Prince of Wales drove when he was at Oxford. It's for you,' he pulled off a glove, dipped into a pocket and produced an envelope, 'and I was instructed to hand this over to you.'

David took the envelope mechanically, recognised the insignia on it and just managed to stammer, 'Thanks very much. I'll come out with you if you'll hang on a moment.' Then he turned and raced up the stairs.

Richard had sported his oak so was by no means pleased when he burst in crying, 'This is a bloody miracle. Will you please come and see what I've got? He's sent me a car like his.'

Richard turned crossly, 'For God's sake what are you

116

raving on about? Who sent you what car?' He spoke to himself.

David was reading the note which said quite simply, 'Trust it gives you as much pleasure as I had from mine,' and was signed Windsor.

'Good God!' he cried, 'he's sent me a car like his. I haven't even looked at it yet. I wanted to tell you first so don't be curmudgeonly. Come down with me, it's outside.' There was no more work done that day by either of them.

The name David Kincale began to be known rather well. By the end of the first term David and his old Daimler were sights to be shown to girl friends when they visited. Somehow David and Richard were asked about together without any suggestion that their relationship could be homosexual. Oxford accepted their explanation, repeated separately and jointly, 'We were at prepper together, then at Gordonstoun and by the greatest good fortune we got here together – we just suit each other.'

There was such an imputation – once. The pair drove the perpetrator, protesting, to a field well out of College jurisdiction and handed him a pair of boxing gloves. The Camstock twins drew up alongside 'just to see fair play'. David proceeded to knock the man out cold, after which he tended the resultant black eye with raw beefsteak and the whole party went amicably to dinner at the Hind's Head, at Bray.

Both David and Richard were roped in for freshman trials, at which the latter distinguished himself on the rugger field, became a 'marked man' and half way through the term was picked to play Cambridge in the inter-varsity match. Richard won his blue and that became a night on the town to be remembered. David, deeply engrossed by now and achieving an almost unbelievable three sessions a week with his tutor, was embroiled in political history and even his scout commented upon the number of books to be dusted. He came into his own athletically in the Trinity term, playing in both the cricket and tennis teams against Cambridge. 'One all and two years to go,' was his only comment to Richard.

In their second year both boys spent the Long Vac with the Kincales who were in Europe for the last time before setting out on their long-planned flight round the world some months later.

When the question of a name for their aircraft came up, David said, 'Why not call her "Diana" after you, Mum?' and Michael nodded approvingly.

'"Diana", she shall be,' they agreed.

They went over the itinerary in detail from the first leg. They would take off from Darwin and cross the Timor Sea to Java. The salon of the Provençal *mas* they had rented was christened the Lesser Sargasso Sea by Richard who was eternally recovering and re-folding maps and charts when not participating in long, argumentative picnics on the yacht Michael Kincale had chartered. The famous pioneer flyer, Graham White, joined them on these expeditions, pored over the maps and was heard to say wistfully, 'You two make me envious. What an absolutely spendid project! How I wish I were young enough to join you!'

It was altogether a very happy time. Even Fluff joined in briefly when they brought the yacht round to drop hook in the tranquil bay of Cap Ferrat. Their visit almost coincided with the arrival of the Duke and Duchess of Windsor who were to stay in a nearby villa. At the last moment their plans changed. Diana Kincale was most disappointed since she was curious to meet them.

The third and last year at Oxford was far and away David's favourite. His talent as a public speaker was considered remarkable in one so young; his charm and appeal in debate carried the day with almost monotonous regularity until in his final Michaelmas term he was elected President of the Union, amid many greybeard predictions that, 'Young Kincale will make his mark, have no doubt about it; he will go far, brilliant feller, shouldn't wonder if he pulled a double first either.'

The lack of surprise was justified. David scooped up a double first in philosophy and political economy, despite being simultaneously enmeshed in his first really serious love affair. He had been invited by the girl's parents to join their Ascot house party, but he elected to stay for the degree-giving ceremony. His illustrious girl friend drove off in a huff. The Kincales had telephoned David regretting their date of take-off coincided with the night before he was to receive his degree. Richard's parents drove over to Oxford to see their son be given his more modest first in English Literature. Fluff had long kept this special day free from other engagements.

After night after night of Commem balls and other parties, the undergraduates were required to present themselves, clean, sober and in their right minds at the Sheldonian Theatre that June morning. This august building, designed like a classical amphitheatre with its high painted ceiling and erotically decorated frontage, was exactly suited to the costumed pageantry of the strange and almost farcical medieval performance enacted there each year.

It seemed out of time to the two young men who watched the beadles scuttling about like water beetles grasping silver wands, some with enormous brass badges clamped to their arms. They darted between a seethe of scholars in scarlet gowns and rabbit fur and students in white bow ties, and threw anxious glances from time to time at the Vice Chancellor seated on his elevated throne. David stifled a giggle as he spotted two proctors, archangels of University discipline, the tassels of their mortar boards dangling over their eyes like carrots on strings tempting donkeys to assume a spanking pace.

The actual ceremony was taken at the gallop. A testy verger mustered and marshalled the undergraduates, his black gown fluttering. A Latin incantation was then delivered at a cracking pace. Sometimes the proctors

119

bowed, sometimes they snatched at their mortar boards, sprang from their seats and marched up and down the hall in anticipation of any dissenter who wished to register a protest by plucking at those gowns. Further Latin admonitions were delivered swiftly until at last – like the final gallop at a hunt ball – the candidates were chivvied forward to kneel before the Vice Chancellor and be banged tenderly upon their young heads with a Bible. At a proctorial hustle they were prodded to their feet again and propelled post-haste towards the door through which they trooped out into the yard, flushed, triumphant and looking inordinately young and pleased with themselves. Then as if all were a chimera, the cast of proctors, doctors and beadles faded away as if they had never been more than mere thought forms upon the ether. The new graduates formed groups and stood chatting in the sunshine while proud parents took photographs.

With Fluff between them David and Richard marched him back to their College entrance, just as their taxi drew up. The boys left Fluff while they thudded up the stairs for the last time to collect their impedimenta, shake hands with their scout and bid the porter a slightly valedictory farewell. They were in frantic haste for Fluff had warned them that he had to be back in London by 6 pm and there were only minutes in which to catch the appropriate train.

David had read in the morning papers a report of the tremendous ovation which his adoptive parents had received on their take-off from Darwin. Now he was impatient to read the latest news about that perilous first leg of their long flight.

'Must just get a paper,' he gasped, as the taxi braked outside the station. 'Rikki, get me a ticket, will you?'

As soon as David had gone, Fluff told Richard, his mouth grim and drawn, 'They're missing. I deliberately didn't tell him before his degree ceremony, but now I can't hold back any longer.'

'Oh, no, sir! But surely there is a chance, isn't there?'

'Of course,' Fluff agreed, 'but even so it's a terrible time for David.'

'Why didn't you tell me?' David asked quietly, at Fluff's elbow. 'I had a right to know.'

The front page headline flared:

INTREPID KINCALES FEARED LOST OVER TIMOR SEA.

'Because,' said Fluff even more quietly, 'I wanted you to have your moment. It made not one iota of difference to the situation, old chap, and could not possibly help in any way for you to know beforehand.'

David's expressionless face softened slightly. 'Good old Fluff,' he managed. Then holding out the papers, he said, 'I think . . . it's all over bar the aftermath . . . they've found a patch of oil but no sign of any wreckage . . . what a bloody, bloody waste . . .'

CHAPTER X

'The moving finger writes and having writ
Moves on; nor all thy Piety nor Wit
Shall lure it back to cancel half a Line
Nor all thy tears wash out a Word of it.'

– Edward Fitzgerald – Rubaiyat of Omar Khayyam

FLUFF TOOK THE pair back to Albany, gave them a stiff whisky apiece and then telephoned his old friend, Lord Beardmore. He conveyed the Press magnate's verdict as best he could to David. 'I'm very much afraid there is no hope; they've found a bit of the plane with its name.'

All David could say was, 'Mind if I go out for a bit?' leaving Fluff and Richard staring at each other helplessly as men do whose lives are pledged to no displays of emotion.

David walked. He crossed Piccadilly and cut through the little sidewalk by the Ritz to St James's Park. He stood for a time watching the ducks, listening to the cheeping sounds which herald roosting, before moving off again across Hyde Park Corner towards Kensington Gardens.

His mind was out of kilter with the shock but even so his reactions seemed to run through his head like tramlines. On the one hand he experienced thankfulness that Michael and Diana had never known he did not want their way of life, the homestead in Queensland. On the other, his inheritance reacting, he was infinitely relieved he would never have to face the issue with them. Even his insistence on following the Aristotlean principle of 'Know thyself' yielded to the unavoidable logic of the fact he could not, since he was debarred from ever knowing who he was, or what his real parents were like. His belief that he was Fluff's son went down that night,

122

for he faced the truth that no son of his would ever experience relief at having escaped a painful issue. To David, Fluff was *sans peur et sans reproche.*

Even later, when the tarts came out and accosted him as he walked down the park side of Park Lane, David let his own thoughts run without analysis. At length he came to a decision concerning the future. 'Never go back' was to be his *leitmotif* from that night onwards. He would never return to the homestead. He realised that his adoptive parents' immense wealth would come to him and through this he would have the means to do what he most desired. He would turn the station into a co-operative, with the one proviso that the actual homestead never be occupied again by any private person but be used for the care of handicapped children. The picture of Billy-Boy with his crab-like gait was strong in his mind and he determined there would be some place where such children could grow up in happiness and with the finest care and education his parents' money could buy.

From this point David never questioned that both Diana and Michael were dead. He returned to Albany, where Richard was waiting for him. He told David what he already knew: that it was all over. The BBC had telephoned asking if David would consent to being interviewed. To Richard's astonishment, David agreed and made the appointment himself.

David sat facing his interviewer at a round table adorned by the bulb and the statutory glass jug of water and a tumbler. His mouth quivered as he noticed this, remembering how Gilbert Harding had sipped some water during an interview when he was profoundly angry. He had spat it out saying in furious tones, 'And what's more, they have to give me the water in which Reith put his teeth during the Duke of Windsor's Abdication speech!'

The interviewer mistook the quiver so began mildly. He thanked him for coming 'at such a time' and continued, 'You were Mr and Mrs Kincale's adopted son, were you not?'

Something clicked in David's head. 'Yes, indeed,' he replied. 'I do not know who my real parents are but I do know that no one was ever more fortunate in having such enchanting, happy and devoted adoptive ones. I have had a wonderful childhood and a marvellously stimulating boyhood. I've only just come down from Oxford. My parents gave me the best both of themselves and the good life they made in Australia.'

'You will go back and take up the reins yourself now?'

He had played for this question. 'Oh, no,' David countered. 'When you have been supremely happy anywhere and that happiness ends you must never go back.'

'You mean you will sell the estate.'

'Station,' David corrected him. 'No, I shall do no such thing. I believe that in any enterprise where there are what are loosely called employees, the management gets the staff it deserves. My adoptive parents were adored by the people who worked with them, so I intend turning the entire station into a co-operative for those families who served my parents. All except the homestead.'

'Your parents' house?'

'Yes. I plan to make that into a home for handicapped children. You see I have been left a considerable fortune by my adoptive parents and I think that is what they would wish me to do.'

The interview continued but nothing further of any import was said. David had made his first contact with the great British public at a time when disillusionment was rife. The next morning his picture was in every newspaper and the sacks of mail began accumulating. He had embarked on the one great adventure of his life: friendship with the little people.

There were lawyers to see. There were interminable telephone calls from Australia. Cables poured in, including a number from members of the Australian cabinet, and a heart-rending one from the mechanics and their womenfolk. The Queen sent her condolences too. This gave a wry twist to Fluff's mouth but he made no comment of course. Neither did he pass on the initial approaches concerning memorial services in London and Brisbane. He knew that in David's present frame of mind he would have refused to consider the latter anyway. He and Richard took turns with the telephones in his Albany chambers, holding back the Press and meanwhile sorting out the mail.

There were touching letters, and avid ones begging for assistance from so rich a young man. Ingenious as many were, Fluff was well equipped to deal with them. He insisted that they were all set aside to be sent to the Begging Letter Society. When David protested, Fluff explained quietly, 'If they are genuine, you will have them back – that I promise. Then you can do what you like. If you are interested, I'll tell you of Lord Nuffield's experience. It was what decided him to give only to recognised charities. If I am right about these,' he waved a disdainful hand at the offending pile, 'you are doing that already with the station and the homestead.'

Richard meanwhile was in a quandary. His editor on the Birmingham newspaper clearly possessed friends in high places. Shortly before coming down from Oxford, Richard had received a letter from this man, saying that no less a person than the great Press baron, Lord Beardmore, had expressed a wish to see him.

He mentioned this to Fluff who promptly rang his old friend, who had played such a great part in the pre-Abdication period, and requested a *'bisque'* for this important interview.

'Tell 'em both to come,' the old man insisted. 'Tell 'em my penthouse, top floor, and say one o'clock. It will force that ward of yours to step out again if only for an hour or two. Make it next Wednesday.'

It was the very last thing that David wanted. This

Richard knew well enough but when Fluff replaced the receiver, he was able to say, 'Right, one o'clock next Wednesday. Fancy your getting into that *sanctum sanctorum.*'

Before they set off, Fluff briefed them, saying to Richard, 'I can suppose you know already that this could be the forerunner to becoming one of the old man's "boys". He has a coterie and sometimes there are females too. The final seal of approval is when he invites anyone for a stay at his Riviera villa. It's about my favourite on that coast. It sits like a small white palace overlooking the Plage de la Garoupe which provides his chosen gossip columnist with a most convenient eyrie. Val Smith settles his vast belly in a creaking wicker chair, produces his binoculars and subsequently murmurs, "Excuse me, sir," if he spots a likely target sunbathing or sipping a Bloody Mary.

'But make no mistake; momentous decisions are taken there and as a journalistic training ground the *Clarion* is unique. You must realise it is an immensely powerful newspaper, with an enormous circulation, and headed by an equally powerful man – one, moreover, for whom the British public has a great respect. They have always relished eccentricity.'

David reflected upon this last statement but clearly was undecided about it. 'Why, sir?' he shot back, 'It's the first unlikely remark you have ever made to me.'

Richard who was watching the two men intently realised that this had at least roused David. He saw Fluff nod and heard him say, 'I do believe it is vital that you understand. I am of course speaking of the collective eighty per cent. Any sign of anything which offends the in-bred remnants of their old puritanism causes them to turn and rend, for it is totally contrary to the dictates of their tribe. It equally applies to those whom to them represent the high and mighty.

'Let me give you an example. The great British public adored old "Tum-Tum" and they revelled in his peccadilloes because he remained unswerving in his devotion to the Crown and in his sense of duty which earned him his other nickname "The Peacemaker". But the eccentricities of which they are perpetually disapproving – both among themselves and the privileged – were what caused them to stone Wallis Simpson's windows. It was summed up for me by a bus conductor who, when asked his opinion of the whole sorry affair, said, on the day of the Abdication, "I wouldn't 'ave minded a bit if she'd only 'ave buried the others decent."'

David whistled softly. 'Powerful stuff, sir!'

'Indeed yes. Make no mistake, the pair of you are stepping into the corridors of powerful influence. Many are called there but few are chosen, so if you, Richard, are offered something, you are extremely fortunate. As for you, David, neither you nor I can suppose you are being asked because Lord Beardmore knew Diana and Michael – had that been the reason, it would have been an entirely different venue. It is solely because his interest is aroused *vis-à-vis* the *Clarion* and his other newspapers.'

'Do you think he wants to make me a journalist too, sir?'

'I do not,' Fluff was emphatic. 'I merely say you have caught his eye. You must remember that even to me you have not given the slightest indication of what you mean to do.'

David stood up, thus he looked down on his only replacement for any kind of relative. Factually he was now completely alone and if he fulfilled his declared intention, he was also a man without home or roots.

'Then let me tell you,' he began and Fluff, looking at him, experienced a shock of recognition despite the almost total lack of physical resemblance. David then declared himself and the muffled thread of sound which reached them through the curtained windows seemed to be an echo of the sounds which had reached his father and his guardian when King Edward VIII had stated his case in 1936.

'I shall stay in England,' he stated. 'I have no concrete reason for doing so – just a shrouded certainty that it is what I must do. Call it a premise of my own destiny. I want to become a politician. I am not thinking as clearly as I might so forgive me if I put this badly; but this has been my ambition since I could read and think for myself. There is an undercurrent here now which I have never detected in all my reading of England's history. Something is going on which gives me cold shivers down my spine. You can ascribe it to some foretaste of evil if you wish. Anyway I want to find out what causes it.

'In a constitutional monarchy power becomes vested in the media, high finance and the ruling government. I have come to believe that the media reports everything with one eye on the main chance which is according to their publication's policy; and that high finance, whose middle name is devious, keeps the wheels turning while Parliament busies itself in the main nest-feathering and vote-catching with some pretty liberal forays into downright corruption.

'Let me qualify that. I am well aware of the meretriciousness of generalisations. There are some very fine men too but they are few and gradually diminishing in number. There is something else motivating the unlovely trio which makes me fearful for this declining nation whose greatness is being eroded now. So at the risk of distressing you by my perfidy, I intend to find out what that something is regardless of whether or not I'll be labelled a turncoat.'

Richard already knew David's views to some extent so remained silent. Fluff just nodded, wondering if it were possible to experience a greater weight of responsibility than that which this young man now laid so squarely on his shoulders. 'And what do you want from me?' he then asked a trifle sadly.

'Introductions, sir – the opportunity to meet politicians – I've scarcely met any except in Australia.'

'Have you decided which party you want to try for initially?'

David hesitated. 'Let me put that differently. I am sure that there are two men with their hands on their respective tillers who are totally uncorrupt.' Fluff waited. David elaborated, 'The Prime Minister and the current Liberal leader; but while the former is a splendid character, he is too much of what is really meant by the term a gentleman to succeed in stemming the tides of what I fear.'

'So?'

'I should like to meet your friend, Dylan Caradoc-Evans, who leads the Liberals. It would constitute a beginning.'

That night, when David and Richard had returned from the House where they had gone to listen to a debate, Fluff handed David some envelopes he had extricated from the usual substantial evening delivery. 'Excuse me, sir. Let's see what these are all about.' He ripped open an envelope with an Australian stamp to find another inside addressed to him in Diana Kincale's handwriting. He slit this open carefully, withdrawing a worn sheet of paper dated January 3rd 1937. He read:

Diana dear,
You must understand that in the matter of your and Michael's adopting the as yet unborn child of those other friends, I am acting for both sides. The real parents are as dear to me in their own ways as you know you have always been. I scarcely need labour the point that adoption is always a lottery; but in this case I feel that if you two are to have complete peace of mind I owe it to you both to put on record *what* the real parents are, though I can never disclose *who* they are as I know you understand.

I have thought about this very carefully and what I write now comes from someone who has always loved you. I think I always will. This I know you do not reciprocate, though it may probably explain why I have never married. I suspect you know this too and therefore it should not prove difficult for you to accept that all I now write is

129

the simple truth. Your child – if you decide that he or she is to become so – is of fine lineage. I assure you that the baby whom I shall hand over almost immediately after birth is an aristocrat. I chose you and Michael in the absolute certainty that you would provide an upbringing properly compatible with his or her origins. Even so, I feel that unless you do accept that the in-bred instincts of this child will be compatible with your own, there could never be any true harmony between the three of you. I now offer you this assurance too. There is one more important point – that after the birth I shall obtain from the Swiss authorities a birth certificate for the child, naming you and Michael as the parents, and registering the birth at the clinic, where the child will be delivered from the mother who resides there now *in your name*. Thus it will be British since although Michael has spent so many years in Australia, he still retains his British nationality.

Whether you then decide to disclose the facts, as you know them, to the child is a matter between you in which I take no part, save that I will confirm whatever you say, secure in the knowledge that all tracks are completely obliterated. If you agree, I shall stand guardian in order to meet the unlikely event of anything happening to you and Michael before the child comes of age.

So, my dear, with the greatest hope that what we propose will ensure the lasting happiness of all concerned, I am

Your very devoted
'Fluff'

Pinned to this letter was a scribble from Diana:

My darling boy,
I had intended to give you this when you were with us at Christmas but Pa persuaded me not to do so. You know how he preaches about letting sleeping dogs lie!

God bless you always
Mum

Richard was the first to speak. He was sitting on the floor, with his knees hunched up and his arms linked across them. 'I wonder why they ever told you you were only adopted.'

'Because,' David said quickly, 'they were that kind of people. It would seem to them the right thing to do.' His face was taut with pain; so indeed was Fluff's but as he had been standing at the window, the two young men were unaware.

'And the rest of your post?' Fluff enquired when he had himself in hand again.

'A letter from my popsie, apologising for going off in a huff just before the bestowing of our accolades. I was supposed to go down to her place for their Ascot house party and later go with her people to shoot grouse on their Scottish moors.'

'Indeed, and who might she be, pray? This is the first I have heard of her.'

'Daphne Fanshawe, in her first year, reading law. I took her to the Commem balls. She's a good looker too; you'd like her, I think.'

'I'm sure I would,' said Fluff so non-committally that it drew the semblance of a grin from both of them.

Then Richard put in his oar. 'She's pretty good value actually, sir. Her old man's the Fanshawe of Fanshawe's chain groceries, but she's nothing like as smashing as my little number.'

David stared down at him. 'Who on earth? It's the first I've heard of this!'

Richard agreed, 'It's a pretty recent thing. We went punting after the last ball . . .'

'And never said a word to me. Well, I must say.'

Richard forged on. 'I'm supposed to be taking her out to dinner tomorrow night. If you can spare me, I'd like to see her and then I'll bring her back here.'

'You go,' David said tartly, 'and bring her back so that we can inspect her. I say,' he pulled up and asked in an entirely different tone, 'it's not serious, is it?'

'Could be.'

'Ye Gods!' exclaimed Fluff. 'You mercurial children. I'm delighted you've got a little playmate of course, Richard, but what interests me far more is that neither of you have said anything at all about your luncheon session with old Beardmore.'

'What would you like us to say, sir?' asked David somewhat facetiously.

'Well, what happened of course,' retorted Fluff.

'The whisky was superb malt, sir, and there was a lot of it. We were very much up for inspection with no verdict delivered either way. When the port went round, "the Lord" had me up to sit beside him. He was gruffly condoling first go off, then he wanted to know what I intended doing, so I told him, "I want to go into politics," and he seemed to lose interest.'

'When it came to my turn, sir,' Richard reported, 'he asked me what I had written. I told him about my spell in Birmingham and that I had edited the *Cherwell* in my last year – and that I had had a few rejection slips from his editors to boot. He then suggested, "Why not write something for old Scruffy over there?" The moment his name was mentioned, the man they called Scruffy Stevenson got up and came and sat on his right. Then "the Lord" said, "I've told this young man to write you a political piece, Scruffy – just as an exercise." Then Scruffy began asking me some questions, so "the Lord" wandered off. I didn't even notice, it was such splendid fun talking to such a cracking fine journalist. What he doesn't know about the political scene and its backwaters isn't worth knowing.'

'I know,' Fluff spoke gently. 'Will you do it?'

'I've already started, sir. All I had for a briefing was to write something about the overtones and undercurrents of the present situation, but just imagine if it came off!'

'It'll come off,' Fluff reassured him. 'And now if I can bring you back to immediate problems. David, I think you should lay down your own lines a bit. Let me put you up for some clubs – I've been remarkably remiss where that's concerned – and I suggest you do a round of the more reputable estate agents to see if you can find a small house in the Westminster area. It's a convenient locale for a base. You could spend a few weeks in redecorating and furnishing if needs be. Enlist the help of your popsie if you've decided to forgive her.'

'Yes, to the clubs, thank you, sir,' David said promptly. 'Capital thought, too – a little house. Rikki, how would it be if I found one with sufficient space for you to have your own flat? Would you like that? No – think about it before you commit yourself. But,' he turned to his guardian, 'no to the popsie. I think I may have other fish to fry, but that is not for discussion now.'

'It seems to me,' Fluff said lightly, 'that one way and another the pair of you are growing up.'

By the time the roast chestnut vendors were back against the kerb-side in Leicester Square, David had found the house he sought. He gave Harrods instructions to have the items named on a list crated and despatched to him from the homestead. He chose Diana's spinet, Michael's desk, the Gainsborough and the two Breughels, the contents of the library, the silver, the Rockingham dinner service, the Leeds and all the Meissen, Michael's gold collection including all his coins and his mother's jewellery, about which he had undefined but sentimental intentions.

The house of his choice lay just off Smith Square on the corner of Tufton Street and thus close enough to the House for him to hear the Divisonal bell. It was large enough to provide very adequate private quarters for Richard too. David also acquired two lock-up garages nearby where he installed his old Bentley and the Daimler, which he had collected from Oxford. When asked about his future home, he delighted in replying in the curious terminology of his estate agents. 'It's a late Georgian house, a gentleman's bijou residence on four floors with a small garden.'

A horde of decorators swarmed about brewing up tea in the grate of his future drawing room and playing brag, with occasional forays with paint brushes to restore the house to its original black and white freshness. Prowling in Brighton's Lanes, David found a beautifully modelled brass hand which he chose as a knocker for his newly painted front door.

133

Until the house was ready, David installed himself in rooms in Jermyn Street and was quick to remind his acquaintances that he was 'on the sunny side'. It was from here that he strolled one crisp October evening to meet Fluff. Wholly due to his guardian's far reaching influence, David had been admitted to both the Bath Club and to Boodles. It was to neither of these, however, that he made his way now. He was heading for the National Liberal Club so that he might meet the current leader of the Liberal party. It was his intention to go in by this 'side door' as he called it, always acknowledging that he would cross the floor later.

When Fluff asked him, 'To what party?' he replied, 'Look, sir, if you can't beat 'em, join 'em, so let's postpone the evil day for as long as possible, though I fear it will prove the only course open to me if I want to get at the truths.'

Always, in the back of his mind, Fluff was keenly aware of the appalling impact this would make upon his real father.

Richard meanwhile was in a state of euphoria. Scruffy Stevenson had bought his article, having hacked the first draft to pieces, made Richard re-shape it and then subbed it again. Finally he was the proud recipient of a cheque for thirty guineas and had the ineffable joy of seeing his name over a leader page article in the great *Clarion*.

Richard went down to Fleet Street the following morning, intending to push his luck further by playing Oliver Twist but he encountered Scruffy coming through the swing doors of the newspaper building. 'Hi, Llewellyn,' he greeted him, 'Come and have a beer.' Richard obediently followed him into the Wig and Pen.

Scruffy bought two pints. Saying, 'Let's get out of this mob,' he then shouldered his way to a vacant table, settled himself much like a bear in a sandpit and took a mighty swig. Banging the tankard down, he delivered himself of what to Richard was sheer music. 'How would you like to join us and be my leg man?' he demanded. 'I'll give you a helluva life, keep you up till all hours and generally run you ragged; but I think if you can stay the course, I could turn you into a first rate political reporter and "the Lord" has no objections.'

Richard made no effort to dissemble. A huge grin spread slowly across his face. One hand went to his dark hair which he rumpled abstractedly. 'Fids, fids,' he exulted, 'I gloat, sir, when do I start?'

'Now,' said Scruffy tolerantly. 'Go and get us a couple more beers.'

Richard left an ecstatic note for David who was out. He hastily packed a few things in an overnight case and caught the next train to Wales. That night, amid general rejoicings, he told his parents, 'I've got a thousand a year and reasonable expenses. David's lent me quarters in his new house. Scruffy says he won't pay taxis so, as he wants everything back almost before he's asked for it, I shall have to buy a small car to run around in. David's only got a terrific old Bentley and an even more terrific Daimler and they're both petrol cormorants, so I thought a Mini would be my best bet.'

His father smiled back across the polished oak of their dining table. 'I'll stand you that,' he undertook, 'and I can manage five hundred a year until you get on your feet without going bankrupt.'

His mother fussed a little. 'What about this flat?' she asked anxiously. 'You'll need everything, won't you? We must go up into the attics tomorrow morning and see what we can find. I know your father insists that we have enough furniture for two houses and my linen room is more than amply stocked.'

In the morning Mrs Llewellyn shooed both her menfolk off to find something for the pot. They took guns and spent a muddy and highly satisfactory morning roaming the small estate. Their net bag was a hare, two brace of rabbits and a brace of partridges but Richard's mother was well pleased and thought privately that he was looking very handsome.

135

Before Richard caught the afternoon train back to London, some family furniture had been found for him. Richard urged, 'Please don't bother with any carpets, mother. David's carpeting the whole house in one colour, he says it's much the easiest way – a sort of mushroom – which will look nice with lots of white paint. He asked me to tell you both to come up and stay so we can do a threatre or two just as soon as we are dug in.'

Recklessly splurging on a taxi, Richard got back to Jermyn Street just after seven o'clock. A note was propped up in the usual place against the rather dreadful clock in their rooms. 'See you later. Gone to the Liberal Club with Fluff. Keep everything crossed for me. D.'

Dylan Caradoc-Evans' face was so familiar that David reminded himself that he must not greet him as an old friend because he had not even met him yet. Sprawled in a huge armchair on the far side of the room, he looked more like a theatrical exaggeration of an absent-minded professor than a loved and respected politician. With his spectacles half way down his nose, he was listening to what his companion was telling him with many dramatic gestures. Caradoc-Evans, David also registered, wore the manner of one willing to listen but already determined upon the application of a cane to yet another manifestly delinquent political backside.

David recognised his companion too, but deeming him to be more a firebrand than subversive, dismissed him as inconsiderable to his purposes, while chuckling inwardly at what the *Tailor and Cutter* must surely have written about their joint sartorial sins. Their hair was sparse but erupting grey to the collar line; their clothing rose and fell about their spare bodies resembling deflated flying suits. Knitted ties failed to fulfil their function of drawing into some sense of order the nondescript shirts which had seemingly been bought from some country market stall while canvassing.

As David crossed the great pillared room, many eyes

followed him. This was becoming par for the course, not on the score alone of his good lucks and sartorial fastidiousness – modelled on his Uncle Fluff – but through the attentions of the media.

'One appearance on that damn' "telly",' Fluff said with distaste when David greeted him and sat down, 'that interview has made you into a public figure before the "off". You're already being discussed.'

'Why, sir?'

'Why indeed! Trivially, because of your appearance – you'll be labelled or libelled "Dandy" any moment. Seriously, this notice is also because you spoke pridefully of your British passport and called it your passport to British politics – a fateful sentence, my lad. That, combined with what the more revolting sections of the British Press call your "charisma" will I surmise bring more offers for your hand in marriage than a Miss World. Nice planning, you young devil!'

They sipped their dry sherries while Fluff kept a close, if unobtrusive, watch on the progress of the Lib/Lab exchange. As soon as the two men separated and the rangy figure of the Labour hothead splay-footed towards the door, Fluff rose and led David over.

His career had begun. Via Dylan Caradoc-Evans who made it plain – at least to Fluff, during the evening – that David's radio and subsequent television interviews had impressed him enormously.

Fluff summed it all up for David and Richard in the privacy of his chambers some days later by stating, 'You made a wise choice, David. Dylan's a feller of the utmost probity, but he sees in you a God-sent chance of injecting new life into his sadly ailing party. What happens next is wholly up to you.'

After a long weekend at the splendid old Welshman's rambling house in the border country of his own constituency, the Liberal leader put his young protegé to work at party headquarters, saying, 'You will now set about producing bullets for our Members to fire while we wait for a suitable constituency.' So David researched with frenetic diligence, shaping his material into speech form with such ability that a new HQ phrase became common usage, 'Give it to young David Kincale and let him sort it out for you.'

One year later David was able to write one of his regular report letters to the Duke, which began, 'At last I have managed to get my foot onto the very bottom rung of the ladder. Last night much to my own surprise I was elected Liberal member for Sutton and Cheam after two recounts with a majority of seventy-seven. This is not bad because I had to overturn a Conservative majority of over 11,000. At the worst it confirms that the first section of the British public that I have ever tackled places some credence in what I say. Even so I do not think that I shall stay Liberal for very long. Dylan Caradoc-Evans is a perfectly splendid man whom I think, sir, you would enjoy, but there is a Harold Macmillan streak in him which makes him too much of a *preux chevalier* for him to sweep to power through the morass of politics today.

'It may amuse you, too, that thanks to the extraordinary attention of the media since probate was granted and I came into my parents' fortunes, I have acquired a fan club of screaming teenagers who hang about outside the house with autograph books! I am now properly installed here with Richard in an upstairs flat. I have an excellent man who combines the duties of butler and valet for me – Fluff found him of course – and a cook-housekeeper who always reminds me of Jemima Puddleduck. She really does cluck over me and is apt to walk into my study when I am working late with horrible offers of malted milk drinks and homilies about burning the candle at both ends. She also has traits of disloyalty which I foster; on one unforgettable occasion, standing with arms akimbo, she told me, "Mr David, sir, (meaning you) he never ought to have gone and I never cease to grieve over him,'" at which I read her the riot act and raised her salary.

'So I am very well served, particularly by a brace of

very able secretaries who happen to rejoice in the Christian names of Doris and Elsie and so have quickly become the Waters' daughters to everyone here. I imagine you will remember the famous Cockney act of Gert and Daisy.

'Reverting to the party, the trouble is that our leader is very poorly served and every time I try to construct a cabinet from my colleagues, I find myself woefully defeated.

'Richard knows I am writing and he asked me to send his humble duties, together with my own.'

As he sealed the envelope, Richard appeared round the door. 'Oh, I'm glad you're up,' he said, throwing himself into an armchair. 'Can we talk or are you still working?'

David looked at him thoughtfully. 'I suppose you know,' he observed mildly, 'that you have got lipstick on your ear.'

'That's very possible,' Richard agreed, reaching for the malted milk. 'You see I am engaged to be married and I thought you'd like to be the first to know. I shall expect you to be my best man. I'm in a daze actually, having pulled off the best double of my life tonight. When I turned my copy into Scruffy this afternoon, he tore it to shreds as usual, gave it back to me to rewrite and just as I was leaving, he rapped out, "Before you do anything else, go and wash and brush your hair. 'The Lord' wants to see us in ten minutes and he doesn't take kindly to being kept waiting." He didn't say a word going up in the bloody lift and I honestly thought I was due for the chop, instead of which "The Lord" promoted me and doubled my salary . . . so you see before you a fully fledged Parliamentary Correspondent.

'And so,' he added rather anti-climatically, 'I rang up Joanna. We had dinner together at Baldwin's which nearly cleaned me out. I popped the question and she accepted me. We're going down to stay with her parents this weekend.'

139

Part III

CHAPTER XI

*'Forgetting those things which are behind, and
reaching forth unto those things which are before,
I press toward the mark.'*

— Holy Bible

CLEARLY AT 'THE LORD'S' behest, the *Clarion* played up
the news that David was to be Richard's best man. There
were paragraphs describing the bride, Joanna Wynne-
Owen, as 'a rising young sculptress who has recently
had a highly successful exhibition at the Cavendish
Galleries'. Then it was reported that David's wedding
present was a small house in Chelsea, with more references to both his immense fortune and his charisma.

The little Welsh village seethed with reporters and
photographers and it was rumoured that a television
crew was expected to film the event for the local network, whose chairman was Lord Beardmore. Any hope
of the quiet wedding planned by the brides' parents had
to be abandoned. A totally bewildered Mrs Wynne-
Owen, carrying a sheaf of papers, burst into her husband's study crying, 'Goronwy, we shall have to hire a
huge marquee for the reception and another smaller one
for the Press and television people. We simply cannot
get them all into the house.'

It became obvious that Lord Beardmore had an axe to
grind in all this, for with careful timing he then leaked to
his own writers the fact that the honeymoon was to be
spent at his Riviera villa.

Two hours before the ceremony a dense crowd had
gathered outside the old church. The solitary village
policeman had to fight his way to the only telephone box

143

to ring through to Newport for reinforcements. They arrived, siren blaring and weaving an erratic course between the stream of cars in order to reach the eye of the storm.

Richard's parents were rendered speechless by the spectacle. They stood in the porch watching the best man step out of the driving seat of his shining old Daimler, resplendent in his wedding garments, topper in hand, the sun glinting on his fair head. The waiting teenagers rushed him, screaming. Frenzied policemen linked arms to hold them back. David made his way towards the church waving and smiling. 'For God's sake, hurry, man!' urged one distraught copper, 'we can't hold 'em back much longer. Indeed to goodness, this isn't Cardiff Arms Park.' David kept his cool, honed now to an awareness of what all this signified for his intended future until, safe within Sanctuary, he mopped his brow and moved up the aisle, very much master of the occasion.

Inwardly David was deeply depressed. For months he had been seen in the lobbies and pounced upon, or sidled up to, according to their technique by prominent members of the Labour party who by this time were openly wooing him, avid for an alignment of David's charismatic popularity with their side. Now as he stood waiting to support his friend at a ceremony he feared would leave him completely isolated, save for his share in the life of his guardian, David experienced a desperate sense of loneliness. He also knew that sooner rather than later he would have to disclose to his leader his irrevocable decision to cross the floor, something which he dreaded but realised that he must do. He was as miserable as his Jonathan was beatifically happy. David had helped Richard dress, poured champagne for both of them, checked on the ring, chivvied and joked as if he were as carefree as the bridegroom himself, while really feeling, as he had confided in Fluff, 'like bloody hell'.

Fluff sat among the distinguished guests, wondering if the very best thing for David would not be the catalyst of yet another visit to Paris and his parents. At that moment there was a distraction. The very fraught cleric moved forward. The exhausted organist, who had been playing for over an hour, made swift transition into 'Here Comes the Bride' and she did: tiny, composed, her small pointed face very serious behind the lace of her family veil. Even David's pulse quickened at her appearance as she drew level with her bridegroom, but the pair of them seemed totally oblivious of all the fuss. Their minds and hearts were clear, their movements unflurried and when eventually they returned from the vestry and moved slowly between their friends, they held hands like children. Handkerchiefs were dabbed at many moist eyes. The two mothers were weeping happily but they regained control by the time they faced the barrage of photographers outside. Cameras whirred as groups were formed and re-formed.

One of the fans screamed, 'Kiss the bride, David . . . Daaavid . . .' Quite simply David turned to Joanna who stood on tip-toe to give him a loving kiss. The crowd roared its approval. David managed at last to reach his car where Fluff joined him. As they started to edge forward, fans were clinging like leeches to the doors.

A gloriously comic note was struck when the local policeman spotted his own fourteen-year-old daughter in hot pursuit of the Daimler screaming, 'Daaavid . . . Daaavid . . .' He raced after her, his helmet rolling onto the road, as he yelled, 'Myfanwy, come here or I'll tan your behind for you.' His Myfanwy had by now reached the car and was hanging grimly onto the folded back tonneau cover still shouting, 'Daaavid . . . Daaavid.' One ham-like paw plucked the besotted girl off like a burr and dragged her back the way she had come. The policeman retrieved his helmet from a highly amused spectator, clapped it back, crimson-faced with combined anger and embarrassment, and elbowed his way through the crowd with his leg-flailing daughter firmly under one arm and muttering, 'What your Mam will say, I don't like to think.'

During the reception Lord Beardmore ambled towards Fluff and David. Having greeted them, he said, 'I want a word with you both in private. Is there anywhere we can go here?'

David answered promptly, 'Just follow me, sir,' and led the two older men across the lawn into a small room on the ground floor of the rambling house. He closed the door, saying, 'No one will bother us here.'

'Right, then.' The old peer sat down, knees apart, hands upon them, 'How long is it going to be before you cross the floor, young man?'

Fluff smiled. 'Trust you to crash your fences,' he said affectionately.

'I'm interested,' snapped the Press magnate. 'The air is thick with rumour and conjecture. No one knows what you're up to, Kincale. You're devious, y' know, damn' devious. I must suppose you are not wholly unaware that we are going through a somewhat difficult time. We seem to be drifting dangerously. The murmurs of discontent threaten to become shouts the way things are going. Mark my words, at the next General Election Labour will come to power. What are *you* goin' to do?'

David parried, 'Am I permitted to ask, sir, why you wish to know? You are unquestionably *not* a collector of snippets for your papers, so there must be some more deep-seated motive for your kind interest.'

The old man flashed back, 'Are you trying to be sarcastic, young man?'

'God forbid, sir! No, just factual.'

'Meaning you won't open up unless I do?' Lord Beardmore was glowering now under those bushy eyebrows. David met his look and held it.

'Exactly so, sir,' he then answered.

'Ha!' his interrogator relaxed, 'I'd have despised you for any other response. Are you in town in the next few days?'

'David's driving me back to London when this affair is over,' interpolated Fluff. 'Can you by any chance dine with us tonight?'

146

The endearing gleam which was so much a part of the man lit up his wrinkled face. 'I'd be delighted. Would nine o'clock suit you?'

'Perfectly.'

'Then perhaps you will let me propose that you are my guests. I'll lay on a private room. Right then,' Lord Beardmore rose to his feet, 'nine o'clock, the Savoy. Go in by the river entrance – it's less conspicuous.' He left Fluff and David staring at each other with some amusement.

It was a heady evening for David. When it was over, he and Fluff turned out of the Savoy and strolled along the Embankment towards the Westminster house. The ex-King's one-time equerry was genuinely startled by what had passed between Lord Beardmore and his ward. Fluff was a forward-looking man by nature, training and his war experiences; but even he had never envisaged that the baby he took to Diana Kincale and the nanny at the Dolder Hotel in Zurich would ever embark upon such a course as had been outlined to him tonight.

Rigidly suppressing everything which was churning in his mind, Fluff said, as they crossed Parliament Square, 'One thing troubles me though, David.'

'And what's that, sir?'

'I take it you value your curious friendship with the Duke of Windsor.'

'You know I do.' David stopped in his tracks and gazed at Fluff. 'What a very odd thing to say.'

'Not at all; I merely wish to point out that this is going to come as a bit of a shock to HRH.'

'Then I'll take up their invitation. I'll fly over and explain it to him myself,' David said briskly. 'He'll understand, if I manage to put it over properly. She's never there to luncheon, so we can play a little golf and then I'll tell him in the club house while he drinks that dreadful tea.'

'I see,' said Fluff resignedly, inwardly wondering why the devil no one had ever remarked upon how very royal this monarch's offspring could sound.

'No need to get angry,' David turned his smile upon him. 'You were stuck with him, sir; now you've stuck yourself with me because you loved my Diana mum.' As he spoke it flashed through his mind that this might at long last be the one moment when he could pierce the impenetrable armour and ask the forbidden question. 'And I may as well say it now, I wouldn't be a whit surprised but absolutely delighted if I did find out that you were my real father. In fact I couldn't think of anything more splendid. No,' as Fluff opened his mouth, 'just let me finish. Rikki and I have discussed this often. He thinks the same as me. You needn't answer me of course; I know you won't anyway unless you want to but please just don't give me a lie . . .'

It could scarcely be said that Sir Frederick Musgrave could be the worse for drink on two sherries, a glass or two of fine wines and a couple of brandies. Even so he experienced all the sensations. Big Ben seemed to turn turtle, the pavement to rock under his feet and his own voice sounded very far away and blurred saying, 'My dear chap, I cannot begin to say how much your conjecture flatters me. I too would be delighted if it were the truth but I can promise you it is not so. Will you accept my assurance and my gratitude.'

'Oh, hell,' replied David. 'Yes, of course, sir. Only, what a bloody shame it isn't so.'

If anything had been needed to stiffen Fluff's resolve to see this developing drama through to its unpredictable conclusions, this was it.

After a brief pause the two men continued their walk until David slipped his key into the lock, saying, 'You haven't seen my drawing-room since the stuff came from the homestead. Do let me show it to you. I'd value your opinion, sir.'

Driving down to London Airport, parking the Daimler, before finally gaining the privacy of privilege in the VIP lounge, the question squirrelled in David's mind, 'If not Fluff, then who?' Throughout the flight, abstractedly studying the winking bubbles in his champagne glass, his mind acknowledged that this too was a desperate disappointment. 'After all if I had to be a bastard, it would have been almost like having royalty for a pa if it had been Fluff,' ran his thoughts. Then the stewardess murmured, 'Fasten your seat belt please, Mr Kincale; we're just coming in to le Bourget,' and he resolved never to think of it again. In the end he had no need to bother, but that lay many tomorrows away.

He hailed a taxi at the airport and gave the address, at which the ancient cabby cracked hoarsely, *'vraiment'* and *'tiens!'* which made David laugh. As they sped along in the traffic's mainstream past the now familiar landmarks, David began checking his baggage. The Hermes wine leather case with his initials on the tab — that would be all right, his man had packed his 'gear'. His golf clubs were beside him. The special Virgin Tea of China he had ordered from dear old Mr Laity's shop in St Ives was on the seat beside him with his wine leather briefcase and a small parcel containing 'her Meissen pugs'.

The long cardboard box, heavily bespattered with customs and airport labels, was there too. He had had the flowers flown in from Guadeloupe and collected them at London Airport. The box now lay across one of the bucket seats; on the other his feet in Lobb brogues were resting comfortably. Then panic assailed him. Had Bronson remembered to pack the photographs Fluff had made him have taken by Patrick Lichfield — just in case HRH might want one . . .? Realising he could telephone his home and have these put on the next plane if they had been forgotten, he reflected again on what Fluff had said concerning the Duke's deep-seated antagonism towards the current men of the left.

'Neither monarchs nor those dethroned or abdicated should become fiercely political animals. He is simply choosy. He has much respect for little Clement Attlee whose weasel-like appearance was always so completely deceptive. He feels warmly about Hugh Gaitskell whom he genuinely admires and even cherishes a real affection still for old Ernie Bevin; but what he calls "the present lot" displeases him mightily. He said to me, "I see the whole pack of them as nest-featherers and rank opportunists. I have an uneasy conviction that the more dangerous elements among them could wreak havoc in Britain."'

David jerked back to the present as they halted at the gates, received their *laisser-passer* and went slowly towards the house past the notices, *Beware of Small Dogs – Drive Carefully.*

The great double doors opened as David hopped out of the cab and paid his reckoning. Turning, he said, 'Good afternoon, Hale. I trust you are well,' to the butler, and then to the hovering footman in dark blue livery with silver buttons, 'Hello, Sidney, and how are you?' drawing a smile of welcome from them both. Hale relieved David of his coat, hat and gloves. Indicating the flower box, he said, 'I would like to take that myself please, Hale, and those two small parcels,' and then he followed the coloured footman to the Duke's study. The Duke and Duchess were sitting by the fire with their pugs.

'Ah, there you are,' the Duke looked up. 'We were just discussing you.'

David went through the motions and then picked up the flower box. 'I wonder,' he said with just a touch of diffidence, 'if you care for the *Roses de Porcelaine*, madam. I sent for some for you.' He held out the box. This went down very well. Then he put a small parcel on the drum table beside the Duke, saying, 'Some special tea from old Laity's shop in St Ives, sir, and – er,' – he was back with the Duchess – 'these are for your collection, madam.'

'David,' she protested, 'what a naughty extravagance! Now please sit down. You're giving me a crick in the neck. I do declare you have grown again. How tall are you now?'

'Six foot two, madam.' He disposed of his long legs and accepted a cup of tea which he detested.

150

'And how is Sir Frederick?' Thus the opening gambits, but when she rang for scissors and Sidney came in to cut the string and unwrap the tissue from the long-stemmed flowers, she was really pleased. 'We had a few given to us in the Bahamas,' she told him, 'but I have never seen them since. David, look, they are exactly like shaded pink porcelain and they last for weeks and weeks if you remember to snip the ends and have the water refreshed daily.'

He was off to a good start; but no sooner was he chatting amicably than he remembered, 'I say, sir, I've made a bloomer. I've left your crumpets in my coat.'

The Duchess insisted, 'Please don't bother now. We can have them tomorrow. I want to tell you something. We are having a ball given for us tomorrow night. There are a number of French politicians coming to dinner here first as I thought you might like to meet them. The Jebbs will be here too and they've all expressed a wish to meet the rising young politician who made such a brilliant maiden speech. You see I *have* followed your progress closely!'

David murmured his thanks, wondering why the hell she bothered. Then the Duke who had first obtained his wife's permission to smoke his pipe puffed away contentedly and asked, 'Do you think you can do much for the Liberals, David? I always imagined they are a bit moribund despite that excellent man, Caradoc-Evans.'

David nodded. 'Thereby hangs a tale, sir. Frankly I don't think much can be done. The present mood of the country finds them − otherwise engaged.' He quickly turned to the Duchess, 'I am not keeping you from your hairdresser, am I, madam?' He was anxious to turn the conversation.

'Fancy your remembering!' she exclaimed − once again pleased − as she glanced at the exquisite little pearl and enamel fob watch which was the sole adornment to her little black suit that David had already decided was like no little black suit he had ever seen Englishwomen wearing. 'My word, I am a little late already,' she ran on. 'I shall leave you in the Duke's hands,' so saying, she rose and David escorted her to the door. Then the two men were alone together.

The Duke said, 'Nice to have you back and congratulations on your maiden speech. It's not often the British Press breaks into eulogies. I remember Duff had a similar *tour-de-force* with his. The Press raved.'

'I read his book, sir,' David carried on. 'It was, as I remembered, called *Old Men Forget*. Incidentally, I saw Lady Diana recently and she looks wonderful for her age.'

'She was the toast of the town when I was young,' the Duke reminisced. 'She had beautiful, enormous blue eyes; but of course they were not a patch on Wallis'.'

David's brain clicked back into position. It was all unchanged – she was still his one true love. It was there in every word he spoke, every glance towards her . . . 'I wonder,' he speculated inwardly, 'if I shall ever fall in love like that.'

Just before they went up to dress and while the Duke was still sipping his customary whisky, his son, rather shyly, explained his latest project.

He began, 'I have decided on a personal venture which is derived from that little handicapped child of the outback called Billy-Boy. It is just possible, sir, you may recall what I told you about him on our homestead. You do? Oh, good. Well then you will also remember that the actual homestead is now a centre for just such Australian children. It struck me recently that it wouldn't be a bad idea to start working towards a chain of them throughout both France and England too.'

Once launched upon his project, David shed his initial diffidence and began enlarging upon the scheme while the Duke lay back enveloped in an aura of tobacco smoke, totally absorbed and bereft of any of his usual restlessness.

David went on, 'I thought I might be able to find some handicapped chaps who would be willing to take part in the running of my homes too – not that of course they

152

would be called homes because "home" seems to have an unwanted, sort of left out connotation to it. Actually I wanted to know what you would think of my calling them The David Kincale Training Centres for Handicapped Children.'

'Capital,' the Duke nodded. 'Where do you intend launching the first?'

David flushed. 'Well – er – here, sir,' he said, 'right here in Paris and I wondered if you would consider it monumental impertinence if I invited Her Royal Highness to be our leading Patroness?'

'Fiddlesticks!' David was assured, 'I am sure Her Royal Highness will be delighted.'

At that moment Sidney appeared in the doorway with the pugs on their leads. This was always the absolutely last warning that His Royal Highness was expected to put himself without any further delay into the hands of his valet.

'Damn!' exclaimed the Duke, rising even so. 'All right, Sidney, you can walk those dogs now. Mr Kincale and I are going up immediately.' As the footman left them, he added, 'We must talk more of this. You can be sure of our support anyway. Now come along, there's a good feller, we simply cannot be late tonight.'

He was, as he told his reflection, 'off floosies', reminding himself of what he thought of as the 'primped and painted little darlings at the Mill'. He merely shrugged off the pending encounter, knowing that the worst whoever it was would be beautifully dressed and able to chatter away easily. So, when he hurried down the short flight of the rather fine staircase into the breathtakingly lovely salon, he was ill prepared for the meeting with his 'floosie'.

A girl was standing beside the Duchess at the far end of the room looking up at the twin minstrels' galleries and saying in what registered to him as a dark brown voice, 'It's quite beautiful, madam,' which was trite enough except that she sounded as if she really meant it.

153

'Ah, David,' said the Duchess and made the introduction. 'Mr David Kincale, Lady Mary Harland,' adding as she sat down on a satin-covered gilt chair, 'David's just arrived from England. He's a very new politician.' She chattered on, while the pair just stood looking at each other, as if neither believed anything of what they each saw.

The girl recovered first. 'How silly!' she laughed, 'we're staring at each other. I must admit I didn't expect . . . er – that is . . .'

'Nor did I,' David agreed, without allowing her to finish.

'You weren't like this with my pretty sub-debs at the Mill,' the Duchess rallied him. 'He was charming and chatty, Lady Mary, and absolutely bored stiff with both of them. Now you two look as if you had seen ghosts. Have you met before perhaps?'

'Never,' said David emphatically, adding softly, 'more's the pity,' as he deliberately crossed over to sit down beside her.

Then the Duke came in and under cover of the general exchange David managed to study the girl at his side. He could see that she was tall – made to seem more so by the little Duchess – slender, with long slim legs, absurdly long and curling eyelashes fringing her enormous green eyes.

By the time they went in to dinner, he had himself in hand again and was able to devote a fraction of his attention to the exquisite food and wine. He asked her at one point, 'Do you care deeply for what you eat and drink, Lady Mary?'

She responded to this somewhat pedantic question enthusiastically, 'Deeply. I am a disciple of Brillat-Savarin – a slave to my own palate. I echo even in *my* inexperience Her Royal Highness' precept, "The first mouthful is always the best."'

'That's a good girl,' the Duke endorsed warmly. 'I am a laggard in such matters. I only hope that what you are quoting isn't true where I am concerned.'

Lady Mary had clearly dined with them before because she asked, 'Do you mean your large breakfasts, sandwich luncheons and plain dinners, being in direct opposition to "*dites moi ce qu'il mange, je te dirai ce qu'il est*"?'

'I hope so,' said the Duke with such feeling that they all laughed. He defended himself, 'I'm not as dull as those three make me sound, I hope.'

The Duchess said lightly, 'Of course you're not, darling, or I would never have married you; but I must admit I do enjoy men who love fine wines and they mean little or nothing to you, do they?'

'Not really, but you must agree that my taste in women is superb.' He lifted his glass to the Duchess and the pair facing each other smiled.

David was thinking, 'Now those eyes are hazel, but they were green and that hair is like a copper beech leaf in the sun.'

'What are you thinking, Mr Kincale?' the girl asked and David a trifle wildly replied truthfully.

'Well, so it is,' the Duchess agreed. 'I wonder, has your family a touch of the Irish?'

'Not that I know of, madam. We're Leicestershire through and through with just a leavening of French, *pour me sauver*, I always say, being a fervent Francophile.'

In the ducal limousine, bowling towards the theatre, David sat as far back as he could to watch as the lights played on this girl's remarkable hair. He expected so little that for the moment he was bewildered. There was the usual stir when they went through the foyer, pausing two or three times to greet acquaintances, introducing the young pair with them. When they reached their *loge* and were settled behind their hosts, David realised that the Duchess really enjoyed being recognised.

'Can you two see all right there or would you like to come and sit here, Lady Mary?' the Duke leaned back.

'Certainly not, sir, thank you,' said Lady Mary quickly.

'We can see perfectly and besides everyone would be so disappointed.' To David, she whispered, 'Do you know if it is *de rigueur* to ask if they would call me "Mary"? I rather think not, you know.'

David whispered back, 'Sorry I don't know either but I must conclude it is all right because they call me David.'

'Ah, but how long have you known them?'

'Ever since I was eight,' he admitted.

'Well, then you see it's not at all the same thing.'

Suddenly the Duke turned round again. 'What are you two whispering about? I think I heard some of it. If I did, the answer is certainly – Mary. Isn't that right, Wallis?'

He explained and the Duchess said lightly, 'How charming of you, my dear; most certainly we shall call you by your first name if you wish.'

Quite suddenly the staring and the stiffness disappeared. By the end of the second interval they were chatting away eagerly. When they reached Maxims and were shown to their table, David stood over the Duchess and asked, 'Madam, will you dance?'

She answered a trifle tartly, 'Go and dance with Mary. I know you're dying to and anyway we can dance later.'

Lady Mary stood up, bobbed and in moments they were on the small floor. Their table had been set for eight; on their return the empty places had been filled and more introductions followed. From that moment and until he let himself into his own house again, David moved in an enchanted world.

He learned during that first evening that Mary and her aunt were staying at the British Embassy. So, greatly daring and having already found out her home was in Quorn country and she hunted with them regularly, he asked her to ride with him the next morning. When she accepted, he said, 'I will find out if it's all right tonight. The Duchess seldom appears during the day and I am only pledged to playing golf with His Nibs during the luncheon hours.'

'His Nibs,' she pounced. 'Is that what you call him?'

David had the grace to colour. 'I'm sorry, of course not.

It's just that – er – well, my guardian was his equerry once and my running mate, a Welshman called Richard Llewellyn, and I always call him His Nibs, when we're alone. You are so easy to talk to, it just slipped out.'

'You're easy to talk to, too,' she answered softly. 'You must tell me about your Richard Llewellyn and about your guardian. You're over twenty-one, aren't you?'

'Yes.'

'I'm only nineteen,' she volunteered.

'Mary dear,' the Duchess' voice cut across these exchanges, which made the pair start guiltily.

When much later the Duchess danced with David, she teased him, 'My choice this time is somewhat more successful, isn't it?'

'Oh, yes,' David said quickly. 'She's quite lovely and so intelligent too.' Then losing his cool again for an instant, he added artlessly, 'I'm having a lovely time.'

'You don't play enough,' she told him, delighted at her success. 'You must come here more often.'

The Duchess danced beautifully; David scarcely felt he was holding her, but he was too tall for her so she did not dance with him for very long. Walking back to their table, it suddenly struck her that for the first time in her life she had danced with her own son and there was a wry twist to her mouth as she sat down.

Typically plans ran like a flame through her mind. 'I'll have him here more often – he is so good looking – and besides he wears his clothes superbly and has lots of money. Really he's a very eligible *partie*. It will be fun . . .' She was off pursuing the *leitmotif* of her existence and presently moving around in the Duke's arms on the crowded floor, she whispered to him, 'He's really rather a credit to us, David, don't you think?' but she flinched when she saw the sadness in his eyes and did not press him for an answer.

Just before the party broke up, David seized an opportunity to ask the Duke, 'Is it all right, sir, if I take Mary for an early morning ride?' and was able to go back to her, lean over her chair and murmur, 'permission granted

157

His Nibs says he will give me the stables' telephone number before we go to bed so I can ring them in the morning. He'll lend me a car to come for you. What time shall we make it?'

'I can be ready by eight o'clock.'

And she was.

Blatantly they inspected one another in the sharp morning light. Blatantly they looked again as having handed her into the saddle, he swung himself up and gathering the reins, moved off beside her.

'Want some coffee?' he asked her as they reined in by his borrowed car.

'In a café? Nothing grand. Then I would – and some croissants.'

The Duke had insisted on sending one of the footmen to accompany them, saying, 'He can take your mounts back to the stables for you,' almost as if he guessed they would want to talk somewhere together before separating.

They found a small café, ordered *deux grandes tasses de café au lait* and had a basket of croissants set before them. It was the kind of place where the butter was parcelled up in little papers, so David undid about a dozen and put some on her plate. She removed her bowler and veil, shook her head and the copper beech leaves flew out. They sat close together in a remote corner of the city of lovers and just before it was essential they left, he laid a hand across hers under the table and said rather hoarsely, 'I shall count the hours until tonight.' He had explained both Fluff and Richard to her and she had promised to come and see his 'little house in Westminster within the sound of the Division bell'.

As he stood beside the car outside the Embassy, he asked, 'What are you wearing tonight? I would love you to wear my flowers or at least do something with them.'

'Bliss, David. How very kind! I'm wearing white, a silk jersey thing Mummy had Mainbocher make for me – sort of Greek – and I'm putting my hair up too.'

David played a shocking round of golf. He wondered how he could possibly force himself back into the state of mind which had been so wholly his when he came out of the Savoy after the dinner with Lord Beardmore. He was also burping slightly, having – as he discovered when he called for the bill – scoffed seven very large croissants and about a pound of butter, to say nothing of four big cups of coffee.

'Wind?' the Duke enquired mildly, sipping his special tea.

'Croissants, sir. Mary and I went into a café and what with talking and one thing and another, I ate seven croissants.'

The Duke regarded him thoughtfully. 'It's the ''one thing and another'' which concerns me. She's not for dalliance, need I remind you?'

'No, sir,' David confirmed, 'you can rest assured . . .'

'Thought I could. She's a discontented gel by the way. She doesn't care for doing the season, such as it is from all accounts nowadays. She takes photographs. Try to see some. They are rather good. I think she'll want a career presently.'

'What will her parents say?'

'I cannot tell. I only met them once when they were passing through Paris on their way to Davos. The mother's been a beauty – made her curtsey to me, by the way. The old earl is a difficult feller. Crazy about horseflesh, hunting, collecting Stubbs and slaying pheasants. I don't think either of them would mind. Their son was killed in an accident. Mary's the only one left. They would want her to be happy.'

David listened feeling as if nails were being hammered into him. It was so clear that this little idyll was fated to be no more, for what could a man embarked upon such a course as his have for such a girl as this?

He heard himself saying, 'There is another rather more serious matter I would like to discuss with you, sir, if it wouldn't bore you.'

The Duke looked at him a trifle sharply for a moment. 'You're nervous,' he shot at him.

'Yes, sir.'

'Why pray?'

'Because I expect when I've told you, you'll want to chuck me out lock, stock and barrel and never darken your doors again.'

'Fiddlesticks!' snapped the Duke, so like old Queen Mary for an instant that David was nearly brought to laughter — but not quite. For he was ready now. He waited while more hot water was brought. He watched the Duke's straining ritual, and then when the cup was re-filled and ready, the Duke told him, 'Fire ahead, David. At least you can talk to me.' He bit back the words he very nearly added.

David had stiffened in his chair. 'Am I allowed to ask, sir, that what I have to tell you is strictly between Your Royal Highness and I?'

This time the silence lasted for quite a long time. Finally, a trifle sadly, the Duke affirmed, 'It will remain so until further notice, you have my word for it.'

CHAPTER XII

'The light of Lights
Looks always on the motive, not the deed,
The shadow of Shadows on the deed alone.'

— William Butler Yeats

THEY DINED BY candlelight which sparkled on the jewels of the women and on the embroidery of their gowns. They sat below the famous painted ceiling with its ribbons and flowers, intertwining. Their background was composed of the delicate blue of the *boiserie* which Wallis had brought from the Château de Chateloup, interspersed with *chinoiserie* wallpaper. The tables were covered by the fitted tablecloths which were the Duchess' hallmark. On this occasion gleaming satin was masked by exquisite lace. Upon it the candlelight danced and postured on a multiplicity of wine glasses at each cover, on the dazzling silver gilt and on the patina of the 18th century Lowestoft dinner service which was once the property of Queen Alexandra and bore King George IV of England's crown and cypher.

There were six covers set at each round table. As dinner progressed, the Duke and Duchess moved, so that by the time the *Soufflé glacé Pompadour* was served, they had spent time with all their guests.

Mary was sent in on David's arm. As he looked down at her as they moved towards the dining room, he said softly, 'My orchids must be very proud tonight.'

Her hairdresser had pinned the flowers across the back of her upswept curls. Around her throat and one wrist she wore her mother's emeralds which were a perfect foil for the china whiteness of her Mainbocher jersey dress. She flashed him a brief little smile of acknowledgment.

As they entered the famous dining room, she murmured, 'Fairyland, isn't it? She does flowers superbly. I believe she studied when she was in China and now with the world's flowers at her disposal, the result is magical. Even so, she complains bitterly when she is compelled to buy them from the Paris shops. "No scent at all," she declares, handing over a huge scent spray filled with Diorissima, "so give them all a jolly good squirt from this."' They had reached their table. As the footman, wearing the royal ceremonial livery of scarlet and gold, held their chairs and they sat down, she added, shaking out her lacy napkin, 'If she hadn't married him, she might have been a very famous interior decorator.'

He nodded. 'But have you noticed that our gifted hostess is not really interested in great paintings or really fine furniture unless it's gilded, painted or otherwise tarted up?'

This evoked a little laugh which bubbled up and was instantly suppressed.

On her right a distinguished-looking elderly man with silvering hair turned to greet her, saying, 'Good evening, Mary dear, looking lovelier than ever I see.'

She replied, 'Hello, Nikki,' and then across herself she effected introductions, 'Mr David Kincale from England; Mr Nicholas Guttenberg from Zurich.'

'Cue for a bit of Mr Coward's dialogue, eh, sir?' laughed David.

Nicholas Guttenberg nodded, amused. 'I ask, "How was England?" You say, "Rather chilly England".'

David joined, 'How was Switzerland, sir?'

'Very small, Switzerland . . .' he broke off, then added, 'what an enchanting play that was. I hear it's to be revived again. You know for my generation that balcony scene was one of the most charming of love scenes. Romeo and Juliet were so overdone I have always felt, knowing this to be *lèse-majesté*.'

David nodded, 'Lovers are surely too inhibited for all that rhetoric. At least at first . . .'

'Exactly so.'

Mary put an end to this exchange, exclaiming, in mock disapproval, 'Talking across me, gentlemen! Really! Anyway you can tell that to the Master himself. He is joining us, I believe.'

The Swiss shook his head. 'That, my dear, is the delight of round tables. Wallis never fails, does she? The world's most exquisite hostess.'

Honours having been done, he devoted himself to Mary for a while and David turned to his left. For some to him unaccountable reason the Duchess had placed him next to Miss Elsa Maxwell, at least according to her place card. She was deep in a scandalous conversation across the table, so David had time to look around him and having had no luncheon, to devote himself to the exquisite *Caviar en gelée* on his royal plate.

It had already become very apparent to him that this royal circle was – if this evening was truly representative – a microcosm of the glitter and dazzle of the ball which was to follow and the company the Windsors kept. The Duke was now seated with his new found court, among the gossip-column aristocracy of retired manufacturers and brokers, real estate barons, bankers and cosmetic makers. 'Jet-setty,' he thought, 'not at all *le gratin*.' Then, ashamed by his silent criticism, he turned again to the girl at his side and found to his relief that she had returned to him.

'Brief me, do,' he asked softly. 'Who is your friend?'

'What the international gossip columns label a Swiss gnome. We always call gnomes "gernomernies" at home. Do you?'

He replied gravely, 'Garden ones – yes, of course – the ultimate in abomination, but I take it you mean a financial one.'

'Just so. He is probably the biggest of them all. He carries such secrets around he even has to have a permanent bodyguard.'

'Really. Why?'

'Those paradisical things called "Numbered Accounts". He would – or rather could – be richer than Croesus; own the world in fact, if it wasn't for one thing.'

163

David frowned. 'Meaning what?'

'Just a little matter of fastidiousness. He could as soon practise blackmail as you could subscribe to parliamentary chicanery.'

'He's in love with you,' David said abruptly.

'Oh, yes; but something more – he's a very dear and kindly friend. He has been a family one for ages. He and Daddy were at Eton together and he comes to stay with us quite often.'

David's food suddenly tasted like ashes in his mouth. He said, 'Far too old for you of course.'

The taste came back with the next mouthful as she agreed, 'Of course, silly. Do you know I've only ever had *Sole Lucullus* once before?'

By 10.30 they were back in the great salon and then the Duchess beckoned to David across the room. He joined her, only to find himself being led around, moving rather like a pawn in some wholly incomprehensible game, until he realised that he, a minnow among such glittering fishes, was being displayed. He found it totally distasteful.

Once he caught the Duke's eyes on him, a curious expression in their blueness. David just smiled back, disengaged himself and moved in his direction.

'How are you enjoying all this, David?' the Duke asked.

'Marvellous, sir,' he mimed rubbing his stomach for an instant. 'Your dinner was worth my luncheon time austerity. I was ravenous, you know.'

The Duke turned to his bemedalled companion and said in German, 'This young man took pity on me. We played two rounds of golf at luncheon time, so he missed his feed bag altogether.'

David made a suitable disclaimer in the same language. The Duke raised a surprised eyebrow and was about to comment when he saw that the Duchess was beginning to rally her guests. Then Elsa, with a great burp, announced, 'I'm going ahead of all you dear people; now don't be late – the traffic's terrible tonight.'

Soon all the guests were flowing out into the great hall in a flurry of furs and fans, and the cars were drawing up one by one.

As he handed a princess in and followed her, David felt a piercing wave of longing for his adoptive parents, reminded by some trivial incident of a dance they had taken him to where they had all sung silly songs driving home and ended up in the swimming pool. He felt himself abruptly in alien territory; besides which Mary had gone off with 'that Swiss' and he was suddenly at sixes and sevens with himself . . . none of which showed of course.

The rest of the evening was spent predictably. He was caught by the cameras when standing talking to the Duke. He danced with a great number of women, most of whom extended invitations to him with a light 'let Her Royal Highness bring you – I'll telephone her.'

When once again dancing with Mary, with the scent of her hair in his nostrils, he calmly steered her off the huge ballroom floor to ask behind a bank of oleanders, 'Can we – dare we – go?'

Mary looked at him thoughtfully. 'Where?' she temporised.

He told her what he wanted, straight out. 'I'd like to wander about a bit with you on my arm, perhaps to Les Halles, hear some of the pithy comments those wonderful old boys are bound to call after you, fill your arms with flowers and then go into somewhere like the Veau Noir for a bowl of *Soupe à l'Oignon*.'

That decided her. 'One never leaves before the royals,' she reminded him primly. 'I'll find my wrap and meet you under the fountain on the left at the foot of the staircase. Give me about five minutes.'

He was pacing about when she reappeared. He caught her hand, tucked it under his arm and they strolled out into the night, past the inevitable crowd which had gathered. Then he put her into a taxi and they drove away.

165

'I shall send flowers and a pretty little note,' she told him. 'I shall say – so remember to back me up – that we went for a stroll and I caught my heel and broke it off . . . she wouldn't ever expect me to come back all dot and carry one. It's the perfect alibi for such gross bad manners.'

It was after this that they returned to serious talk together, strolling between the aisles, bandying words as he had predicted, bartering for an armful of flowers, stroking the little dog on his chair outside the restaurant and ultimately finding a table, remote and perfect for them, where chin on hands they talked into the dawn, oblivious of the marketeers who came in for their coffees splashed with cheap brandy.

The next day David flew back to England and reality. Before he left Mary gave him the address and telephone number of her flat in Berkeley Street and her home in Yorkshire. In turn he had handed over his card. She told him, 'I shall be back in a week or two,' adding the magical words, 'then I want you to come and meet Mummy and Daddy . . .' which was at least something to look forward to in the future.

Richard was still on his honeymoon; Fluff was away on Ducal affairs, so when David let himself into his Westminster house, he was feeling unaccountably depressed.

The morning brought Bedlam. 'Hen', as he had re-christened his housekeeper, came in as usual with his breakfast and the morning papers, saying, 'Good morning, sir and welcome home.' Having taken in the disorder as she crossed with his bed-table, she turned round and began reducing the chaos of half-unpacked suitcase and tumbled clothes.

David began leafing, as usual, through the papers. 'God's bloody flaming boots!' he exploded suddenly. 'The pox-stricken, leperous bastards! How the hell have they got onto this?'

'Hen' stiffened like Lot's wife, stared at David and

166

opened her mouth to expostulate as David leapt out of bed, yelling, 'Get out, Hen, I must dress.' She waddled mutinously out of the door and went bumbling down the staircase, muttering, 'Well, I never, a nice performance I must say. I never would have believed it . . .'

Nor did David believe the gossip columns on which his eyes had alighted, as he flipped through the papers. Richard did not know. Fluff would never tell; and there was no one else he could think of who could have 'leaked' the information, yet there were the headlines blaring out, *Promising Young Liberal Quits Party* and *Where Now, David?* with, worst of all, a picture of him chatting to the Duke under the bannered question, *Is millionaire David Kincale resigning from Liberal party to become International Playboy?* with a report that 'David Kincale dined with the Windsors before attending a Gala Charity Ball given in their honour by international hostess Elsa Maxwell.'

David stood still for a moment, trying to collect his thoughts. Then he grabbed the telephone and dialled Dylan Caradoc-Evans' private number. When he came on the line, David said, 'Good morning, sir. I apologise for troubling you at this hour but have you seen the papers this morning?'

The familiar voice replied levelly, 'I have.'

David drew a sharp intake of breath before continuing. 'I want you to know that I have never given anything to the Press nor have I said anything. May I come round and explain please?'

'Of course you may. I shall be at headquarters at eleven. Please meet me there.'

Stammering his thanks and just about to replace the receiver, David heard, 'Are you still there, David?' He affirmed he was and the question came down the line, 'Just tell me one thing now – is there a germ of truth in what the beggars are saying?'

'Yes, sir. I'm afraid there is.' The line went dead. David rooted among the papers on the floor until he found the *Clarion*. This he combed through, but failed to find a single reference to himself. Tying his dressing-gown around him, he ran barefoot down the stairs to make his most abject apologies to 'Hen'.

Before he was out of the bath, there was a telephone call from the Labour leader. When his man told him, David shouted from behind the bathroom door, 'Tell him I have gone to see Mr Caradoc-Evans and you will get in touch and see I ring back.'

Then the redoubtable Sven Jorgensen, Editor of the *Clarion*, came on the line and David took that call.

'Let's cut the preliminaries,' Jorgensen began mildly. 'Have you been indiscreet, David?'

'Not a bloody thing,' David snarled back. 'I give you my word on that.'

Jorgensen's voice lightened. 'Well, then, Playboy, you'd better get down here as soon as you can and we'll try to put out something factual. "The Lord" on the Penthouse floor is not pleased, I think you ought to know.'

David sighed. 'Look, sir, I'm meeting Mr Caradoc-Evans at eleven o'clock. His opposite number, if you get my meaning, has already been on and I've stalled him until I've seen my present boss. Can I buy you some luncheon afterwards?'

'Where do you suggest for privacy? Behind the High Altar at Westminster Abbey? That's a nice venue for a snack.'

'What about coming here, sir? Plain food, good wine and bodyguards like starved cheetahs.'

'Excellent; but first we'll have to kick out some copy before we eat. We must make the early editions of the evenings and it'll have to be checked by His Holiness.'

David put back the receiver in a somewhat lighter frame of mind. While his man helped him dress, he reminded himself that the only thing which really mattered now was treating the 'grand old man' as decently as possible. 'The Other One', as he thought of his future leader, 'will be purring anyway!'

After as distasteful a morning as David had ever spent, he came back to his house with a piece of paper in his pocket which bore a copy of the statement Mr Caradoc-Evans would circulate to the Press, plus an invitation to spend a few days with the old man as soon as time permitted. David had exerted his charisma in no uncertain manner while feeling like Miss Dorothy Parker when she reviewed a book by A A Milne and confessed to her reading public, 'tonsant weader frew up'.

The 'Waters' Daughters' – Doris and Elsie – stayed until midnight during which hours the telephone rang incessantly. By the time David closed the front door behind them and drew the bolt, it was all over. Elsie had typed and Doris had posted David's letter of resignation to Mr Caradoc-Evans and tomorrow his name would be put forward with the proposal – a foregone conclusion this – for him to stand as Labour candidate for a thoroughly safe seat at the next General Election. The announcement of this was to follow exactly six weeks later. The hustings loomed ahead.

David sat up late that night writing his 'Mrs Collins' to the Duchess and his confidential report to the Duke. In the latter he wrote, 'I am only so thankful, sir, that you permitted me to outline my plans to you instead of playing that second round of golf. It really would have been too horrible to contemplate if I had not told you first. As it is, I imagine Her Royal Highness will be quite revolted by my actions, especially as she has been so very kind and hospitable to such a sprat among her very eminent whales! I hope that Your Highness will graciously permit me to continue my reports to you. But most of all I want to apologise for the implicit impertinence in labelling (and libelling) me "playboy" when in Your Royal Highness' company. When I look back on your years of devoted service to this country . . .'

David continued in this vein for several pages, sealed the envelope and only then glanced at the little gold travelling clock which had been Diana Kincale's. It stood on his desk beside the photograph of them both standing laughing beside the aircraft in which they had flown to their deaths. Its hands declared it to be 1 am.

The telephone rang again. Wearily, David lifted the receiver to hear a soft voice asking, 'Oh, were you asleep, David?' It was Mary. She said, 'I'm coming back to England. I know what happened. I want you to know I feel you have some very deep-seated reason for what you have done. No, I have no intention of trying to pry; but it's made me do some pretty serious thinking about my own life. Can I come and see you and explain myself, because I believe you know someone who has offered to help me?' In the event she never came because she learned her mother was seriously ill, so she went directly from Paris to her parents' home in the country and it was two years before they were to meet again.

As they talked on, David felt as if he was emerging from a labyrinthine tunnel into the light. When they had agreed to dine – at his suggestion – in a private room two days later – with a slight argument as to which day that was in the middle of the night – he said goodnight to her and sat on at his desk staring at the picture of his adoptive parents. Finally he told them, 'I think you two would have liked her very much indeed,' and went around turning off the lights.

He met 'Hen' in the doorway. She was upholstered in a quilted dressing-gown, tied across her generous middle which he thought affectionately made her look like a Michelin tyre advertisement. She carried a small silver tray with a cup of the dreaded malted milk.

'Feelin' better now, Mr David?' she enquired.

'Much better,' he said smilingly. To prove it he drank the beastly stuff in one gulp, returned the empty cup and she reminded him, 'Now you can sleep well after all them muckrakers have done to you. Don't forget Mr Richard and Mrs Joanna come home tomorrow.'

CHAPTER XIII

'For this could never have been, not ever,
'til the Gods and the years relent, shall be . . .'

— Algernon Charles Swinburne

IT WAS OCTOBER and a surly little wind rampaged among the remaining leaves, chivvying the fallen along the street like a cross nanny chasing her charges home.

Below David's windows, six men from the Council were totally absorbed in their work of brewing up yet another billy can of tea under the tarpaulin they had erected with infinite care when they first appeared two days before. In that time, David reminded himself, they had between them managed to lift six pieces of kerb-stone, which they had leaned against his railings together with a dozen paving slabs – par for the course these days, he accepted. When they had removed the slabs as far as the corner of Smith Square, a man arrived in a car and instructed them to put them all back again. This was deemed to be wiser than facing yet another strike by trying to dismiss the men.

Mary's taxi grated to a halt just beyond the tea party. She stepped out, a lady from the pages of France's *L'Officiel* fashion glossy magazine, dressed in a soft sand colour from the suede coat slung across her shoulders to the high-heeled, high cuffed suede boots. For contrast there was the glitter of gold chains over her cashmere polo sweater and the brilliant copper of her low-swinging curls. David was confident that any 'telly' lovely swathed in mink and flashing her diamond loot would look dowdy by comparison.

As the bell pealed, David turned away from the win-

171

dow, calling out, 'All right, I'll open the door, Bronson.'
This was the first time he had seen Mary since Paris. Her
mother had developed cancer and lingered before her
death. Only when the inexorable shades had closed over
her once elegant head did Mary consider herself free to
leave her father and return to London.

David followed her up the staircase.

'I match your decor,' she exclaimed. 'Clever me! I only
got in an hour ago. The train was late so I merely dum-
ped all my stuff at the flat and came straight to you. We
have *so* much talking to do.'

She was achingly beautiful. He took her coat, laid the
soft suede over a chair and came back to the fireplace
where she stood looking round.

'You're an extraordinary man, David Kincale,' she told
him. 'This is not at all the bachelor pad I expected. I suppose the spinet was your mum's. That rose! Is it Corot or
Cortot? I always muddle those two, but it is quite
exquisite. I pity the poor gal who inherits this. She'll
have nothing to do – not even the flowers. Who does
them?'

'Bronson and I,' David admitted. 'The old boy said a
hilarious thing this morning. He looked at me solemnly.
You'll agree he is rather like Mr Pickwick. He said, "You
know, sir, we had better be careful or we'll be mistaken
for a couple of those homosecticides!"'

Bronson entered the room amid their laughter carrying an ice bucket and a small tray. Mary chatted away to
him easily while he opened the bottle, filled their glasses
and proffered cigarettes which were refused. Looking
vastly approving, as if indeed she were a bowl of milk
punch, Bronson took himself off on his customary exit
line, 'Will that be all, sir?'

Mary looked at David over the winking bubbles. 'I
feel like a character in a Victorian melodrama, wanting
to say, "Alone at last!" It's been a long, sad time, David;
and for you such a fraught one, with such dramas and
now the hustings again. Oh, Lord! Am I to be allowed to
help?'

He smiled wryly. 'Not bloody likely,' he retorted, 'and have your father deepen the melodrama with, "Never darken my doors again." Remember, my lady, I'm Labour now.'

She flopped down onto a dusky orange sofa and waved one elegant leg. 'Unboot me, please,' she asked. 'I like stockinged feet best.' Running straight on, she told him, 'I have decided you must have your reasons but that you will be pretty close about them.' As the second boot slid off, she flexed her toes and added outrageously, 'Even to me.'

Without leaving any pause for David to take up such a deliberate challenge, she resumed, 'Daddy was really rather nice about it if you must know. When I told him I intended coming here, he said he had met you once at White's or the Garrick or some such male gossip shop. He told me he had formed the opinion even then – his own words, David – that you are "a Coming Man" – which is open to free interpretation I will admit; but then dear old Daddy is totally archaic; really just one long cliché with a fat bank balance and a very useful handle to his name.'

David stood, the second boot still in his hands, looking down at her. 'Mary,' he warned, 'if you persist with this carry on, I shall probably rape you before dinner. There is only so much I can endure. Put your legs down this instant.'

She responded to this order by standing on tip-toe to link her hands around his neck and whispering, 'Then please kiss me – just for starters. I'm right off all this chastity.'

They sprang apart as the door opened to re-admit Bronson with another scuttle of coal for the fire. When he had stoked it, he straightened up and addressed the girl, 'Excuse me, my lady, but Mrs Binns and me wondered if you and the master would care to have dinner here by the fire. If you please, my lady, cook would also like to know if you care for oysters.'

'I adore them,' she replied. 'They're more beautiful than any religion. David, who said that? Was it Saki?'

'It was,' he agreed. Choking back laughter, he wiped his mouth and saw the resultant carmine on the white lawn. 'You might have warned me,' he reproached her, scrubbing away with the handkerchief.

'I didn't give you time, sir, for which I apologise,' Bronson murmured. 'Shall we say nine o'clock? Mrs Binns will come in a few moments beforehand and take you to the toilet, my lady.'

Mary had the grace to colour slightly as she thanked him, but when the door closed once more, she and David exploded with laughter. 'He's not real,' she choked, 'he's simply . . . not . . . real.'

'He's incredible,' David agreed. 'Fluff found him for me.'

They sobered fast; there was too much at stake and their laughter faded as she drew him down beside her on the velvet. 'How much will you tell me, David, of what you plan to do?'

'Little or nothing,' he regretted, 'but knowing what is meant by the term I will give you an "opinion" and ask you to comment on it, if this won't bore you.'

This she ignored, saying, 'It's just the *why* of your apparently blackleg gesture that still foxes me.'

'I think I must have been sired by a man who was either a politician or a statesman.'

'What's the difference?'

He shrugged. 'According to the Oxford Dictionary a politician is primarily "a crafty intriguer", whereas a statesman is not necessarily so, but is "one skilled in the management of public affairs". In the final account all party politics stink; but until an acceptable alternative can be found, we're stuck with them. Even so there are people in high places who foresee a total collapse of the democratic system. I think they have a fancy for tying this island to the coat-tails of this European Economic Community they're talking about. If that comes about, we shall get dragged into it and we shall lose by it all the way along the line unless our men in power are strong enough to bargain for an adequate cut of the great fat Franco/Germanic cake, which I very much doubt.

'For Britain, decimation is the name of the game. It is happening already, as you know . . . the loss of her possessions and the awful corrosion of the national character too. Joe Public is beginning to lose his backbone. Idleness has become the God of the market place; potential employees only ask two questions today: "How much will I earn and how few hours will I be expected to work?" If the answers don't please, they go back to the dole and tax-evading, casual jobs.

'Even the best of 'em are hamstrung by the taxation on overtime. As an electrician told me recently, "It's no use trying to work overtime when it's all bloody well taken in taxes." He makes a valid point.

'Look at the crime rate. It is rising all the time with the age group descending to the lesser teens, simply because the young have no inspiration, no incentive. With threats of nuclear war far too many of them now shrug and mutter, "What's the use? We may be bombed out of existence any day."'

David paused a moment and then resumed. 'Even so, I could still have sufficient faith in this marvellously resilient nation if it were not for my conviction that underneath it all — burrowing like some monstrously evil mole — the Communist bug is very actively engaged. Somewhere, somehow, there are already men deeply bitten by that bug, already nourished on subversive muck, men trained to infiltrate and suborn while being paid handsomely for so doing.'

Mary nodded. 'Of course, David, but let me go further and say that in my opinion we *are* Communist-riddled already. In fact I strongly suspect that even some of the chaps you've joined are in up to their necks.'

'But have you any proof?'

'No, of course not. Nor have you!'

'There you have it,' he spread his expressive hands and then thrust them deep into his trouser pockets. 'So, my beautiful lady, we come back to the cliché more hoary than any your belted earl of a pa has ever uttered.'

Her face stiffened. 'Oh, David, you mean . . . if you can't beat 'em, join 'em.'

He used one of Fluff's phrases. 'Exactly so.'

'And what now?'

'Ah, that's the unanswerable one . . .'

Her eyes were suddenly very green and glittering. 'You mean, "So far and no further, Mary," don't you? *You're including me out,* that's what you're really trying to tell me, isn't it?'

'Of course,' he said simply. 'There is no place for you, my lovely. Do you remember at the Elsa Maxwell ball when Noël Coward went over to the piano? He strummed a bit and then he sang that little song of his from *Private Lives* which you and I have never even seen . . . "Some Day I'll Find You".'

Mary nodded mutely.

'You slipped one hand round the back of your little gilt chair and I took it. *Then* I knew that I'd found you . . . but that it wasn't any good to either of us.'

'But why not, David?' This came out as a cry of despair and was to remain so in his mind in the years ahead.

'Because,' he told her harshly, 'only a fool trails sables in a cesspit. I do not know where I am going, so how can I hold your hand and lead you into an unknown destination?'

There was anger in her voice now. 'Do you suppose,' she asked furiously, 'that I can now invoke a sleep and a forgetting? My family motto is "to have and to hold". And you may as well know, damn you, that I have absolutely no intention of making a well-bred exit from your life. I refuse to behave like a gentlewoman. It's just not on, David. For the last three years – ever since I came out in fact – I have had my own cold grey dawns at the utter futility of what's expected of girls like me.

'Of course, at the beginning all the play and the privileges were rather delicious; but my mind was made up for me when we were in Paris – no, not by *you* but by

176

your friends, the Windsors. I knew I was through with it all when I saw for myself what wealth and privilege had done to two ageing romantics – an ex-King and a woman of boundless ambition, both now embittered by their own errors of judgment but still inextricably bound because of them to a trivial merry-go-round which will ultimately fling them off to meet eternity. I determined then to have no more of it. If you analyse what has happened to them, despite his royal aura, they are condemned to pursue that endless round of theirs in the company of brittle actors, American industrialists and second-rate titles.

'Then you come along; a modern Don Quixote, hell bent on tilting at windmills, but when I offer myself as your Sancho Panza, you turn me down flat, saying in effect, "Oh, no, Mary, you must stay mouldering inside your social scene in the safety of your father's home." That's what you're telling me. Well, let me tell you my social scene is only a substitute for the real thing these days and I am sick to death of it. Somehow I must do something with my life, if not with you, then elsewhere,' she rose abruptly, green eyes blazing. 'We both seem to be erupting with quotations tonight so here's one prophetic one for you. Try it for size. "Some little talk awhile of thee and me . . . and then no more of me or thee," but tag on, David, if you please, "for some time to come . . . maybe".'

Before he could stop her, she had snatched up her coat, bag and boots and was out of the door down the stairs, slamming the front door behind her. David rushed to the window just in time to see her flying up the street in her stockinged feet, yelling, 'Taxi . . . taxi!' and waving one boot in the air.

Then Bronson came in wheeling his trolley on which were their oysters and thin brown bread and butter.

CHAPTER XIV

'. . . plunge into disaster.'

– Harold Macmillan

HE KNEW BETTER than to follow his urge to dash down the stairs in pursuit as he heard her voice crying 'Taxi!' and saw her running up the street. He knew that whatever he said now would only stiffen her anger; even worse, he realised, he must not let himself capitulate just as she had said 'for some time to come'. He faced the fact that he must now try to force himself into protecting her by remaining apart until he had achieved the objective to which he had been dedicated since his boyhood.

Upstairs Bronson removed the trolley and carried the contents down to the basement kitchen where 'Hen' sat in her rocking chair twitching.

'What in the world is going on?' she demanded querulously.

'They've quarrelled,' he told her. 'She's run off. In her stocking feet too and he hasn't called her back, nor run after her like I expected he would.'

'Hen' bristled. 'It doesn't make any sense,' she said crossly, rocking to and fro. 'Is it just a lovers' tiff, Mr Bronson? For if ever I saw two people head over ears in love it's them.'

He shook his head. 'It's more than that. There's some deeper reason, you mark my words,' he said as he sat down heavily beside her.

On the ground floor David was now sitting in his study. It had that air of suspended animation common to such rooms when typewriters and dictaphones are shrouded and wastepaper baskets stand empty. David was struggling to come to terms with what he now saw was inevitable. Mary's words came back to haunt him with their inherent promise of future happiness together. They rang in his head, 'for some time to come . . . maybe', torturing him with hope, then forcing him to acknowledge the total improbability that such a girl – brilliant, beautiful and so agonisingly desirable – would fritter away her years in waiting, while he contended with what at best must prove a labour of Sisyphus.

He had made little headway yet; but as things stood now, his success so far had at least put him within grasp of a cabinet post. This achievement he knew was the open sesame to finding out all the things he needed to know.

He made himself envisage what he thought lay ahead, reminding himself that it had all been *his own choice*. He had plotted and schemed, often sickened himself by what he was doing, but he had gone doggedly forward living an increasingly solitary life, as the friends he would otherwise have made and enjoyed were becoming dangerous to his 'cause'.

It went right back to the time when Labour cabinet ministers first began singling him out for attention. Even before he was appointed Postmaster General the label 'a coming man' was hung about him. When talking to Richard in the little Chelsea house he had likened this to 'a tin can tied to a cat's tail'.

It put an end to one particular pleasure, for no 'coming man' in the Labour Party could have the freedom of the *Clarion's* penthouse meetings with Lord Beardmore and Sven Jorgensen, for both of whom David felt such respect. He missed these meetings and the cut and parry of general talk in that 'holy of holies' when wit and the space of 'in' quips seasoned their exchanges and world affairs were debated with cynical cracks which would have shaken the *Clarion's* readers out of the allegiance.

As time went on, loneliness closed in on David. It was his *casse noisette*. Fluff was increasingly abroad, ostensibly on the Duke's affairs, and only the little house in Chelsea remained open to his ward — and that by stealth. David was well aware the close friendship between Richard and himself could damage his standing with the prime gossips of the party, if it became known, leaving himself open to allegations that he was hand in glove with the *Clarion's* bright young star in the firmament of political reporting. He always warned the Llewellyns before arriving at their house, never taking one of his own cars, just picking up a cab and stopping it a stroller's distance from his objective.

It had already made him feel a bit of an outcast, but at least he could hold onto the consolation that he was progressing nearer and nearer towards a cabinet appointment. Then, he murmured ruefully, staring down at the tooled leather on his desk, *'Après moi la deluge'*, after which, if they all survived, he would be free to marry whomever he liked, just as he would be able to choose his own friends.

He sustained himself with such thoughts, as indeed he had during the time since Mary and he had met in Paris; but when he opened the door to her that evening and followed her upstairs with his heart racing, he forsook all reason and for a few heady moments let go, surrendering himself to the ineffable luxury of being a young man very deeply in love.

He would write to her. At least he could do that although Richard had always warned him of the dangers implicit in 'putting anything on paper'. He walked with danger anyway so what matter! So thinking, he extracted a sheet of his personal writing paper, wrote in the date and began, 'My own darling Mary . . .' Even as he did so, all three people in the house were roused by the sound of the front door bell and a loud knocking with the great brass hand.

'That'll be a telegram,' said 'Hen', sounding triumphant. 'Maybe she's thought better of it, eh, Mr Bronson.'

He made no comment, but when he had climbed the

stairs and opened the door, he saw that it was not a telegraph boy but a messenger from the House who stood on the doorstep holding out an envelope.

'Evening,' said the man. 'From the Prime Minister.'

Bronson took the envelope, said 'thank you', closed the door and walked into the study.

'I'm sorry to disturb you, sir,' he apologised. 'A messenger has just brought this from the Prime Minister.'

David took the envelope from the proffered tray, waited until he heard the door click behind Bronson's departing back and then ripped it open. He drew out the single sheet and stared at it disbelievingly. He read it through. He laid it down unable at first to grasp the contents. Then he snatched it up again. This time phrases leapt unrelated from the papers which shook slightly in one unsteady hand . . . *Cabinet reshuffle . . . regret to inform you . . . my colleagues and I have mutually agreed . . . in the present situation . . . need for an older man . . .* it slid from his fingers onto the desk, falling over the four words David had written, 'My own darling Mary . . .'

He was out! sacked! They had put in an older man. He was no longer PMG but just a young man relegated to the back benches. The immensity of his dismissal at this time seemed to him like some monstrous game of snakes and ladders. He was almost home, then with one more shake of the dice down he went, back to where he had started, from within a hand's grasp of success to total failure. What was more outrageous, no reason was given other than 'a change of policies'.

He *knew* he had served the party well, while admittedly furthering his own ends. He knew he was admired, written about, photographed, interviewed. Only last week old Joe Blundell had said jokingly over luncheon in the House, 'Our Dave's the pin-up boy of the party and that doesn't do us any harm, bringing a bit of glamour to us as it does, so long as it doesn't turn his head, eh lad?' . . . *and now this.*

He was totally bewildered. His daily diet of praise,

admiration and success had ill prepared him for such a setback. It took him some time to grasp the reality; then a coldness ran through his bones and he shivered. *Had they found out something?* It took him a little while to deal with this one too; but finally his own reason began to reassert itself and he sent fear packing simply because, as he made himself see, *there was no one.* They could not know.

He began pacing up and down and the two old dears who served him looked up at the ceiling, then back to each other.

'I'll put the kettle on. I don't feel like sleep yet. Do you fancy a cup of tea?' 'Hen' asked.

She made the tea, sugared their cups liberally and they sat sipping. Big Ben began to strike another hour and this time they counted the twelve sonorous strikes.

'You know,' 'Hen's' worried eyes met Bronson's over cup rims, 'it's like it was during the war. I could always tell when old Ben struck nine if the news was going to be dreadful . . . more 'n ever I feel in my bones something's very wrong.'

David paced to and fro in the study. By this time his mood had changed again from fear to rising anger. One thing was certain, he would ask the PM himself what was the reason for this summary and unheralded dismissal.

He began looking back more closely. Stray glances came to mind, little gestures of irritation, odd cracks, always emanating from 'old Devious' . . . half jesting remarks like 'our capitalist leftist' . . . 'it's all very well for our David, he's so bloody rich' . . . and 'you cannot understand our need at times to supplement our incomes, you bloated plutocrat'. That was when it dawned on him that the PM had never quite extended the same rough camaraderie towards him as had been shown by other leading members of his government.

David evoked his leader's image as he had seen him in the House the day before. He had realised that the PM was becoming slightly bent and that there was a jaundiced tinge in that hitherto ruddy countenance. This time his pacing halted by the drinks cabinet. David opened it, poured himself a stiff whisky – which he never touched normally – and stood sipping it, his mind now racing.

What if the motive were compounded of jealousy and resentment? Just supposing, because the PM knew his health was imperilled, he had allowed such destructive emotions to cloud his judgment. David knew the party needed him, if only as the one sure way of having oil poured on troubled waters. But supposing this man was fearful that his own powers were weakening at such a critical time, then could his vanity transcend his common sense? David knew that his vanity was enormous. If he saw David as a usurper, then could that have made him succumb to the temptation to get rid of him before he acquired real power despite the gamble implicit in this dismissal?

David emptied the glass, resumed his pacing assailed by the one dominating thought in all this speculation. Whatever the PM's real motives were – for he was certain it had been *his* decision – it made very little difference. He, David, was out of the corridors of power. If he remained with the party, he could still be used to employ his persuasive talents in unruly situations. It would be easy enough to persuade him if only because friendly overtures and requests for help to him in his new lowly status would automatically carry the inference of a pending 'come back – all is forgiven'.

Big Ben struck one o'clock. By now the PM's announcements of the cabinet re-shuffle would be written into the morning newspapers. A few hours more and the world would know the golden boy of the Labour Party had been weighed in the balance and found wanting. It was his first experience of failure and nothing in his life had equipped him to handle it.

Back he went to his desk where the PM's letter lay across the one he had begun to write to Lady Mary. He pulled this out, stared at it for a moment, then crumpled it up and threw it into the wastepaper basket, realising as he did so that it must be destroyed. He fished it out, put it into a large pewter ashtray and set fire to one corner with his lighter. 'Symbolic,' he thought grimly, watching the paper curl, flame and blacken. He took a vicious pleasure in grinding the charred remains to powder. He tipped them back into the wastepaper basket and said aloud, 'And that's that. Goodbye, Mary.' Then he buried his head in his hands and let despair engulf him.

What use was there in writing to her now? The years stretched ahead of him unrewardingly. His hope of reinstatement, possibly to be hinted at in the future, had, in reality, little chance of success. If he reasoned correctly, the PM wanted him out and out he might well stay until . . . he scarcely dared think of that 'until' for the country whom he sought to serve.

He failed to hear Big Ben tolling the night away. He longed for someone in whom he could confide; but with Richard and Fluff away, there was no one, so he fought his battle alone. By the time dawn came fully, he had done the best he could. One thing he was determined upon, he *would* see the PM but whatever came out of such an interview, he would then write the swine a letter in which he accepted his ruling without question and merely wished him to know that his own devotion and loyalty to the party remained unswerving, whether he enjoyed the responsibility and confidence implicit in a governmental appointment or remained in the comparative anonymity of those back benches.

The full force of the storm broke over him as the newspapers screamed their headlines: DAVID KINCALE OUT . . . CABINET RE-SHUFFLE REPLACES DAVID KINCALE AS PMG . . . DANDY KINCALE RELEGATED TO THE BACK BENCHES. His telephones began ringing as the Press pounced. Photographers besieged the house. A tearful and enraged Gert and Daisy repeated the statement he had authorised them to repeat to everyone. As he wiped their tears between callers, murmuring words of consolation, he rallied them with his ironic, 'The PM giveth, the PM taketh away. Ours not to reason why. For goodness sake, cheer up. We shall live to fight another day,' realising as he spoke that he did not believe a bloody word of it himself.

Eventually he went out, thrust his way through the clamour of Press and photographers and drove to the House where he had to force his way through a huge crowd. There were shrieks of 'It's a shame,' reiterated chants of 'We want David', so in the doorway, he turned to smile and wave before ducking inside. The shouting continued. He learned later that his supplanter, the new PMG, was booed by David's fans. Then he braced himself to take his new place and an unexpected spatter of applause broke out as he came into the House. Mr Speaker called, 'Order! Order!' The applause died but David felt a huge upsurge of gratitude and it heartened him.

Late in the afternoon the PM sent for him. As the door closed behind him, his destroyer said blandly, 'Sit yourself down, David.' Then he leaned back in his chair, adding, 'Well, David,' and the issue was joined.

David spoke quietly, beginning, 'I want you to know, Prime Minister, that I have not asked to see you in order to waste your time by questioning your decision. This, as I expect you know, I have told the media. I only want to know if you will tell me why.'

'Of course,' the other nodded, 'very right and proper. I knew you would ask for this meeting and I felt sure you would agree that my answers would be preferable in the spoken word.'

He paused while David, as he told Richard later, felt sure he could hear the feet of Ananias thundering in his ears. All he said was, 'Can you tell me where I have slipped up, sir?'

The PM replied, 'You have not slipped up. You have done extremely well. Your political conduct has in fact been exemplary. You have served the party splendidly.'

'Then what . . .'

'Now look, son.' The man chose to be avuncular which

David thought ill became him. 'It is nothing to do with your *political* record, either inside the House or out of it, but . . . you will forgive me if I speak quite frankly.'

David merely nodded.

'It is the company you keep, old lad, as a matter of fact . . .'

Here come the lies, thought David.

The PM repeated, 'As a matter of fact when the issue was joined, I may as well tell you I was all for having a heart to heart talk with you to try and exert my powers of persuasion, but my colleagues were adamant. It is just the company you keep, old lad. You must see that from our standpoint this has always been a stumbling block for us.'

David echoed disbelievingly, *'The company I keep?'*

'Well, yes, old son. Take, for example, the Harlands. That man is a thundering nuisance to us all. He's always stirring up trouble for us in the Upper House, asking awkward questions. Let us face the facts. The old fool is an out and out die-hard Tory of the very worst kind. So what do you do? You choose his daughter, Lady Mary, as your girl friend. You must have realised this would make trouble with my colleagues.'

'Christ!' David exclaimed. 'It never even crossed my mind.'

'It must have done. Come now, David. A girl like that, hobnobbing with royalty in which many of our party place very little credence, I may add. She is a blueprint of what so many of us abhor. Rich, pampered, the darling of so-called society, living a life of Riley which is abhorrent, in particular to those among us whose early life was compounded of privation, struggles, unemployment and class warfare. Then as if all this were not enough to make you steer clear of her, we learn – never mind how – that she is now going to work for that bastard Beardmore of the *Clarion* whom we see as the most dangerous man in Britain to our cause.'

It needed every shred of David's newly won self-mastery to stop him from rising from his chair and striking the Prime Minister. Fluff Musgrave's description of Lord Beardmore ran through his mind, 'the staunch and loyal defender of all that is most precious in our English history'. These words streamed through David's consciousness even as he fought for self-control.

'Besides,' the PM added, 'he's still a randy old sod. I'll wager he would never have taken the girl on in the first place if she hadn't been a beauty. That appointment was the last straw. Despite *my* opinion of you I had to agree that my colleagues had justice and reason on their side. Try to see this dispassionately.'

His eyes fell for a moment on David's clasped hands on which the knuckles stood out whitely, but he looked away instantly and continued, 'We all had the highest hopes for your political future. We hoped that one day you would become our Chancellor of the Exchequer.

'Remember when you crossed the floor to join us, what was the tenor of press speculation? That you were fed up with politics, had your head turned by the nobs and were dubbed "playboy" after attending that charity ball in Paris with the Windsors. I rode that little storm because I believed you were destined for great things in our party, but my colleagues continued to mistrust your social background. Your guardian belongs to that same set. He still plays equerry to an ex-King in fact. I tell you, David, if you had deliberately wanted to queer your own pitch while becoming increasingly successful politically, you couldn't have done so more capably than by the company you keep.'

He paused, shifted some papers about on his desk and then added, 'About the only thing which could save you now after all this foolishness would be if you could prove that your real parents were dockers or workers at the coal face.' Having so said, he laughed.

David stood up, well aware that what he had set out to do was so much in jeopardy now, that he must walk like Agag, if he were ever to do what he had told Gert and Daisy, 'live to fight another day'. All hung by as slender a thread at this moment as that Damoclean sword.

'I only regret, believe me, Prime Minister, that I cannot furnish you with such evidence,' he managed through stiff lips. 'All I can do is say that time will prove where my loyalties lie. I shall of course remain in the party and at all times exert my utmost endeavours to proving to you and your colleagues that I merit future reinstatement.'

The PM held out his hand. 'And let me wish you the very best of luck, old lad,' he said.

Somehow David shook that hand, somehow he left the room, but he never could remember who showed him out or where he went until he felt the bile rising in his mouth. Then he turned into the nearest lavatory and threw up.

Part IV

CHAPTER XV

*'The Gods are well pleased when they see
great men contending with adversity.'*

– Robert Burton

DAVID READ THE announcement of Mary's departure
from England in the Cassandra-like comment made by
the *Clarion's* leading gossip columnist. She was heading
for India armed with cameras and introductions. She
was reported to be planning at least two years abroad. In
the interim David realised he was no longer *persona
grata* with the Windsors either, at least so far as any
appearances at 'her' house, No 4 rue du Champs
d'Entraînement, or at 'his' house, the Moulin de la
Tuilerie, were concerned. The Duchess had sent him a
curt little note of congratulation on his PMG appointment, but since then her silence was eloquent. She
clearly had no wish to include him in her parties and,
after all, to what else could she invite him?

Even his correspondence with the Duke was subject
to censorship from Richard, who flatly refused to let him
put anything in writing which could conceivably be held
against him in the admittedly unlikely event of such letters falling into the wrong hands. What David *had* told
the Duke constituted the only secret he had ever kept
from his precious 'Dolly' on whom he continued to dote,
besides everlastingly showering her with valuable
jewellery. David likewise withheld from Richard the
extent of his confidences to the Duke, believing he not
only disliked him – though not nearly so much as his
Duchess – but also that he mistrusted him. David had no

such fears himself, a matter on which he often reflected without arriving at a satisfactory answer.

By this time Richard was back and a meeting had been arranged at the little Chelsea house. Fluff was still absent, his whereabouts unknown. David had never felt so solitary as the day he went to see the Llewellyns. As his taxi rattled along the Embankment towards Chelsea, he did the best he could to set aside his thoughts and fears in anticipation of being admitted once again to that very happy household. He paid off the cabby and began to walk the rest of the way as usual, reliving the game of happy families he had played with them before he received the PM's letter.

Joanna had produced their son and heir the previous year. She sailed through her pregnancy looking absurdly young and pretty, enjoying the best of health and stubbornly insisting on having her baby at home. During this time David had spent every spare hour of his crowded life helping her to decorate the nursery and in so doing, managed to wreck several pairs of trousers as he papered and painted with her. Bronson became sufficiently incensed to take himself off in a huff and return with a painter's white coveralls which he presented to David – with the bill.

The only squabbles in the nursery stemmed from the unending stream of bulky parcels which David carried into the house. He called this 'baby loot'. Joanna nagged, wailed and invariably lost the day, since she had provided the weapon David used to break down all resistance. With monotonous regularity, he told her, smiling, 'Darling Joanna, you really must understand that it is only right and proper for godfathers to contribute pre-natal gifts with which to honour their godson's arrival in this vale of woe. *You* announced your pregnancy – *you* invited me to stand as godparent. As you sow, so shall you reap, madam. Now open this up and see what bliss I've brought today.'

Thus they ended up playing with the huge fluffy

sheep dog which was nearly as big as Joanna, the Harvey-sized white rabbit with ears which wiggled, the complete orchestra of musical monkeys and all the other enchanting toys David ordered from Paris.

'No one,' he declared, unwrapping a floppy lioness with a tasselled tail, 'makes cuddly toys like the French. I'll buy my godson's presents over here when he becomes a jet plane, flying saucer or helicopter buff, but while he is rattling and gurgling . . .'

'He!' Joanna exclaimed crossly, 'and godson indeed! Be reasonable, David. Whatever will you do if I have a girl?'

'Adore her; buy her jewellery probably . . .' David looked up from the lioness. 'See how safe he is, even the eyes can't be eaten. There's nothing he can swallow on any of the toys. I checked very carefully.'

Out would flash the dimples as she smiled down at his fair head indulgently, bent over the lion . . . elephant . . . whatever. She even started urging Richard to 'hang around, my love, and see if you can waylay David. I've cooked masses for all of us and you know how he loves my Rabbit Pie . . .' or 'Steak and Kidney Pudding'. They would eat together at the bamboo dining-table in the little dining-room which was thronged with stephanotis, mandevillea and smilax, with whom Joanna had endless one-sided conversations.

David once came in to hear her saying reprovingly, 'One more season without so much as a bud and off you go to see God who will also be gravely displeased with you — so come on . . .' The extraordinary fact was that after such reproofs, as David told Richard later, 'the damned things rush into bloom. Your wife is a witch.'

As they ate, on the From-David-With-Love white dinner service with the painted parakeets and butterflies, they would laugh and chat happily. Afterwards David and Richard would sprawl by the fire and talk of what Joanna always referred to as, 'You know what, but it's all as clear as mud to me.'

'I am a spy,' David would tell her solemnly, 'just like

193

Burgess,' to which she would retort, 'Silly!' and settle to her knitting of tiny garments.

When the baby came there were four hours of panic while Richard ran true to form and paced the sitting-room carpet like a demented puma. When the doctor sent him flying up the stairs with wobbly knees, he tip-toed in, only to find his love propped up, rosy-cheeked, her curls tied with a bewitching blue ribbon and beaming at him. He reproached her, 'Well really! Here am I worn to a shadow with anxiety, while you sit there looking as if you had belched our baby into the world. Darling . . .' They clasped each other in total rapture.

Richard enraged the nurse by enquiring, 'Is he deformed? Have you checked everything?'

She told him indignantly, 'Of course he's not deformed, Mr Llewellyn. He's a beautiful baby boy.' Then she put the crumpled bundle of fleecy shawls into his arms.

'Gosh, you're ugly!' he said, peering at the cross little face. 'Bald as a badger too. We'll have to lavish love on him, Joanna. God knows no one else will!'

This so upset the nurse she snatched the baby back again and marched off in a pet.

Presently David was admitted and was told they were christening their son, Richard David. So of course he returned the next night bearing half Moyses Stevens for 'Mini-Mum' – her new name, plus a large bundle of Dutch gilts scheduled to mature in twenty-one years' time. He announced, 'I'm putting down some port for his twenty-first birthday. Rikki, have you entered him for Gordonstoun? One can't be too careful these days, you know.'

A week later he arrived with a large white box under one arm. Joanna was downstairs by now, sitting by the fire with her baby asleep on her lap. He lay face downwards, dribbling contentedly. David told her, 'It is always considered proper for a gift to be given to clever mums, so here's yours. Please try it on for size.'

Joanna scratched excitedly at the tissue paper, saw

194

what was folded below and turned an enraptured small face to him, saying, 'Oh, David!' in tones of absolute awe.

He patted her hand. 'Do you know when I was very small I adored the feel of my Diana-Mum's furs? I used to rub my face against them.'

She made no reply – and no demur either. Richard walked in on them to be greeted by his spouse, 'Hello, my love! Look what David's given me as a whelping present. Someone once told me the best way of wearing mink was inside out, when starkers and in bed, so we must try.'

David started out of his reverie as he came alongside the Llewellyns' garage doors. He gave a quick glance to left and right, then slipped inside and began edging past Joanna's little car to reach the back door.

'How will it be now?' he wondered as he paused with his hand on the sitting-room door.

As if in answer Joanna's voice floated downstairs, 'If that's you, David, go in and mix yourself a drink. I'm just coming down.'

She sounded so unchanged, so normal and cosy that David felt a constriction in his throat. He did as he was asked and the next thing he knew as he stood, drink in hand, was soft arms reaching up to him from behind and her voice murmuring, 'Why have you waited so long? Darling David, do come and sit down; you're too tall for me to reach properly.'

He swung round, lifted Joanna up, stammering as he kissed her, 'I thought . . . I'd better give you time . . . I decided to wait until I heard from Rikki.'

'He'll be here in a minute. What did you think would happen if you had come straight here after that awful shock?'

He put her down gently. 'The answer to that, my little one, is that I didn't think then. I was just afraid.'

'Then you're a bigger fool than I dreamed you would ever be. I don't know what you and Richard are up to. It

195

is not my scene. I only know he loves you, I love you and Richard David loves you and we know that whatever it is, you'll come out on top in the end.'

This shook him more than all the events of the past few weeks. She saw it in his face, so she just pushed him into a chair, sat down beside him on the floor and took one hand in hers. 'You must have been so terribly lonely! Presently you must tell us everything, but not until Richard comes. I've cooked you your favourite dinner and you're going to eat every scrap of it. You're so thin, David darling! You'll have to have "thirds" all the time until you put on some weight.'

She chattered on, then reaching out to a nearby small table, took some photographs of Richard David. 'Look at your beautiful godson,' she wheedled. 'I had these taken last week to surprise you when you came.' She drew the photographs from their envelope and was in the middle of showing them to him when they both heard a key turning in the lock and Richard came rushing in.

It was all a joyous escape from reality and neither of them would even allow him to mention what had happened until after they had dined. Then Joanna led them back to the sitting-room and stood hesitantly for a moment.

'Is it "secrets time" or may I stay?' she asked softly.

David answered her. 'You stay, my pretty. From now onwards we have no secrets. At least, if Rikki agrees.'

'No more secrets,' Richard agreed soberly. 'We'll share everything from now onwards. You talk first. Tell me exactly what happened. I only know as much as the public does which is virtually nothing. When you've done, I'll tell you what has been going on in my camp which may brighten your life just a little. Wait a bit though, I expect you would like me to pass on a message about Fluff. "The Lord" said to tell you he's coming back on Wednesday. He had a telephone call from him, something to do with your Windsors, I believe.'

David spoke hesitantly at first but presently got into his stride while Richard watched him critically. When

David talked of his meeting with the PM his remarkable gift for remembering dialogue came into full play and he repeated the entire conversation. He concluded, 'And, by the way, Mary and I had broken with each other beforehand. This only set the seal on our separation.'

Joanna was crying silently. She blew her nose like a child and said, slightly muffled by the handkerchief, 'It'll all come right in the end. Just you see if it doesn't.'

'It's still a perfectly bloody set back,' Richard said gloomily. 'You know, "The Lord" has a theory, which I may add he shares with Sven. I'll give you the details in a minute but the nitty gritty is this: nothing has changed. We pursue the course we have already decided upon. "The Lord" said that with his jaw at the pugnacious and the cigar charging across his mouth like a drunken torpedo.'

David actually laughed, but not for long. It petered out as he asked, 'With me bogged down among the rank and file?'

Then Richard made a startling comment. 'They don't want you there. You don't belong and they know it.'

'They've been so amazingly friendly,' David mused. 'That's what puzzles me.'

'So would you be if you suddenly had a super star abruptly plonked down beside you.'

David stared at Richard. 'You mean it's just taking out insurance against the day when I'm reinstated.'

'I'm glad you're waking up at last!'

'But look, that's just not on. What could Old Crafty possibly do to justify such a complete *volte face*? He's got such a great opinion of himself, how could he ever admit he was wrong, which is what would have to happen for me to get back.'

'Think, David,' Richard urged. 'Think, man. Who did you say had asked you to dine with him informally?'

David did not answer.

Richard sighed. 'I can see I shall have to lay it on the line for you. Old Crafty is rumoured to be a sick man. He doesn't look good to me, but then of course he never did.

Even if he's not sick, there are those who feel he has lost his nerve, or he may just envisage a more advantageous course for himself by pulling out. One way or another I think he'll go. I agree we will have to watch his timing pretty closely. But we are unanimous that all you have to do now is just hold on and stick to the line you have established. Above all come back here after you have dined with old Pemberton and report in your own inimitable fashion every word of your conversation, no matter how trivial it may seem.'

By the time David slipped out through the garage doors and began walking along the Embankment, Richard had given him his news with a warm and encouraging personal message from Lord Beardmore. There was only one thing he did not tell him. Lord Beardmore had also pointed out to Sven within Richard's hearing, 'Even with David relegated to the wrong side of the tracks, he is still furthering his own cause. He has time on his hands so see to it that he uses it to forge ahead with those Cottage Industries and his Training Centres for Handicapped Children. They bind him to the rank and file with what will one day prove to be "hoops of steel".'

For his part David memorised and duly repeated to Richard all that passed between himself and the Chancellor of the Exchequer. The older man was cheerful, friendly and slightly paternal in a way which David described as not unlike when he was asked to tea by the Head after a beating. He added thoughtfully, 'The old boy seemed very interested in my Cottage Industries and in the Centres. He even asked if I would show him round one of 'em and he put some very pertinent questions to me about what they cost me to run, how I staffed them and how I placed my trainees when they had mastered whatever it was they were learning.'

This brought a grin to Richard's face but he quickly suppressed it as he made a mental note to tell Lord Beardmore as soon as the opportunity arose.

After leaving Richard and Joanna on that occasion David felt the need to stretch his long legs so he walked home. It was a clear night. The dark velvet stretched over his head into infinity. It was radiant with stars. Below him the great old river flowed steadily as it had done through countless centuries bearing those in despair to the malevolence of Traitors' Gate; yet, he reminded himself, those far above him in greatness had emerged therefrom to see their lost causes come to triumphant renascence ... Elizabeth, that 'Lion's cub' who had survived to take the English throne and hold it magnificently ... Charles James Stuart, the hunted fugitive whose bitter years of exile had ultimately conquered banishment until he too rode back triumphantly along what had been his *via dolorosa.*

David experienced a sudden wave of confidence. What he already knew and what he feared seemed now to become an assurance that if his cause were just and his suspicions founded on fact, *his time would come too.*

A hoarse 'Hello, dearie, like a bit of fun?' from a tired whore at his shoulder startled him.

'Sorry,' he told the woman. 'No thanks!'

He turned away and resumed his walking. The light from a street lamp fell on his fair head and 'Who should be so lucky!' the woman called after him as he quickened his pace.

Her words stirred in him a fitting reminder of the immensity of his problem as once again he felt a burning sense of urgency assail him. He began reflecting on the anomalies of his situation as represented by his fall from power *vis-à-vis* the growing friendliness of his fellow back benchers. It seemed to him that so many of them went out of their way now to talk to him, to pause at his solitary table when he ate in the House of Commons dining-room to make some insidious remark which led to their casual 'Mind if I join you?' as if a conspiracy was afoot to make him feel wanted.

It fitted as ill with his situation as the unswerving loyalty shown to him by his fans. Their letters poured in

199

after the event, many of course couched in terms of devotion to himself, but quite a number urging him to 'hang on' declaring openly they had lost faith in a Prime Minister who had shown himself to be completely inadequate in failing to recognise David's importance to the party. There were cabinet ministers too who seemed to go out of their way to be friendly.

It was all most odd. The requests for him to appear on radio and television now multiplied too. He was almost more in demand than when he had held office. Curiouser and curiouser, he thought.

For his part, once he had wrestled with the initial shock and the inner revelations of his interview with his Prime Minister, he spent an increasing amount of time fostering his Cottage Industries, dipping deep into his own pockets to launch new ones, give help to his chosen young men of ideas and enterprise. In every public appearance David parried all attempts to draw him with a deprecating little smile and a reiterated, 'I serve my party in whatever capacity I may.'

Now, as he walked home, he suddenly remembered what the Governor of the Bank of England had said after failing to stop the two per cent increase in the Bank Rate so soon after the election. 'We have seen into the abyss. It is an uninviting prospect.' From thence he reviewed the sequence of events and how the City's fairly sanguine attitude changed to Stygian gloom after the famous statement, 'We shall squeeze them until their pips squeak,' meaning the wealthy.

Following this elegant prediction the 'Haves' were panicked by the ever-increasing rumours of a wealth tax. Business was hit by the Corporation Tax. The City in fact grew to regard the Labour Party as playing the role of an invading army, which, as Richard observed grimly, 'Unless we are clean round the twist is precisely what some of them are.' The High Street 'have-nots' wore out shoe leather searching for 'loss leaders' with which to make ends meet; their ever-accelerating grousings narked their menfolk and the unlovely pot began to simmer. The total abandon with which the Government borrowed from the International Monetary Fund forced higher and higher taxes upon the everyday necessities of life.

Then the brain drain began wreaking its havoc as disillusioned men succumbed to the obvious temptations of additional scope, income and creative opportunity in the New World, and off went some of the country's finest brains. Very soon afterwards it became plain to see that the rich had had enough. When a man could and did pay £1.27 tax in the pound on the highest level of his unearned income and 95p in the pound on earned income, the millionaires fled abroad. As one embittered man told David, 'We are being turned into a nation of fiddlers in order to protect our families and our heirs. There *are* ways and means and we have now become so desperate we take them while bitterly resenting being forced so to do. England is in a parlous state. When we see the reckless abandon with which money is being frittered away, mis-spent and mis-directed, we can no longer tolerate the situation.'

In one week alone over a hundred million pounds were siphoned into tax havens. This modern 'flight into Egypt' merely changed places, becoming instead an exodus into certain Caribbean islands, Monaco, the Channel Islands – anywhere in fact where there were no death duties and taxation was minimal, or in some instances non-existent. The Republic of Eire hit on a happy way of wooing, by offering total tax exemption to 'creative writers'. With their customary logic the Irish excluded writing they deemed non-creative, into which category even the most exhaustively researched 'source books' were relegated. It was all relatively unimportant since this was the only country which failed to hold its 'refugees'. Having sampled the life, they either returned to Britain to pay their monstrous taxes or moved elsewhere.

Simultaneously, the pall of lethargy and bitter discontent spread over the so-called working man, faced with excessive prices for a pint of beer, his 'smokes' or a seat at the local cinema. The nation's staple diet began to suffer too. A steaming newspaper parcel of fish and chips was no longer a bargain, while once humble monk fish more than quadrupled in price overnight because a television cook showed it on the 'box'. When she complained to the fishmongers, they told her, 'Blame yourself, ducks.'

There was hidden peril too in the fish and chips shops' substitutions of reconstituted dehydrated potato chips, rich in dangerous additives, while salmonella-infested chicken portions were foisted on the ingenuous public due to the hugely increased price of fish. Richard found this out from a permanent civil servant whose job it was to reject any poultry suspected of salmonella poisoning from sale in the middle and top level supermarkets. Having worked on the informant until he was thoroughly irritated and therefore careless, Richard slipped in his loaded question, 'What happens to the rejects then?'

The man snapped back, 'Oh, they go to the cheaper end of the trade for chicken portions.'

From this alone, in terms of sickness and diarrhoea, absenteeism in schools and factories had shot up.

The brass doorknocker loomed up suddenly in front of David. He groped in his pocket for his key, let himself in and went to his study. He riffled through the messages . . . would he open a constituency fete? . . . address a young Labour movement rally in East Ham? . . . would he be one of the judges at the forthcoming Miss World contest? Once again he wondered that a demoted back bencher was in this kind of demand.

He reverted to his purpose in coming into the study. Earlier in the day someone had sent him a volume of the complete verse of Rudyard Kipling. Flipping through it, he had come upon the poem entitled *The Gods of The Copybook*. He had marked the page and now re-read it.

'In the Carboniferous Epoch we were promised abundance for all

By robbing selective Peter to pay for collective Paul;
But, though we had plenty of money, there was nothing
our money could buy,
And the Gods of the Copybook Headings said, "If you
don't work you die."'

He sat staring over the room with the book on his knees. None of them seemed to want to work any more. They were only interested in the amount of money and the shortness of the hours. If they did in some rare instances want to work more than the system allowed, they merely moonlighted, moving from job to job and paying no taxes at all.

Meanwhile the honest men in Government were being steadily winkled out to make room for the burrowing 'moles' who were slaving away at Britain's downfall; but just how to offset this before it was too late was still only a dream . . . a hope . . . a conjecture . . . as each word formed in his mind, David rejected it, only finding any spur in the last . . . a grail.

Three nights later David dined with Sir Frederick Musgrave. Richard had told him that he was to take a circuitous route into Hampshire. He was given a map and the assurance that 'Sir Frederick is completely in the picture so you will not have to plough through all *that* again'.

David felt a quickening of his blood as he drove down. He was as certain now as he had been uncertain before. Something was in the wind. It was to be his first meeting with his guardian since Fluff's withdrawal from the London scene. He had merely told David that he was feeling his age a bit and had decided to leave Albany. David was filled with anticipation for another evening alone with Fluff and the chance to see his new home at last.

He was driving his latest acquisition: a beautiful, snarling, old green Bentley with great leather straps across her bonnet. Over the years David had developed a passion for buying cars, chiefly old ones, which Richard then took to an 'absolutely wizard mechanic' in a garage at the back of Shepherds Bush, to spend anything up to a year there being renovated. When David had seen his first old wreck of a Lagonda transformed into a pristine black beauty with cream upholstery, he tilted at wind-mills by driving up to the House in it. This evoked some fairly stringent comments. When the PM contributed his mite, David retorted, 'Why not, Prime Minister. Every-one knows I have money and after all *I've* only one house.'

Now as he worked his way along a lane, flanked by splendid oaks, David had his first glimpse of mullioned windows looking out serenely over knot and herb gar-dens in their box enclosures. It was clearly an old hunt-ing lodge, possibly one to which, long ago, the Long Lad himself had ridden with a handful of equally naughty courtiers for some private wenching, general roistering and the hunting of the King's own deer which David's fancy supposed must have been subsequently dressed and roasted on a great turning spit somewhere in the old kitchens.

The light was fast fading as David braked in the old courtyard, coming to rest under a swamp cypress tree of immense age and girth. As the engine stilled, David looked about him appreciatively, thinking, 'There has to be some running water here to sustain that tree!' and in the silence the muted singing of water flowing over stones answered him.

The door had swung open disclosing Fluff with the light behind him, silver-haired, but still very erect and elegant in his braided smoking jacket.

'Hello, old chap,' he moved towards David, a sil-ken-eared spaniel at his heels, 'say how de do to my pooch.'

David bent eagerly to the bitch, saying, 'Hello, girl, you're rather beautiful but then I suppose like all females you know it.'

Fluff wandered slowly round the Bentley. 'She answers to "Folly", but her real name is Mademoiselle

Lolita Salteena Musgrave because she is both a nymphette and not *quite* a gentlewoman. She has an exquisite mouth and is an all round splendid gun dog. This is a very fine motor, David, but has the royal Daimler turned up her toes or been banished like its owner?'

'Over my dead body, sir,' David laughed. 'She is simply being honourably retired after a long and dashing life . . .'

Fluff glanced keenly at his one-time charge. 'Dear me,' he said mildly, 'and if I'm not mistaken, there is also the rejuvenated Lagonda besides that little contribution to political expediency in which you bumble Hamwards. Where do you house them all?'

David told him. 'I have found a marvellous trio of mechanics in a garage behind Shepherds Bush. With the enormous sums such cars are fetching from the Americans, and indeed the Germans too, I am starting my own cottage industry. It'll have to come, sir. Besides, the lure of such motors is sufficient to tide the young 'uns over the apprentice stage, so you see before you a budding industry in refurbished motor cars. It's a miniscule beginning of what must come in soon . . . the revival of scope for the little man – the nucleus of a David Kincale Partnership.

'I've got another lot going in Norfolk with 'withies', another dying craft I intend shall be revived and a third based upon an old man in Somerset who has had a life-long love affair with fine woods and even finer carving. His son who is partially crippled is really a reincarnation of a 15th century cofferer, and they too are taking on youngsters. It's the greatest fun to fund and foster . . .'

'And,' thought Fluff to himself, 'in part compensation for your unnaturally solitary existence . . .'

Aloud he said, 'Come on. I'll show you round. You may be surprised when you see what I had in mind.'

It was a comparatively small Tudor hunting lodge with uneven polished oak floors and some superb tester beds in the twelve bedchambers which must have seen some rubustious days; their adjacent closets had now

205

been made into bathrooms. Below ran a loop and chain of rooms from the panelled, tapestry-hung miniature of a manor house's great hall, the dining saloon furnished with a high table and some fine coffers, a livery cupboard and several back stools or 'farthingale' chairs as they were later known due to their armless suitability for the hoops and crinolines of the 17th century, two small withdrawing-rooms – now the library and study – and a large, tranquil principal withdrawing-room which looked out over a small lake, the knot garden and the encircling topiary.

They returned to Fluff's study where the seemingly unchanged Harris, who had known David since he was a baby, came soft-footed to pour their sherries into old schooners and tell David, 'Mr David, sir, you are in the blue room. I have unpacked you and your clothes are laid out. If you will just ring when you require me, I will dress you.'

'You shall do no such thing, thank you very much,' David replied. 'You have to cope with dinner and if I cannot change trousers by myself at my time in life, things have come to a pretty pass.'

Harris set the decanter at Fluff's elbow and went out, saying outrageously, but with the privilege of an old servant, 'You really are quite a big boy now, aren't you, sir? Thank you very much.'

The scents of the country night drifted through the windows. An owl loosed its mocking call and over the lake the young moon's light pierced the surface of the water. David sighed. 'How did you find this small jewel, sir?'

Fluff replied, 'I didn't. I inherited it and this seemed an appropriate moment so I moved in.'

'Retirement?'

Fluff then dropped his bombshell. The man whose name was AS in the highest echelons over many years, shook his head. 'Start of a new job, dear boy,' he drawled. 'When I saw how admirably suited this little place was to *our* purposes,' the pronoun was not lost on his

206

listener, 'I just moved in. You see, David, I've been in on this little lark for quite a time already.'

'What little lark, sir?' David enquired very politely but his eyes had suddenly become blank.

'We are proposing to call it Operation Phoenix subject to your approval of course. I wonder, do we have it?'

David expostulated, 'Christ Almighty, sir! How did you get in on the act? I've done my best to keep you out of it.'

Fluff nodded. 'I know,' he said. 'You must blame Beardmore who is not exactly ignorant of my activities in the French Resistance. He roped me in.'

'To do what, sir?'

'To contrive with the aid of some of my old companions who were youngsters when we worked together before, to obtain the vital information we now need, whether we get it by fair means or foul.'

David interpolated wearily, 'Even with me stuck on the sidelines?'

He was answered, 'Certainly. Always supposing your present situation to be irreversible.'

'But surely, sir, I mean you're not a young man any more, you are not contemplating active participation in some unspecified cloak and dagger stuff?'

'Only indirectly, alas.'

David flung out his hands. 'What a rod you put in pickle for your back, sir, the day you undertook to stand guardian for me!' he exclaimed.

This Fluff ignored. 'Why don't you just digest what I've told you?' he advised, reaching with unruffled composure for the decanter. 'Dinner will be served shortly, so go up and change now. We have the whole night before us.'

They needed it. Over dinner they talked more of David's 'cottage industries', of the young towards whom such small enterprises were directed, and only once did their otherwise rigidly imposed self-restraint crack when Fluff said wearily, 'Over two million unemployed already and escalating. It must come soon, David; even the police are fearful of a total breakdown of law and order – anarchy in fact. That is the alternative to our intended Operation Phoenix.'

After this they did what they could with the cheese soufflé Harris handed. He returned to the kitchen with two-thirds of it, sat down at the kitchen table and poured himself a glass of wine. 'Pity to waste it,' he told himself, adding, 'they went right off their food they did when Sir Frederick said something just as I took it in.'

Harris served their coffee in the study, set the brandy at his master's side and closed the door behind him.

'Now will you begin, sir?' David asked. 'I'm self-excommunicated you must remember, so please give me a complete briefing.'

Fluff said, 'In a moment. First let me tell you that Beardmore asked me to pass on some private information to you. You see he is also well aware of the parlous situation between Lady Mary Harland and you. He asked me to tell you that she is safe, well and continuing her roving camera exercises. At the moment she is in Switzerland in a house overlooking Lac Léman.'

'Whose house?' David rapped this out unaware he barked the question.

'A Swiss banker. An elderly character like me. He will fulfil certain functions for us presently in his capacity of what the vulgar call a Swiss gnome, one moreover of vast international importance. Concurrently my job is to organise from here a seemingly impossible theft.

'My servants all live out. All are recruited from the ranks of my – er – past. They have cottages and small cars in which to travel to and fro. Thus we are completely separate from the life of our nearby villages, and I have already gained a reputation for being an old recluse who writes. It is amazing the awe still felt by simple country folk for writers. We all meet here until we come upon our hour; that is to say, Beardmore, that splendid man, Sven Jorgensen, and of course Richard Llewellyn. You will read tomorrow of his appointment as

Chief Political Correspondent to the *Clarion*, which has become about because poor Scruffy is a very sick man. He retires almost immediately as he has to have a serious operation from which his chances of recovery are slight.

'Also we shall have an excellent woman, Gladys Crick, with us – minister without portfolio in the *Clarion's* hierarchy. As you know, she looks like a schoolmistress *manqué* and has been in love with "The Lord" ever since she became his personal private secretary which, God knows, is light years ago. In miniscule terms she is like you, David; she can and has coped many times with the most intransigent big guns on the paper, including his somewhat choleric lordship, and all the men love and trust her – as they should, for over the years she's hauled many of them back in the nick of time from fates worse than death.' Fluff chuckled.

'The thing about our Glad which most impresses me,' said David grimacing at the nickname, 'is the fact that absolutely nothing ever disturbs her bland composure. I'm glad she's in on this.'

'And there will be others,' Fluff added, 'but we can go into all that later. Why not come for a stroll and I will outline our final plan of campaign for your approval?'

They went out onto the small terrace, the tips of their cigars glowing in the darkness like giant fireflies.

CHAPTER XVI

'Now is the time for all good men
to come to the aid of the party.'

– Anon

BY THE TIME Harris received Sir Frederick Musgrave's next instruction to prepare for a meeting at his hunting lodge, a torrent of dirty water had run under the frail bridge which spanned the country between turmoil on the one side and anarchy on the other.

Richard's declared conviction that the Prime Minister would pull out had come true. A few months before the rumour began to flare up throughout the lobbies that the Government was going to the country once again. 'Owing to increasing ill health', it was announced as a *fait accompli*, the Prime Minister was retiring and his successor would be the man who currently held office as Chancellor of the Exchequer; but no indications were given as to who would replace him.

When the statement appeared, it was exactly as Richard had predicted. 'Owing to increasing ill health and having been strongly advised by his medical advisers to retire the Prime Minister is resigning, not just from his great office but very reluctanly accepting that he must withdraw altogether from public life.'

Then the new Prime Minister, in a speech rich with unctuous righteousness, declared, 'If we are to succeed in what we set out to do when you voted us into power so overwhelmingly, we feel it is only right and proper to ask for a further mandate at this time. Make no mistake, my friends, we stand now at the crossroads of destiny in our country's history. Either you give us this mandate to

210

take really stringent measures towards a fair division of wealth and property for all, or we shall be compelled as a nation to suffer unendurable hardships.

'Therefore the time has come for us to lock the door against any further depletions of our nation's resources which have already been dealt such crippling blows, both to our economy and to our democratic freedoms. Untold millions have already been siphoned abroad by devious and unscrupulous subterfuges. In order to put an end to this evil and ultimately destructive situation we need your loyal support . . .'

This was the rallying cry to a nation sunk into a morass of disillusionment and disbelief in the whole party political system.

The results were eloquent, with Labour skidding back in what was manifestly a vote of no confidence, a vote based, in fact, on fear of the implicit threats contained in the new Prime Minister's initial and oft reiterated warnings. The poll was the lowest in centuries of parliamentary rule. Only David Kincale swept back with a hugely increased majority.

Within hours there was trouble. The strike by the steel workers which was already beginning to cripple the country flared up, threatening to become perilous. David, still on the touchlines of the back benches, sat quietly, his confidence flowing back now as he grew increasingly conscious of the way he was being watched and whispered about, while the general atmosphere of slightly deferential friendliness became more intense. Then one day as they poured from the chamber at dinner time, Richard whisked past him, managing to whisper, 'Any minute now,' and that afternoon the new Prime Minister sent for him.

David was shown in, asked to sit down and then, bluntly, with no beating about the bush, the question was fired at him, 'How would you feel if I asked you to take a hand in this confounded strike? I must tell you that pickets are multiplying, and have now led to police intervention. Their presence has merely exacerbated an

211

already dangerous crisis. My latest news is that more police are being rushed to the area at this very moment. So how would you feel about going down there and seeing what you can do to ameliorate the situation?

'We all know how great an influence you have brought to bear in the past and your majority in the election has only served to stress the confidence which our voters have in you.' He paused while David's mind raced ahead. 'I too have confidence in you, my boy,' the Prime Minister added firmly. 'You don't need me to tell you the line to take, do you?'

David stood up. 'Then let us not waste time talking, Prime Minister,' he said very quietly. 'Shall I report to you when I get back?'

The older man had a distinct gleam in his eyes now.

'Most certainly,' he confirmed. 'At any hour and do not hesitate to contact me on the telephone if you need me.' Then he leaned back and almost exactly as his predecessor had done, held out a pudgy hand saying, 'Best of luck, dear boy.'

After which he saw David to the door and then went back to his colleagues to report, 'He's gone already; now let us discuss what we shall do with him when he returns.'

By the time David's car reached its destination, a milling crowd of police, pickets and strikers were massed on both sides of the opened gates. Even as the car halted, the mass parted, an ambulance bell tinkled and they all fell back to let it through. One man had already been killed and two others were seriously injured.

David stood up on the front seat of his car. The crowd saw him and someone threw a stone at him. Up went his right hand. He fielded it, laughed, shouted, 'How's that?' and stirred a rumble of uneasy laughter. Then he began to speak. To his own surprise they quietened. On the line, 'Pack it up, chaps. Murder will get none of us anywhere,' he caught their collective ear and on his final appeal to them for 'six pickets and no more violence', someone shouted 'Good old Dave!' and another took this up until suddenly one man leaped into the car over the door and onto the seat beside him. David stood firm.

The man had a megaphone. He shouted through it, 'Do as 'e says, lads. Pack it in. Listen to Dave. 'e really does 'ave our interests at 'eart. My kid's a cripple. What with me out of work, if it 'adn't been for Dave's Training Centres, my Ted wouldn't be what 'e is today. 'andicapped still maybe but starting work in one of Dave's private Cottage Industries, making a decent wage subsidised by Dave 'isself like many others. You can trust Dave . . .'

Beside him David slung one arm around the speaker's shoulders, grabbed the megaphone from him and completed the job of bringing the crowd into line. A small car drew up and out climbed Richard with a photographer. They waited. They listened. They photographed and when the crowd rushed David, even the police fell back as they cheered and lifted him shoulder high. The photographer got that shot too while Richard raced to the nearest call box which had not yet been vandalised to phone the story through to the *Clarion*.

They blazed it across the front page the next morning. They carried the picture of David being borne shoulder high by the strikers; but when it was all over, Richard had to leave his photographer to drive his car home while he took the wheel of David's, because the combination of stone-catching and hand-shaking at the end had rendered one hand useless.

Within hours there was scarcely a soul in Britain who did not know the name David Kincale, nor learn of his Training Centres and his Cottage Industries. Nor did the *Clarion* fail to remind them that this was the man whom the former Prime Minister had sacked as PMG and banished to the back benches. The Press in general told their readers how, despite this, the new Prime Minister had sent for David and how he had rallied to the cause. Only the *Daily Worker* chose to ignore the incident entirely. The other papers wrote of David's wealth but paid tribute to his use of it.

Up and down the country women and girls screamed after him wherever he went, swarming round him and generally indulging themselves in orgies of hysterical adoration.

As they were driving back to London, Richard told David, as if he did not now suspect it himself, 'You're back, old boy. Now we can move in to the kill. They'll have to have you back whether they want to or not; but this time I am certain it'll be a cabinet post.'

Richard berthed the car, hailed a taxi to take David to a doctor who treated his hand. A huge bruise had risen on the palm where the stone had impacted.

'Lucky not to have smashed your hand,' the doctor groused. 'What a dam' fool thing to do!'

To which David replied as he meekly submitted to a sling, 'In the circumstances I am bound to disagree with you,' and he went out grinning.

Once safely inside the Llewellyns' Chelsea house David telephoned his report to the Prime Minister and was told, 'See me at eleven in the morning. I have to be at the Palace by noon. Nice work, old son.'

The details of the new Prime Minister's cabinet were published that afternoon. They had made David Kincale Chancellor of the Exchequer. That was how matters stood when Fluff telephoned Harris and the next meeting was convened for four weeks later.

David was the last to arrive. By the time he drove round to the back of the house, berthing his car in the unoccupied part of the stables, the rest had made their appearances at scheduled intervals in cars which were immediately driven off again.

He let himself in by the back door, crossed through the kitchen into the drawing-room and slipped into his vacant chair. Even before he spoke, his presence seemed to charge the atmosphere. Then, greeting each one in turn, he unerringly found words which brought warmth to their eyes and relaxed what had seemed to him on entering to be an almost unbearable tension.

'Oh, David!' thought Fluff wryly, 'how anyone fails to recognise you, I cannot comprehend.'

'Well met, Lysander,' growled Lord Beardmore, creasing his face in what passed, with him, for a smile.

'I'm sorry to be late, sir,' David smiled apologetically, 'but you can imagine the House is in some disorder over the PM's latest little bombshell.'

The old peer nodded. Then David went round the assembly handing out greetings as if they were accolades. 'Hello, Uncle Fluff. Good to see you again, sir.' ... Laying an affectionate hand on the plump shoulder of the only woman present who was seated next to him, 'And how's our gorgeous Glad?' as he turned to kiss her. 'All the better for seeing you, dear,' she replied serenely, returning the pat. ... 'What a splendid spread you gave me, Sven.' ... and so on to a final, 'Hi there, Rikki, and how's my godson?'

'Going to be a space traveller according to this morning's pyjama bulletin.'

Amid general laughter Lord Beardmore cleared his throat, David caught his eye and asked, 'Is this another planning meeting, sir, or is it mobilisation?'

'Both, but the first item on our agenda is the Royals.'

'Then I have news for you.' David waited a moment and then added reluctantly, 'There is a projected inner cabinet of twelve.'

'Which twelve?'

'*The* twelve, I'm afraid. It is all a matter of timing now. For their part they must try to legislate for what is tantamount to a commandeering of all wealth and property beyond a certain fixed income and a single home apiece which is concomitant with what they call "adequate housing". Eventually it will be illegal to own more than an acre and a cow. In my opinion it is implicit in all their scheming too that the Royals must go. Of course it will be done under the cloak of "for their own safety". We do have a little time because with their financial intentions declared, they can wing off to this latest Russian conference and there receive their final orders. Nevertheless in

215

this year of no grace we must move fast. What is the general consensus of opinion?'

Fluff spoke, 'By your leave, sir,' glancing at 'The Lord', 'my plans will be completed shortly; then it is only a matter of about six to seven weeks before we do our part.'

'Barkiss is in fact willing?' Lord Beardmore met Fluff's eyes, uncertainty in his own.

'Barkiss is indeed willing having been labouring towards these ends for some considerable time.'

A sigh of thankfulness ran round the table.

'But what happens to him?'

'A seat on that plane and his new papers must be ready when he reaches England. It is my belief that he first intended to blow his brains out on completion but on reflection he decided upon a new identity and South America instead. He needs no financial aid, you may like to know.'

'Then all swings upon his one heroic gesture?'

'Not all, but the easier way,' Fluff told Lord Beardmore. 'Less messy too. I merely await instructions to leave for Paris and set all in train.'

After this cryptic exchange Lord Beardmore spoke again, 'David have you anything to add?'

'I have, sir, but first may I review the situation very briefly. As I see it, the only things in this country which are up today are prices, unemployment and ruinous taxation, soon to be drastically increased for many. As Chancellor of the Exchequer – their one major error in appointments for the furtherance of their own ends – I have my hands in the till.

'Thus I have unearthed the equivalent to an IOU. They have borrowed one thousand million pounds from the International Monetary Fund since they – er – we took office. During that time they have indulged in what amounts to some monumental nest-feathering among the hellish twelve. Yet when they took office, the IMF borrowings were zero, and that's a pretty thought to dwell upon, setting aside – because they are unimportant

216

to our work – the other immense borrowings elsewhere. I believe I can eventually work out an awesome deficiency between the total borrowings and legitimate Government expenditures, showing missing sums which seem to have vanished into thin air.

'The unfortunate man in the street voted them back this time – just – because he believed that it was the remaining rich who were now to be squeezed until their pips squeak, only to discover that he too will be equally involved in this *casse noisette* performance which will prove tantamount to the total collapse of our nation. Anarchy is in the air.'

Lord Beardmore picked up his theme. 'The police talk openly of their fears of just that – anarchy! There is threat of a postal strike, and even now a go-slow has been declared by postmen, thus causing a vast overflow to accumulate in the sorting offices. Women's protest marches are increasing woefully. Two policemen died in that Welsh affair despite David's triumph with the mob. Now in London, Manchester and Birmingham the bus drivers are threatening to leave their buses on the roads which will result in traffic chaos on an unprecedented scale. I spoke with the Assistant Police Commissioner yesterday and he insists the situation is verging on the unmanageable. Only last night gangs stoned the police in Edgware Road. As you so rightly say, time is of the essence now.'

'And,' David added grimly, 'the time is close upon us when I must tender my resignation – that is becoming inevitable. My instinct is that just as soon as Fluff can set up his end of this affair, which gives us a *prima facie* case, I must send in my letter of resignation and then apply for the Chiltern Hundreds.'

Sven cut in, 'I shall enjoy setting that up in a big way.'

'Not only you,' Lord Beardmore snapped, 'but every Editor of every newspaper I own.'

David was saying as he closed his notebook, 'You see I have become hoist with my own petard, for God forbid in my present post that I should be a participant in the

217

swindles which are already being mooted; yet I am hamstrung until we get the vital evidence. I have sent you reports on all I know; ten of the Inner Council are the guilty men plus the two loners in the Tory party, but we must prove it beyond any shadow of doubt.'

It seemed to Fluff that history was uncannily repeating itself. In that autumn of 1936 he had been set a seemingly insuperable task by his King. Now the son of that King was looking to him to pull off an even more fantastic coup in order that *his* desires could be brought to fruition. The sole difference was that his kingly task had been motivated only by his devotion to the man – for he actively despised the woman – while this time he not only loved the son but believed passionately in the rightness of what he sought to do. This helped.

When Harris scratched on the door and was admitted in order to announce dinner, 'The Lord' was firing orders staccato at his equally believing henchmen who were scribbling, as Richard later described it, 'like all hell let loose'. They filed in to dinner and when the port had completed its first circuit, Lord Beardmore raised his glass and proposed a toast to Operation Phoenix. Instinctively they rose. As they sat down again, Lord Beardmore growled, 'By rights, David, you should have remained seated – after all you are the bloody bird.'

CHAPTER XVII

WITH HIS LONG legs resting across one corner of his stratified desk, Sven Jorgensen pontificated to the *Clarion's* Chief Political Correspondent, Richard Llewellyn. 'When the Labour Government first came into power, they were a reasonably honest if misguided lot. What Sir Winston said fitted the bill. Bloody hell, you're too young to remember! I'll quote, "Mr Aneurin Bevan and the Labour party are like ostriches with their heads in the sands and their thinking parts exposed to the British public." That may not be exact, so check it in *Hansard*.

'As time passed, the "moles" began to push their dirty little snouts above ground. How and when they were suborned, we may never know. My own opinion is that they were "sleepers" roused a long time ago when the word was passed for them to re-awaken. I further believe that their indoctrination began in their university days, but our "moles" were clever, a submerged coterie, content to bide their time but already in the pay of their chosen masters – hooked in fact. I also think the links forged between them and those traitors who defected were sedulously maintained.

'So much of this is speculative still, but for what it's worth, I'll lay it on the line for you.'

Richard sat with his elbows on his knees, his eyes terrier-bright and intent. Outside the chimes of Big Ben vibrated. It was midnight.

Sven dolloped a generous measure of whisky from his

flask into two paper cups and then resumed. 'The known twelve traitors burrowed their way into parliament. Nine went burrowing on into the Government and finally into the Inner Council. Happily, the tenth was the man who is now Chancellor, our David. Thus we are kept informed of their intentions. As to the other two *known* traitors, they regrettably belong to the party now in opposition, but because of their existence, along with only God knows who else not yet uncovered, the whole democratic system is at risk.

'Concurrently other like-thinking bastards began their appointed tasks of obtaining a stranglehold on the country's industries. Gradually they were able to tighten the screws and so suborn the honest men among them; men eager to work and of indisputable loyalties. They dedicated themselves to sowing the all too fruitful seeds of subversion, encouraging go-slows and, of course, engendering endless strikes. It has all been done in such a way that even the staunchest of loyalists are forced to go along with them or else put their own jobs and those of their wives and families at risk.

'Intimidation is the name of that game until hugely diminished productivity – so brilliantly satirised in that Peter Sellers' film *I'm All Right, Jack* – has brought the whole nation to the brink of bankruptcy.

'To complete the havoc, untold millions have also been siphoned off into some foreign banking house, to which their masters have also been diverting their payments, begun when those sleepers were awakened. From the standpoint of total disillusionment – to say nothing of their anger when they learn how they have been duped – *we need only obtain the evidence of this to turn every man and woman's hand against the lot of them.*'

While Sven Jorgensen was summarising the British crisis for Richard Llewellyn, Sir Frederick Musgrave was preparing to fly to Paris. The Duke had become very frail. The trouble with his eyes, depleting as it was in itself, had led to other even graver causes for alarm concerning his state of health.

Before he left Fluff spent an hour with David.

When he rose to go, David asked, 'A moment more please, sir. I want you to give the Duke the facts as we have discussed them tonight. I hated deceiving you concerning what I had told him but I was reluctant to involve you – so I said nothing. It was only when I realised that the Old Man had drawn you in so deeply, that I realised it was pointless to hold back any longer. *I told His Royal Highness what I intended doing even before I crossed the floor of the House.* I believe this is the only secret he has ever kept from his Duchess.

'Now I would be obliged if you could see your way to bringing him up to date. You say that time is running short for him, even as it is for us. I – er – would very much like him to know what we have discovered and also what we must still discover before we clean out this Augean stable.'

The older man's eyes were very warm now. As he stood, he fancied he could hear again the words spoken to him by his King in Buckingham Palace all those years ago. He heard his own voice asking, 'In total secrecy, sir, while you and Mrs Simpson are standing centre stage with the spotlights of the world upon you?' and he heard the King's reply again, 'Exactly so, my dear Fluff. How do you fancy your chances?'

Fluff went down the steps of the Westminster house to his waiting car and told his chauffeur, 'Heathrow, if you please, Terminal One.' Then he lay back and closed his eyes.

He had come full circle. It only remained for him to reverse the roles, to play messenger to the King's son and at the same time set the machinery in motion which would put the missing information into his hands.

Before leaving London, he had obtained Lady Mary's address and sent her a cable which would, he knew, bring her to Paris to meet him.

There was only one more meeting at the hunting lodge, this time without a host. When David walked in, the inestim-

221

able 'Glad' sat tranquilly on Lord Beardmore's right. Gathered round the table were not only Richard and Sven but also Joe Grantley, said to be the finest layout man in Fleet Street; Henry Scull, the Night Editor, whose huge experience dated from before the Abdication, Will Scranton, whose columns were generally regarded as equal in brilliance to those of the great Cassandra; old George Studely, the venerable and venerated leader writer, and Edward Graybourne, the *Clarion's* financial wizard. All the biggest guns were in fact assembled about 'The Lord'. Their faces were eloquent of what they had learned from him in the past hour.

The chair at the head of the table was vacant, and Lord Beardmore motioned David to take it as all the others rose. He slipped quietly into the empty place, conscious of ten pairs of eyes studying him. He dredged up a smile, murmured, 'Please be seated,' and at a nod from Lord Beardmore, leaned forward, hands clasped on the table and kindled answering smiles by saying, 'You do me great honour, for which I thank you. Am I to understand we now represent the d'Artagnan spirit?'

'Not bad,' grunted Lord Beardmore, 'one for all and all for one. Who is the one, may I enquire, in our context?'

'The monarchy,' said David. 'God willing, and above all other considerations the time has come to recognise our greatest asset, to put an end to carping criticisms and to acknowledge to the world that we, their people, know them for what they are – the most selfless, courageous and hard-working of us all. In order to do so, we must vitalise the nation and totally exterminate this canker from our midst.'

Ten men met in a small, dejected room among the back alleys of Montmartre. Nine of them had worked before for the man they knew simply as 'Marc' when they were striplings in the second year of the German occupation of France. Now their hair was tinged with grey, but they had long ceased being desperate fugitives and over the years those that had survived had prospered.

'Marc' had been speaking for almost an hour. There was no furniture in the room, only flaking paint, grubby windows, a broken sash cord dangling from one, so that they sat cross-legged on the floor, except for two who leaned on the lip of the narrow stone mantel-shelf. Some were Swiss and some were Frenchmen, so what 'Marc' had to say was said in their common language, French.

'Marc' reached the end of what he had to tell them. Pausing only to light a cigarette, he then laid it on the line for them, adding, 'On the face of it, it seems unlikely that you would wish to attempt such a venture.'

The nine just smoked and waited.

'Do I continue?' He was brief and to the point. Finally he unrolled some plans, spread one out on the dusty floor and said, 'You go in here, you get to here, and then you blast your way through to here – this is your objective. I still do not know whether it will be necessary for you to tunnel. It is still on the cards that you may be admitted but after that you use force.

'The moment you are out again, you all blow except for one, and put as far as possible between you and the – er – seat of the crime. We draw for the one who hands over. He goes by the fastest possible route to a rendezvous which only he will know. An aircraft will be waiting. It is vital that this meeting takes place by 2 am. Now the exercise becomes like all the most romantic spy stories because your pick-up is a beautiful redhead. Once the papers are in her hands No 10 blows too. I shall in due course distribute funds. Remember you will all need very fast, very reliable cars; all must be destroyed immediately. What a great advantage to us that there are so many excellent lakes in Switzerland.'

'Marc' opened his slim briefcase, extracted nine spills, the men drew for them, unfolded them, handed them back and 'Marc' burned them in the squalid little grate.

'I remind you that in this instance *I cannot be your Redeemer*, and the sentences, if any of you are caught, will be very stiff indeed for men who are no longer young. Now as to dates, the present estimate is for between six and seven weeks from now. Much has been done already but there is still quite a lot of ground to be covered before you receive your signal. I shall stay in Paris now until this little sortie is concluded, so you all know where we make contact.'

She came into the Ritz bar, halted and looked around her, thus giving Fluff time to see her before she strolled across to join the young man who waited for her. She was hatless, her long burnished copper hair worn loose and curling. Over her shoulders she had slung a sable-lined cream cloth coat.

She hitched herself onto a stool behind him. Presently the barman put two drinks before them. The young man said something, paid and they picked up their glasses and began searching for a table. She passed Fluff who, glancing up from the paper he had not been reading, rose exclaiming, 'Lady Mary, what a delightful surprise! I thought you were in Cambodia.' Thus they actually met one another for the first time.

She put out her hand, saying, 'I'm about to embark on a sabbatical. I don't think you know . . .' and she effected introductions. Putting her bag down on the table, she asked, 'May we join you for a moment or two?' They spoke of the Windsors. She explained herself more fully, 'I have to go to Switzerland for my newspaper, so then Claud and I go on to spend some time at Nicholas Guttenberg's fabulous villa on the heights above Lausanne. Lucky us!'

'I know him,' Fluff told her, 'and the villa which is quite exceptional. Is he not a great friend of your father?'

Thus they made small talk, until her escort, glancing at his wrist, exclaimed, '*Tiens, que nous sommes en retard, M'sieu*; you must forgive us but I must tear Mary away. We are promised at the Embassy for a drinks party.'

'I'm staying at the British one. Why don't you call me some time, Sir Frederick?' she asked, smiling warmly at Fluff. 'My cousins would be enchanted if you came to luncheon one day.'

224

It was all so uncomplicated, really. Now it was only a matter of waiting for that signal from Fleet Street.

They stood together leaning down watching the swirling water of the Seine. Fluff had made his Embassy visit and now they were strolling back together, having been to a viewing of some young artist, none of whose talents were noted by either of them. Their thoughts were too deeply concerned elsewhere.

A *bâteau mouche* with its lights glinting through the portholes slid past.

'This is one of my favourite bits of this city,' she confided. 'Paris *vaut bien* so many other things beside a Mass.'

'It has a magic,' he agreed, 'which the French call *inoubliable* but it's untranslatable, don't you think?'

Then the exchange began. She asked, 'Sir Frederick, are you not David's guardian?'

'I was,' he agreed, 'but scarcely now that David has grown so great.'

'How is he?'

'Lonely, very lonely. He spends much of his spare time with Richard Llewellyn and his wife Joanna. They now have three children. David is godfather to the eldest boy which delights him.'

'I suppose he spoils him rotten.'

'Absolutely.'

'Does he still hold the people in his thrall?'

'More than ever, his appeal is magical.' After a short pause, Fluff added, 'He wants your help.'

'Of course. I have longed to help. He wouldn't let me. He sent me away. It has been a long, lonely time for me too.'

'I think,' he told her, 'it is nearly over now.'

The rayed lights of a passing car revealed an almost blinding radiance in her face. He became slightly devious, saying, 'You make me feel I must remind you of what Queen Elizabeth I told Effingham.'

The girl watched him curiously. 'Are you warning me?'

225

'Very much so.'

'Then tell me what the Queen said.'

'She said, "The fate of England this day, my Lord Howard of Effingham, rests in your two hands."' He added, 'Yours are so much smaller, my dear; are you sure you want this responsibility?'

'I have no doubts.'

When he had told her what she must do, she asked, 'When am I to be in Geneva?'

He told her what he had told his old comrades, adding, 'You will receive a message at Nicholas Guttenberg's house. Then, with God's help, we shall meet in London.'

'We will,' she answered confidently. 'Rest assured, we will,' and then to his astonishment, he felt two slim arms about his neck and the soft brush of her lips on one cheek. 'That's a date, I promise you,' and she was gone.

It took four men to heft the machinery from the van into the emptied garage behind the hunting lodge. Harris watched the operation with his usual passivity. He saw his employer pull himself up again into the van, turn to wave one hand and then vanish into the darkness.

Harris led the four back into the house. When he had served them dinner, he brought in coffee. 'I shall go to bed now, gentlemen. I shall leave you to lock the scullery door. All the others are bolted and barred and I understand you have your men already posted outside. I just wondered, is it permissible to give them some refreshment?'

The four at the table were some of those who had squatted on the dusty floor of a room in Montmartre three weeks before.

Lights blazed all night in the penthouse floor at the *Clarion* building. Gladys now slept there but her hours of rest were unpredictable; for each of the *Clarion* men who had last met at the hunting lodge came in to work when their normal duties were over. Thus 'Glad' considered she must be on hand as much for Henry Scull, who as Night Editor worked 'aloft' during the afternoon hours as for Edward Graybourne who joined him around five o'clock.

They worked together at one huge table, entrenched by reference books, ferried to them by 'Glad', who travelled up and down in the lift at what she called 'most unseemly hours'. Will Scranton shared another vast table with old George Studely. Sven, Richard and Joe Grantley occupied a third. 'The Lord' was in his element, seemingly able to dispense with sleep altogether. He moved from one to the other, reading, discussing, suggesting and even – to Richard's intense amusement – ripping the wrappers from cigarette packets before feeding the contents to his men at their clattering machines. Outside the main doors, next to the lift, two men sat sipping tea and appearing to doze. Over their heads the red unwinking eye signifying 'No Admittance' gleamed permanently.

There was a long list on the wall of 'The Lord's' inner sanctum. Gladys affixed it every morning and only removed it into the safe when the last weary man had left to walk out into the dawn, to his car, his home and possibly a few hours' sleep. Down the left-hand side ran a single column entitled Heads of Office and underneath were printed HM Forces; Defence; Arts; Finance; Foreign Affairs; Commonwealth Affairs; Agriculture, Fisheries and Food; Education; Science; Employment; Energy; Environment; Health and Pensions; Industry; Posts and Telegraphs; Trade; Law and Order; Northern Ireland; Wales and Scotland.

The first task which faced the big guns of the *Clarion* and their overlord had been to agree upon twenty names. When these were chosen, dossiers had been compiled in such meticulous detail that nothing concerning any of them was concealed. All the information was recorded and prepared for the final objective: publication in the Beardmore newspapers. Even the most trivial items which could possibly throw light on their characters, instincts, beliefs and principles had been carefully checked, an activity which had occupied a number of trustworthy men over a period of several months. It remained for the inner team to convert the facts into compulsively readable material for newspaper publication. This was what the chosen few were struggling to achieve in the closely guarded penthouse, while David wrestled alone in the study of his Westminster house with his letter of resignation and some highly complex figures. Meanwhile hot and bothered policemen did what they could with the incessant crowds which gathered outside as the general situation worsened daily.

When the 'White Dossiers', as they became known in the penthouse, were ready and David had completed his task, he made a somewhat undignified exit via his own back garden while the 'Waters' Daughters' held a ladder steady for him and he climbed over his own wall clutching a briefcase. He then drew up the ladder and reinstalled it on the other side. After three such climbs, he leapt into a waiting taxi and travelled on the cab floor to the *Clarion* offices. Edward Graybourne, the *Clarion's* chief financial wizard, was waiting for him in the penthouse. The two men went to a small alcove which had been prepared for them and pored over David's photostats and figures, wresting from these their damning analysis.

Edward Graybourne took off his glasses and rubbed his tired eyes. 'Now we will check these final figures again,' he said wearily, 'but this time let us do so separately to see if we agree.'

He finished first, wrote a total on a piece of copy paper, ringed it and began decorating it with an elaborate doodle.

David looked up moments later. 'I make it fifty-seven million and a few odd thousand. Do we agree?'

In answer his companion turned his paper round. The figure inside the doodle was fifty-seven millions. 'Now for the Lord and possibly the benison of sleep thereafter,' he said thankfully. 'Let's have a drink before we carry the news from Aix to Ghent. At least we can drink to the damnation of all such bastards.'

CHAPTER XVIII

'"If seven maids with seven mops
Swept it for half a year,
Do you suppose," the Walrus said,
"That they could get it clear?"
"I doubt it," said the Carpenter
And shed a bitter tear.'
— Lewis Carroll

'MARC'S TENTH MAN awoke from his afternoon sleep in a service flat in Half Moon Street, yawned, stretched and walked barefoot across the carpet to the bathroom. Then, whistling *'auprès de ma blonde'*, grimacing wryly at the implicit age of his selection, he shaved, showered, wrapped himself in a towelling wrap and paddled off leaving a damp trail of footprints as he headed for the kitchen. With meticulous care he measured freshly ground coffee into the percolator, plugged it in and went through to the bedroom to dress.

With a mug of steaming coffee in one hand and a cigarette between his lips he then leafed through his documents, tucked them into the left hand inside pocket of his Anderson and Sheppard tweed jacket, gave a tweak to his Eton Ramblers' tie and sat down on the edge of the bed to wait.

It was 6.30 pm when the telephone rang. He picked the receiver off its hook, heard the pip-pip cease as the caller inserted a coin and recognised the familiar voice of the man he had known as 'Marc' saying, 'Hi there! I am standing on the Piccadilly corner like a frustrated old whore. Come down.'

A grin creased the listener's face, which might easily have been mistaken for Rex Harrison's. Then he went through each room checking, picked up his hat, slung his coat over one arm and went down to meet Sir Frederick Musgrave.

The two men strolled along Piccadilly to St James's, turning into Jermyn Street and thence into Bury Street where they settled at a small table in a corner of Wilton's. They ate a prodigious number of oysters, washed them down with an excellent real Chablis, punished a wedge of Roquefort, and drank four cups of coffee apiece. On leaving the restaurant they headed for Green Park where, walking under the budding trees, Fluff gave his companion a final briefing.

'You are Sir Charles Wedderburn's private pilot, remember. You are flying to Geneva to collect his daughter and her uncle. You will of course by-pass the airport and come down instead in the very large field you will doubtless recall from – er – previous occasions. You are to arrive at 1.30 am and circle once, thus enabling the watcher to switch on her torch. Then it's up to you to make a safe landing. The girl will be waiting. Once she's on board, a man will join you. Take off again immediately he is inside the aircraft and return to the English rendezvous. Offload your passengers speedily. A car will be waiting to take the girl to her destination. As soon as she's gone, another car will appear – a dark blue Porsche with the number HH 1171 and bearing a CD plate. See the man into it and then get the hell out of it.'

Fluff's companion repeated these instructions after which the pair strolled on until they reached Horseguards Parade where a dark blue Porsche was drawn up against the kerb with its engine idling. Its number was HH 1171 and it carried a CD plate. The two men installed themselves in the back seat and the car moved off immediately, turning into Parliament Square and thence across Westminster Bridge.

Operation Phoenix had begun.

The ways of great banks are at all times predictable. The cycles of labour are observed with meticulous punctuality. The reliability of the persons concerned is above questioning: unhurried and imperturbable. The hours

231

go by, with each according to his station fulfilling his or her duties with achingly monotonous repetition. When the cleaners are admitted, they pursue their tasks overseen in the echoing chambers and corridors by the night watchmen, who in turn are fixed irrevocably to the umbilical cord of hourly communication with the forces of security, law and order. On the hour, every hour, they renew these contacts lest all hell break loose and the august portals be breached. Almost instantly another building becomes surrounded and its roofs populated by swarms of armed representatives of security, law and order. Everyone knows this. It is accepted as integral to their daily or nightly working lives. They take it entirely for granted, secure in their own minds in the comfort it gives to them concerning the untold millions which lie cached below in the huge vaults.

So it was with the Banque Internationale et Suisse in Geneva, where its massive overcoat of white stone, interspersed with wide windows caged in iron bars, rose stolidly upon the corner of the rue de la Liberté and the rue Royale. That disarmingly ordinary overcoat concealed an inner lining of such tremendous insulating power – by stainless steel and reinforced concrete – that the absolute maximum of protection was afforded to all the multifarious treasures within. Not least among these, to the men who entrusted them to the care of this august establishment, were the strong boxes hidden below in the utmost security of the great vaults.

In one such chamber rows upon rows of strong boxes soared above each other, holding the secrets as well as the loot of many, while the Banque Internationale et Suisse held their numbered accounts. Only the owners of those strong boxes possessed the keys to open them. None of the numbered account holders ever received bank statements except when they or their accredited representatives presented impeccable credentials and thus were able to receive copies by hand. These they then cached in their strong boxes along with any other papers which they could not afford to run the risk of keeping elsewhere.

The routine of the eminent persons of unblemished

232

international reputation who comprised the Bank's Board of Governors was interesting too. Turn and turn about, according to their mutually fixed roster, one of them ended the day's work each day by remaining behind to admit the two night guards. This ritual was performed at 5.05 pm precisely. Even they were only admitted after close scrutiny of their *cartes d'identité* to which each man's photograph was attached. Five minutes before their arrival the bell in the Duty Officer's private room rang to announce the arrival of the six cleaners, for whom the same scrutinies were observed. These would then be let out by the guards themselves when their duties were completed.

The guards – all men skilled in unarmed combat, although each one was armed – did a twelve-hour stint which, in the case of the night guards, finished at 5.05 am, their last duty being to admit their replacements according to the same ritual scrutinies. Finally they were released, having handed over the formidable chain of keys to their successors. On departure the night guards synchronised their watches with the Duty Officer, and the day guards checked theirs with the night guards. Then one or other of each pair would press the vital button on the hour every hour, thus confirming to Security HQ that God was in His heaven and all was right with this particular banking microcosm.

One fine spring night in early April Nicholas Guttenberg was the eminent governor on whose shoulders the responsibility rested for admitting and checking the guards and cleaning staff. He was sitting in the Duty Officer's room checking, mentally, the somewhat unorthodox arrangements he had made for the night when the main door bell rang. Instinctively his eyes went to the small jade clock beside it. The hands registered 4.57. He rose, walked unhurriedly to the great doors, keys in hand. He bent down to unfasten the first lock and draw back the first bolt, thereafter rising slowly as he turned key after key until he reached the top. Two cleaners in white overalls stood on the steps waiting.

233

'A thousand apologies, *m'sieu,*' said the taller of the two. 'We are almost three minutes early.'

Nicholas Guttenberg made no reply. He inspected them before beckoning them in. He locked up again and with a slightly more hurried gait led them back to the Duty Officer's room. He closed the door and remained standing, waiting patiently while the men stripped off their overalls, disclosing underneath the replica uniforms to those of the official night guards. Then simply nodding his approval, he opened the door for them as the bell on the desk pinged again.

'Take up your positions now,' he said softly.

They obeyed, flattening themselves right and left of the doors which had been opened to admit them. Crossing behind them, keys in hand, Nicholas Guttenberg glanced at his wrist. His watch showed 5 pm precisely. This time six cleaners in white overalls stood waiting outside. He pressed the vital security buzzer and then opened up the door to admit them. Closing it again behind them, he watched the cleaners move towards the staircase leading to their cleaning cupboards. As the last of them clattered away, Nicholas Guttenberg turned back just as the bell pinged for the third time. The two stationary men – 'Marc's' men – remained flattened against the mahogany lintels.

For the third time Nicholas unfastened the doors. This time two men stepped inside, identity cards in their hands. They dropped in their tracks with slight grunts, collapsing onto the tesselated marble flooring. Their assailants bent over, hefted one apiece across their shoulders and made straightway for the room with the little jade clock on the desk.

Here the unconscious men were laid out very carefully, handcuffed, gagged and bound. 'Marc's' men stepped back to survey their handiwork. Nicholas crossed to the desk and from two deep drawers produced two large canvas holdalls. These he handed over, with another bunch of keys. Meanwhile his companions produced cutters and severed the three telephone cords.

234

All three left the room, the door was locked and picking up his hat, coat and gloves from a nearby chair, lifting a small suitcase from the floor beside it, Nicholas said, 'Now you lock me out; but remember, you ring that buzzer every hour, on the hour – one long and three short buzzes.'

The bandit guards saluted him saying, 'Oui, M'sieu le Directeur, d'accord,' as a cleaner moved across the marble flooring carrying a mop and bucket.

Dropping his voice to a whisper, Nicholas added, 'Eh bien, mes braves, merde alors!' and quit the premises for the last time, while the remaining pair mimed locking all securely once more as the great doors closed.

Moments later the doors were opened slightly and the first man slipped inside. At brief intervals the remaining seven entered and stood against the wall while the doors were locked once more. The guards then marched across to the lift, slid back the door and one by one the men raced across to crouch down inside. Nine men in all went down, past the lower ground floor, past the basement and on until the lift came to rest facing the short corridor leading to the vaults.

The two guards stepped out first, inserted the keys Nicholas Guttenberg had handed to them and simultaneously turned them in the two separate locks, using the special combination. At last the doors swung open very slowly and silently, disclosing row upon row of numbered black boxes which rested in niches along three sides of the wall rising in tiers almost to the ceiling.

They were in at last. Coats were removed and folded ready for departure. Wrenches were fished out from the canvas bags and passed round.

'Start at the top and work down. Our friend has put the steps ready as you can see.' The man who spoke was busy rolling back the sleeves of his shirt. 'Touch nothing except those bits of pasteboard and the papers.' He paused. 'Are you all gloved?' he then asked.

Nine pairs of hands were held out, black-gloved and fastened at the wrists with straps.

'Then here we go.'

They worked with the speed of great, past practice, soundlessly save for some heavy breathing for none were young men and the heat was already taking its toll. Box after box was hauled from its niche, handed down, smashed open and the contents riffled. Then each was thrown into a corner where there was soon an untidy pile. The men were all sweating profusely by now as '*de rien . . . de rien*' they muttered tossing boxes aside. Then one of the guards had to be let out to buzz again on the hour. By seven o'clock the atmosphere was heavy with frustration and every face drenched with pouring sweat.

The guard came back to report, 'Cleaners gone. As the Duchess said to her chauffeur, "Darling, we're alone at last."'

'And six hours to go,' someone reminded him grimly.

A few minutes before eight a grey-haired Frenchman with two fingers missing from his right hand – which caused the glove fingers to wiggle ludicrously – held out his discovery. It was a piece of coloured pasteboard measuring around 3½ inches by 4 inches. It was attached to several sheets of paper covered in figures and marked across the top *Number X T 47563*. The men crowded round, staring incredulously at the coloured thing which was shaped like a folded Christmas card. Then turning away, they redoubled their efforts. By twenty past eight they had found another.

'Christ! I'm thirsty,' exclaimed a tubby, balding little man whose silk shirt was sticking to his back.

'Bring down Box No. 97 then; that's the chap, Louis, just to your left. It's full of whisky, paper cups and Vichy too.'

The tallest among them reached out for it from his position on the ladder. Whisky splashed into paper cups. The men drank, wiped their mouths on expensive linen handkerchiefs, mopped off once more and one commented, 'God bless chummy who let us in. I suppose it has to have been him?'

Then a lean elegant man of around fifty with Gucci

shoes and a monogrammed shirt said tautly, 'Ten to go and time's passing, let's get cracking.'

They fell to again. By ten o'clock the tally had risen to four. A fifth appeared inside the next hour and then until just past eleven, when the guard came back from his routine ringing, they had a run of luck and the tally rose to nine. The mess had become indescribable. Angered beyond endurance by the discoveries they had made, additionally frustrated by the ones they had not made, the men began tipping the contents of the boxes out after searching them, so that one corner of the room became a chaotic mixture of papers, notes in dozens of currencies, ropes of pearls and the glint of gold, silver and precious stones.

It was three minutes before one o'clock when the last three turned up. Once more, they all crowded round while the Gucci-shod one counted them out carefully and tucked them down into a leather briefcase.

'Now let's get out,' he said tersely. 'Giles and Philippe, get up and do your pinging on those perilous buzzers. Does anyone know what we do with the keys?'

'Make confusion more confounded by locking every- thing up and then losing the keys in the lake.'

Once more sweat was wiped from faces now streaked with dust as well. Once more coats were donned, hands passed rapidly across untidy heads, gloves stuffed into pockets until, as before, nine men and one briefcase soared upwards in the lift and walked calmly out the way they had come into the night. Turning their heads to left and right, one spied the back of a plodding *gen- darme* moving steadily away from them up the hill. Unable to resist the impulse, he blew the retreating back a kiss before melting away into the darkness.

They had drawn lots for who would keep the rendez- vous. It fell to the tall, thin one they called Jean. He now ran to the street corner, glanced hurriedly around and turning left jogged along until he came to an empty house with an adjoining garage. He let himself in, went down some side steps by the kitchen door into the garage, pressed yet one more button and, vaulting into the driving seat of the low black Alfa Romeo, he tucked the briefcase uncomfortably under his narrow hips. He switched on the ignition as the up and over doors swung high and in seconds the car was purring out and away towards a rendezvous with a jet aircraft and a lady.

Lady Mary Harland spent the evening with a film star in his chalet overlooking the lake. She was in sparkling form, looked entrancing and thoroughly enjoyed both her dinner and the assembled company. At midnight however she complained of a slight headache and after a plethora of regrets, she was put into her host's chauffeur-driven Rolls and taken back to Nicholas Guttenberg's villa where she was staying. She let herself in, grateful that the housekeeper was already in bed. She dismissed the drowsy butler and hurried to her room. Here she changed into jeans, a sweater and soft-soled shoes, grabbed her thoroughly unsuitable sable coat from which she refused to be parted, picked up her dressing case and went down again into the hall.

She extracted two notes from her shoulder bag and left them propped up against the gilt clock on the console table. One was a pleasant apology with a very adequate tip for the housekeeper. The other was a note to Nicholas, written with the thought in mind that it would be read by many other persons than the man for whom, in this instance, it was not really intended since, with any luck, she would see him within the hour. It read:

> Dearest Nikki,
> Lord Beardmore telephoned me. He wants those pictures yesterday! So I am leaving in ill-bred haste. I heard Tommy saying he was flying to London tomorrow at the crack so I shall try to hitch a lift with him. Failing that I'll use public transport. Please ask me again. I've had a blissy time and am only so sorry to go like this but He Who Must Be Obeyed does have a first call on my extremely well-paid time.
>
> Lots of love and gratitude,
> *Mary*

...

Having completed her chores according to Fluff Musgrave's instructions, she let herself out and stepped into the Mercedes which was standing in the drive. Once she had parked the car at the airport, she set out to walk to her rendezvous. About a mile towards this objective, she found a bicycle propped against some railings. Murmuring, 'Eureka!' she appropriated it and pedalled off into the darkness with her dressing case across the handlebars, and the sable tails of her coat knotted across her stomach. As she rode, she tried to resolve what she must do with the tell-tale bicycle on arrival and at the same time experiencing considerable regrets over the sables which were becoming intolerably hot.

Finally she reached the field, edged herself and her stolen bicycle into the shelter of some bushes and sat down in a mercifully dry cow-pat to await her signal. This did little to improve her temper either. Having scrabbled in her handbag for the powerful torch Nicholas had provided, she had decided that the aircraft was not coming when she heard it overhead. She crept out, listened, then switched the torch on and off and again waited. The volume of sound multiplied unbearably. Presently the pilot made a rough but safe landing. Then he leaned out and over the engine she heard him shouting, 'Mary, are you there?'

She showed herself, heard him whistle and then asked apologetically, 'Can you help me to dispose of my bicycle? You see, I pinched it. Would you – er – by chance have room for it in your aircraft? I feel it might be a bit tricky to leave it here.'

'Too right,' the pilot agreed fervently. 'I can't get it in like this though. We'll have to take the wheels off and turn the pedals inwards.'

Mary nodded. 'Thanks awfully. What can I do to help?'

'Fetch it – fast, lovely lady,' he retorted. 'Then shade your torch and switch it on. Your job is to hold it steady while I do the unpicking. *And we shall have to hurry!*'

She obeyed him, hauling the offending vehicle from

its shelter. Then the pilot went to work. He had stowed the wheels and was just turning the pedals inwards when the flash of headlights showed up in the lane.

'Our friend,' he grunted. 'Come on now, one good shove and it's in. Just in time or born in the vestry,' he then snarled, almost falling in after the frame as he put his weight on it. 'Oh, the hellishness of inanimate objects!'

The headlights had vanished but they heard the sound of running, stumbling footsteps. Suddenly and silently, the man called Jean loomed darkly on their left. 'Lady Mary?' he whispered.

She, in reply, switched the torch full onto him, saw clearly that he was her man, spotted the briefcase, saying as she took it, 'I am Lady Mary Harland. Nice work, if I may say so. Is it all there?'

'All twelve,' there was a note almost of complacence in his voice, disembodied again in the darkness as the torch was switched off.

Mary laughed.

The pilot shouted, 'Come on! We simply can't wait any longer for your other chap.'

'I'm here,' said Nicholas Guttenberg, stepping out from where he had been hiding. He held a gun in his hand.

Mary stretched out a hand to haul him into the aircraft, leaning back to give him room and at that moment three things happened simultaneously.

Nicholas said, 'Nice work, Jean, you'll be hearing from me.' The man vanished immediately into the darkness. Mary hauled, overbalanced backwards. Nicholas turned in the entrance and a third man suddenly appeared. With a gun steadied by both hands he levelled it straight at Nicholas.

There were two almost simultaneous soft plops. The stranger dropped to the ground and lay there unmoving. Nicholas collapsed inside the plane and Mary leapt over him onto the ground. She bent to the fallen man with Nicholas' gun, which she had snatched up as she scrambled back onto the ground, held pointing down at the still figure.

The frantic voice of the pilot shouted, 'Where the hell's that bloody girl?'

Mary hauled herself inside the plane again. The door closed as she shouted back, 'He's dead, shot clean through the head.'

The pilot yelled, 'Ours isn't,' and the aircraft began to bounce over the rough ground. Mary bent over Nicholas, one hand scratching frantically in her shoulder bag for a mirror. She held it over his face. It misted over. The sudden tears dried on her face as the violence of their bouncing increased. With a lurch the plane was airborne and streaking upwards.

A few moments later and the pilot climbed from his seat.

'No panic,' he said calmly. 'The bird's on George and we're all alive. I just want to see whereabouts this chap's copped it because we've got nearly two and a half hours' flying ahead of us and judging by what my No 1 said, my cargo's precious. So be a good girl and slip into my seat. Keep an eye on that dial. Look! This one. So long as it wavers about where it is now, we're on a reasonably safe course but if it drops, just holler and I'll come running.'

Mary obeyed him, using the waiting time to work out the swiftest way to get out of the pilot's seat if the dial did drop.

The pilot straightened Nicholas out. He unfastened his jacket, felt the wetness of blood as he turned this back and saw a spread of the stuff over the man's shirt. Then he found the source. The bullet had gone clean through the shoulder, well above the heart line. He had seen this particular wound on other occasions, so realised that apart from the effect of shock and the loss of blood, there was no immediate danger, but he was not a young man. The pilot reached above his head for the first aid box, made a reasonable job of padding and strapping Nicholas up and was rewarded by a slight movement of the eyelids.

By the time he exchanged seats with Mary again,

Nicholas had recovered consciousness sufficiently to ask rather weakly, 'Did I get the blighter?'

Mary told him, offered him a plastic cup of water and was asked, 'Don't we have any brandy?'

'You shouldn't have any brandy,' came back from the pilot's seat.

'I am not interested in what I should have but what I want. Am I dying or what?'

'Or what,' Mary told him. 'If you behave yourself, don't move and do as you're told.'

He smiled wryly, then said, 'Then let me fill you in. I more or less knew I was being followed but at one point I thought I'd shaken the beggar off. I only hope the rest of the lads got away. Have I been out for long?'

'About twenty minutes,' Mary told him. 'We've roughly two hours to go. So please, Nikki, be reasonable.'

'I will if you tell me every single thing that happened that you know.'

She did her best, coming eventually to the stealing of the bicycle.

'But why,' he murmured, 'a bicycle, dear Mary? Wasn't my Mercedes sufficiently adequate?'

'Oh, Nikki, be your age! Even we couldn't have got it in here and even the velocipede would have left a dangerous trail.'

'Of course,' he acknowledged. 'I must be out of practice.'

She went on with her explanation, unaware her eyes were sparkling. It caused him to interrupt again, saying, 'I do believe you have enjoyed every moment of this appalling escapade.'

'Oh, yes, sheer bliss,' she agreed, 'at least until you got pooped. Now where was I?'

She finished her tale and then observed, 'I always thought after a caper like this one said, "Mission accomplished" or something similar.'

'One does not,' snapped the pilot severely. 'At least not until it *is* and in this instance that will be when I have handed both of you over and taken off myself. Now listen, you two, I'm turning off the cabin lights so you can pipe down, at least until we land.'

'Please tell me one thing first. What is the time now?' Mary asked.

'Two thirty.'

'Then we should be in by four.'

'Yes. A Porsche will be waiting to take you off at once. There will be another car for my other passenger.'

'But one cannot just hand over a man who has been shot without having to answer some very awkward questions,' Mary interrupted.

'The driver will know precisely where to take him without any awkward questions being asked. Beyond getting treatment, you're not in any great hurry, are you, sir?'

'Me?' In the faint light of the approaching dawn Mary looked anxiously at Nicholas' face, which seemed as though the skin had been drawn too tightly over its bones. His voice sounded slightly rasping as he continued, 'Oh, no, my dear fellow. I've – er – well, really all the time in the world so you need not trouble yourself on my account.'

Mary put out one hand as she crouched on the floor beside him. She smoothed his hair in a tender, compassionate little gesture and said very softly, 'Dear Nikki, does it hurt you to talk? If it does, you really must stop at once.'

'It does not,' he said firmly. 'What do you want me to say?'

'Just *why*,' she whispered. 'Can you tell me or should I not ask?'

He shook his head slowly. 'Of course you may ask, my dear. It may seem strange and indeed treacherous to you; but there are some to whom revenge is as sweet a passion as man can experience. You may not know that my mother was actually English. She and my father were separated. He remained behind in Switzerland. I can best explain this by saying that his "sweet passion"

243

was banking – just that and really nothing else attained any significance by comparison.

'When the war came, Mother and I were in Paris. She insisted I should go back to Switzerland, but she stayed on. Then the Germans came. She was caught harbouring an English Air Force pilot. Later I discovered that it was a Russian girl who had informed against her. I only need add that my mother died ... eventually. Before she died, she was tortured in an attempt to obtain the names of the others in her organisation. She resisted ... to the end.

'It seemed to me to be poetic justice for me to begin working for certain men in Britain. I remained under cover, had a good life and made many friends both in France and England. Then one day I met Sir Frederick Musgrave who knew me for what I was, and the rest I think you can work out for yourself.'

He finished speaking, drew a handkerchief from his pocket and wiped her face, down which the tears were falling. 'Don't cry for me, child,' he said gently. '*Mon parti était pris.* If you succeed in what you are trying to do, I shall be content. I am only curious to learn who will assume command.'

'The man I am going to marry, I hope, thanks to you, my very dear Nikki.'

The pilot's voice cut across this last exchange. 'We are coming in to land and there *are* two cars waiting.'

Sir Frederick Musgrave waited on the Essex airstrip after the small jet had soared off into the starlight. Presently a car drew up. In it were two men. One slid out, held the door open for Sir Frederick, settled him and then climbed into the Porsche as the other car turned round and sped towards London. Fluff stood on the pavement for a moment watching its tail light disappear before entering the *Clarion* building. He took the lift to the fourth floor and was admitted to the penthouse.

All the top brass were there but only Lord Beardmore was awake; the rest sprawled in their chairs, spent and

244

waiting, for there was nothing more for them to do for a while. There was a debauched air about the big room with stub-filled ashtrays, empty cigarette packets and glasses littering the tables and waste-paper baskets erupting with crumpled papers.

The old peer stood up and came across to Fluff. 'If we succeed,' he said very gruffly, 'there'll be plenty for everyone to do then. Come into my room. We can talk there without disturbing them.'

They settled in two deep chairs. Lord Beardmore passed his cigar box across to Fluff, proffered a cutter, reached for the decanter at his elbow and poured out two cognacs. 'Where are they now?' he asked, knowing Fluff would understand.

'In the bank, I fancy,' Fluff replied, 'while Mary is just about returning from a dinner party before setting off for the airstrip. Tell me, where are Richard and David?'

'Eh?' for once 'The Lord' sounded abstracted. 'Oh, those two! Llewellyn is due back here shortly; he's been running an errand for me. David's car which I had collected for him is in the yard; he went out about an hour ago, saying he needed a breath of air.'

Their eyes met. Fluff murmured, ' "Conspiracy his time doth take!" ' and the old peer whipped back, ' "But the waiting time, my brothers, is the hardest time of all." '

'Who said that?' Fluff asked curiously.

'A woman called Sarah Doudney in a thing called *The Psalm of Life*.'

'I think,' Fluff mused, 'the best lines ever penned to any sort of time came in a speech Theseus made to Hippolyta in *Midsummer Night's Dream*:

> "Four days will quickly steep themselves in night;
> Four nights will quickly dream away the time;
> And then the moon like to a silver bow
> New-bent in heaven, shall behold the night
> Of our solemnities."

As you will doubtless remember, Hippolyta has already exclaimed, "But O, methinks how slow the old moon wanes!" My God, it does too.' He ruminated, 'I have been thinking too of all those evil men, asleep in their beds and unaware of what Nemesis may have in store for them tomorrow.'

Lord Beardmore reached out, took a firm hold of the decanter again and spoke their *vale* as he replenished their glasses. 'For them, my dear fellow,' he said harshly, 'there will be no tomorrows . . . should we succeed.'

Before he left the penthouse, David had scribbled a note to 'Glad' who was sleeping with her head on Sven's shoulder.

> Gone out to stretch my legs. Tell 'the Lord' if he asks that I shall try to catch Richard when he returns. We'll be at my house if wanted. You know the numbers.

Love,
David

He went down onto the Embankment. Between Blackfriars Bridge and the silhouetted splendour of the Houses of Parliament he recalled his own words spoken in the penthouse during the early part of the previous evening. 'The Lord', eyes glinting under those massive eyebrows, cigar positively bouncing from side to side, had rapped out the question.

'You say you have nothing but contempt for the men in office and out of it whom we all believe to be communists. You say and we all agree of course that such men are striving to bring about a totalitarian state here, to put an end to monarchy and to bring about the final destruction of all that has made this country great for close on a thousand years. You rightly denounce all those who are grovelling in the corruption of local government for the furtherance of their own political or criminal intents. In all this we are, as we have been from the beginning, in complete accord; but what of the rest, David? What of the ordinary man in the street?'

'The Lord's' question seemed in retrospect to be a

challenge. David realised that during their exchange pencils had been laid down, typewriters had stilled, heads had come up and he had made his answer in a sudden hush.

'Well, sir,' he had begun, 'it has always been my contention that blood will out. The splendid motivation which Shakespeare dealt with through Henry V at Agincourt has maybe been silted over a bit by disillusionment out of apathy, but it is my belief that Joe Public is as decent, as courageous and as gallant a chap, *au fond*, as he was at Dunkirk. In fact I shall never lose faith in the so-called ordinary man in the street or in his womenfolk either. The old spirit is all there still, I am convinced, but by God, it will take some rousing after what the poor sods have been through this time. They'll be punch drunk by morning.

'Maybe the world sees our collective "ordinary man" as defeated, paralysed, apathetic. Certainly with inflation rampant, they are locked into a relentless spiral with wage increases chasing rising prices until if left to go on, as they are now just beginning to realise, all will founder into ruin and anarchy. Let 'em think that. They will have to eat craw by tonight, God willing – and if this perilous lark comes off. Then they'll see Joe Public is still underneath the decent, highly moral and respectable royalist he has always been. Give him a smashing incentive and he'll work like all get out. too.'

At that point Sven had cut across his words with, 'Exactly so, my son. We know it and you know it but with respect, are you prepared to take the strain because make no mistake about it, you're the only one who can rouse 'em, inspire 'em and lead 'em. You are their Pied Piper, but are you prepared to take the job and how in God's name would you set about playing such a Sisyphus role?'

David turned and began retracing his steps along the Embankment. He was clear now in his own mind. He was unshakeably convinced that nothing could be more calculated to arouse the fury and support of the most incarnadined shop steward than to learn that he and his brethren had been conned and swindled all the way down the line by the latest batch of 'leaders', who had been ranting on about sacrifices for the common good while stealing from them.

Suddenly, in all probability a natural corollary to the stresses and tensions which had been building up over the years, David Kincale felt a wave of terrible doubt. Should they fail, what then? He shook his head like a diver coming up for air, it was too horrible to contemplate and yet . . .

Behind him Big Ben struck five times, the resounding note rolling out over the sleeping city.

David broke into a trot, came panting up Fleet Street and out into the yard behind the *Clarion* building. A tousled head moved slightly in the passenger seat of his old Daimler, which he had asked to be brought out of hiding in an inexplicable sudden urge to drive the Duke's car again. Richard was back. David leaned over the opened door.

'Come on back and have a bath,' he urged. 'I left a note aloft with "Glad". We'll both think better after a shave and breakfast. I'm fogged over and shrouded in doubts, and maybe you are too.'

Richard yawned, glanced at his wrist and exclaimed, 'Christ! It's five o'clock!'

'That's right,' David agreed, 'one way or another, it's all over by now.'

The rush of air as the open car speeded towards Parliament Square put new life into them. Over the noise of the engine David shouted, 'I've just had a cold grey dawn of my own down on the Embankment but I'm over it now.'

'You'd better be,' Richard shouted back. 'There's a bod sitting on your doorstep that ought to fix you good and proper if I know anything.'

The great car swerved. The brakes shrieked as they skidded to an abrupt standstill. Mary was sitting on a small dressing case with her arms clasped over a briefcase and her copper beech leaf hair blowing in the dawn breeze. 'Oh, I am so glad to see you,' she said thankfully, 'I'm holding twelve time bombs, David darling, and I'm terribly cold. And poor darling Nikki has been shot; but we think he's going to be all right. The pilot who brought us back gave me a number to ring after 5.30 to find out how he is.'

When they had fumbled frantically with the locks and the door swung open, David picked Mary up, briefcase of 'time bombs' and all, and carried her into the house, with Richard close behind holding her dressing case. David bore her up the stairs to the drawing room and she seemed perfectly content that he should do so. Then he put her down on the tangerine velvet sofa, saying rather thickly, 'You realise this has been worn out, re-buttoned and re-upholstered since you last sat there, my darling.'

'Then please don't waste any more time. From now on we stay together.'

She linked her arms around his neck and drew his head down.

They were totally oblivious of Richard. He just stood beaming behind them for a moment, then put the dressing case down and announced, 'Carry on, please. I think I'll go and plug in the percolator your inestimable man will undoubtedly have left ready. Don't do anything I wouldn't – just do what I've done because I can assure you that you'll find it *very* satisfactory.'

They laughed against each other's lips. 'He means marriage,' David murmured, running his fingers through her hair, grasping it, moving his mouth across her tilted throat, 'and that is what I want, my darling girl.'

'Breakfast is ready,' Richard announced from the doorway. 'Is it proper for me to come in?' He found them sitting side by side bent over the opened briefcase.

'I haven't even looked inside,' Mary was saying. 'Is it all right, David? Is it what you wanted?'

249

David turned to look at Richard. 'The lot!' he said vehemently, 'the stinking bloody lot and what's more – of course I never knew – but we've got them by the short hairs. Look . . . photographs . . . dossiers.'

They all began to talk at once. David hastily crammed all the papers back into the briefcase, saying, 'Come on down. We'll phone in the kitchen. We must buzz "The Lord" and take the glad news from Aix to Ghent. Oh, fids, I gloat! Now are the evil ones delivered into our hands!'

David held Mary's hand while he pressed the numbers. With his hand over the receiver, he murmured, 'Imagine anyone phoning him in his holy of holies! What time is it exactly, Richard?'

'6.05 precisely,' Richard told him, suppressing a slight tendency to hysteria.

David nodded, grinning, and then sobered to say, 'Oh, hello, is that you, sir? Good morning. Well, I have news for you. Mission accomplished . . . yes, sir . . . yes, all twelve . . . we're just having some breakfast and then I'll bring the lot up to you *with their pictures* . . . oh, I don't think so, sir, I mean . . . well, after all they have come all this way in good order . . . oh, very well, sir . . . yes, sir . . . as you say, sir!'

He replaced the receiver and turned to the others ruefully. 'Armoured car, Securicor, the whole bit. He's in a fair tizz. Of course one can't blame him.'

Richard sat down with a thud, poured out the coffee he had made and confessed, 'I don't mind admitting it hasn't sunk in yet with me. I think the whole thing is a glorious dream . . . Mary holding your hand, you looking rather like you did at Oxford – you've shed about ten years in the past hour – and twelve duplicate treasures cached in that blooming ordinary briefcase.'

The briefcase in question lay between the marmalade and Mrs Binns' home-made crab apple jelly to which both men were addicted. As they polished off eggs and bacon, a reproachful, dressing-gowned figure appeared in the doorway.

'Ah ha,' said he, 'I might have known. Good morning, my lady. It's been a long time since you ran out of here in your stockin' feet. Good morning, sir. Have you been up all night, might I enquire?'

'Yes, I have,' David replied, with his mouth full, 'and her ladyship has been travelling all night . . .'

'Tch, tch, tch! Such goings-on,' Bronson said disapprovingly.

'Blimey!' exclaimed her ladyship. 'I've only just realised that just over six hours ago I was dining with David Niven who is as devastating as ever and has an equally enchanting wife as you know already.'

'Might one ask where, my lady?' Bronson enquired, appropriating the percolator and going to the refrigerator for a fresh bottle of milk.

'Switzerland – Geneva actually,' she told him, eyes glinting.

Bronson nearly dropped the milk. '*Switzerland!*'

'Yes,' mischief was now sparkling in her eyes, 'I left just before midnight, went back to the house where I was staying, changed, packed and drove my car to Geneva.'

'I see, my lady. Did you have a good flight?'

Mary winked ostentatiously at David and replied, 'You know, you don't really see at all, Bronson. I then walked about a mile along the airport road, pinched a bicycle, tied the case onto one handlebar with my belt and wobbled to a very private airstrip – in a field actually. We then found the bicycle wouldn't fit into the jet, so I held a torch while the pilot took off the wheels and turned in the pedals. Then someone was shot.'

Rivetting as her story was to both David and Richard, the sight of Bronson, thoroughly unnerved, was even more so. He stood at the refrigerator door clutching the tipped up neck of the milk bottle, staring incredulously at Mary, unaware that the milk was dripping slowly over the sleeve of his dressing gown and falling silently onto the rug on which he stood.

'I sssee, my lady,' stammered the defeated man.

'We did discuss jettisoning the damn thing over the sea

251

but it meant opening the door and as we might easily have got sucked out,' here Bronson sucked in his breath, 'we thought the better of it. I imagine by now it is in a rubbish tip somewhere between London and the M4.'

'Why the M4, my darling?' David asked.

Mary could not resist the temptation. She answered him, all the time watching Bronson and the trickle of milk. 'Well, darling Nikki finally decided against blowing his brains out and instead opted for a new identity in South America. Almost the last thing he said was, "Maybe this is wiser, then I can live to fight another day," adding, "if your David ever needs me." Then he kissed me, was carried into the other car and I got into the Porsche and was offloaded here onto that damned cold doorstep.'

'Doorstep, my lady?' Bronson gasped.

'I sat there for ages until Mr Kincale rescued me. I say, Bronson, you're absolutely soaked in milk, don't you think you had better go upstairs and dress. I'll hold the fort for you.'

One glance downwards and Bronson tottered speechless from the room while the unrepentant trio released their tensions in a huge, sobbing gale of laughter. Eventually, wiping his eyes, David asked, 'Darling Mary, was there a single word of truth in all that *farandole?*'

'It was straight reportage,' she said airily, 'except I left out that darling, heroic Nikki kissed me very tenderly before we separated and said there would be a little something in the post for us if you decided to make an honest woman of me.'

Before they left the house, David rang through to the number Mary had given him. He asked, taking a wild shot, on behalf of Sir Frederick Musgrave, if he could have news of their patient. Then he listened, said, 'Thank you very much,' and replaced the receiver.

He put his arms round Mary. 'My love, they say their patient had a relapse shortly after being admitted. I am extremely sorry to have to tell you that Nicholas Guttenberg is dead.'

CHAPTER XIX

*'Am I a harp that the hand of the mighty may touch me,
or a flute that His breath may pass through me.'*

– Kahlil Gibran

FRESH GUARDS LOUNGED on their chairs outside the penthouse below the baleful red 'eye' which forbade any unauthorised person to enter. The trio presented their passes and were admitted. All heads lifted and Lord Beardmore roared, 'Mary, come on in and *give me that briefcase.'*

The scene had changed once again. In place of a disorderly dosshouse of seemingly displaced persons exhaustedly sleeping in a weariness beyond belief, all present were now showered, shaved and watered. Although none of his men spoke, Lord Beardmore was aware as were the trio who crossed towards him of the immense tension and expectation which charged the great room. Eight pairs of eyes watched unblinkingly as Mary held out the briefcase, handed over the key and said, 'Good morning, sir,' as if it were any ordinary day, then went the rounds, saying, 'Good morning, Gladys', for she detested any abbreviations, and continuing, 'Sir Frederick . . . gentlemen,' while 'The Lord' turned the key, lifted the flap, unlocked the inner clasp and withdrew the contents.

Disbelievingly, he began studying a bank statement stamped across the top of the first page with V Y N 429089, to which was attached what looked to the watching men like a small, dark red Christmas card, ornamented across the front flap only with brilliant and convoluted golden lettering, which in the Russian alphabet were the initials KHCC, the abbreviation for Soviet Union Communist Party Card.

As they stared down at the almost total incrimination implicit in this evidence, their trained faces registered nothing but deep attention. Lord Beardmore turned the small card's frontispiece over, thus disclosing on the inside left a most meticulous dossier of the card holder, with on the facing page a photograph. *Total incrimination at last!*

Under his breath Sven began humming 'Land of Hope and Glory'. When he reached 'mother of the free', 'The Lord' snapped, 'Shut up, Sven, though I agree the sentiment is apt . . .' and withdrew a second clip.

As he laid the twelve Communist Party Cards out on the desk beside the documents which showed the numbers very clearly at the head of each other's bank statements, a sound not unlike a soft growl developed until it was silenced by such a volcanic eruption of invective from 'The Lord' that his senior staff stood back and shut up, just staring wide-mouthed and incredulously. Henry Scull caught Sven's eye for a moment, raised one eyebrow and was answered by a thumbs up sign from the Dane.

Their employer was gazing at a very familiar face. 'So,' he tagged on to his epithets, apostrophising the photograph pasted on the right of the red card, 'you double-dyed bastard, you're one of 'em, are you? May you roast forever in the burning pit!' He detached the card, snapped, 'Circulate and return,' and bent over the papers he still held. Fluff glanced at the photograph, turned the card over, read the back heading *Rules* and handed it on to Sven.

By the time Henry Scull returned it to Lord Beardmore, that worthy had himself well in hand but his face was eloquent of such fury as went down in the annals of *Clarion* history – for even his cigar had gone out and he had failed to notice it.

He cleared his throat. 'Gentlemen,' he said, 'these are the latest bank statements of the holder of this card

254

which you have all now examined. The number stamped upon the top page is X T 47563. The amount in credit on February 4th last was £4,500,000.'

'Scum!' snapped Graybourne, as he passed the papers on.

David, a silent watcher, saw 'The Lord's' hand go down inside the briefcase again and choked back a laugh as Sven whispered, 'Santa's dipping deep into his sack, children!'

The silence, the whispered exchanges, the growls of rage continued until Gladys – always the tidy one – leaned over between Lord Beardmore and Sven Jorgensen and rearranged the twelve red cards, in a neat row, thereby seeing for herself a dozen extremely familiar faces. Henry Scull had already jotted down the totals on the numbered bank statements and was now doing frantic calculations on the back of an envelope, unaware that all his companions were busy with a similar ploy.

'Well,' Henry Scull began, looking up to see 'The Lord', hands clasped together on the table, glowering at him, 'I make the total fifty-seven million in all, sir. Anyone else take 'em down?' He glanced round the table, and 'confirmed' . . . 'confirmed' . . . ran like a death sentence around the room.

Henry Scull made one further scribble and announced, 'Give or take a bit here and a bit there, that shows the fairly substantial figure of just about four and three-quarter millions apiece. I'll get the figures out properly for you in a moment.'

'Take your time, we can afford to,' Lord Beardmore assured him.

David leaned forward. 'Just one more thing, sir, that I think you should know. After I spoke to you, I made a stop on the way here. At No 10 Downing Street. I handed in my letter of resignation to the Prime Minister; one of the policemen took it. Then I posted another in the letter box on the corner containing my application for the Chiltern Hundreds. As of now I am no longer either Chancellor of the Exchequer or indeed even a Member of Parliament, but just a private person.'

The bushy eyebrows shot up alarmingly as David continued, 'I might add, as I assume you have been here all night and in your virgin state of incommunicado – leaving your deputy to put your newspaper to bed – that it may be news to you that London is littered with abandoned buses. All the men – drivers, conductors and inspectors – are *out* and the traffic snarl-up must by now be in a fair way to being total.'

Lord Beardmore was scribbling as David talked. Now he glanced up. 'They'll be back presently,' he grunted. 'Glad, take this down. See it goes to all the media with special emphasis on the BBC and all the rest of the TV and radio appendages. Begin, "The Right Honble Mr David Kincale has this morning resigned his post as Chancellor of the Exchequer in the present Labour Government and has also entered his application for the Chiltern Hundreds." Then define what that means, you don't need me to do that for you, check the lot with Sven and then get it off fast. I want it known throughout the world by noon today.'

He turned to Sven. 'As soon as you can get him, speak to George Tandy and get him here within the hour. He must have this in time for the noon edition of the *Evening Clarion*. Meanwhile I'm off to have a bath and indulge in some quiet reflection. From the moment I return, I shall expect Operation Phoenix to be entering upon its second phase.'

He hesitated, then addressed David again, saying, 'Joe Public will read between the lines all right when these,' he slapped his hands down on the Communist Party Cards, 'are ranged across my *Clarion* with the banner headline underneath DO YOU KNOW THESE MEN? They'll do their sums in no uncertain manner.' He was standing now, foresquare and as vitalised as if he had spent the night in his own luxurious bed. 'Oh, and Mary, get these cards photostatted for me immediately please. David, I would be obliged if you would accompany her.

256

Bring the originals back here and hand them over to Glad. Once this is done, I think it would be sensible for you to have a word with our shop stewards. Get 'em round a table and put the fluence on them. The photostats should do the trick but if by any chance they want to see the originals, take 'em under guard.'

Lord Beardmore was half way across the room when Glad returned with an armful of newspapers. She handed him a set and he went off cheerfully, saying, 'Read 'em in the bath,' and then shouting from the door, 'good luck to our side!' before he disappeared.

As Mary and David went down together in the lift, she asked abruptly, 'Darling, won't you have to go into hiding until we're ready? You cannot talk to the Press yet and they'll be around like hornets once they know what you've done.'

He answered with seeming irrelevance. 'I'm going to Paris as soon as I've dealt with the shop stewards. Call it a pricking in my thumbs if you like. It's certainly more than likely *she*'ll chuck me out rather than welcome me in, but I must try anyway. There's nothing for me to do here – yet – and I can get back by tonight.'

'How do you propose to do that? Oh, blast, here's my floor!' Walking along the corridor, David told her.

'Good old Sir Frederick,' she chuckled. 'Are his brigade of old boys in on this act too?'

'Not exactly, rather shall we say I am to be given the assistance of what the public adore calling "our faceless men" – the chaps who never appear in court. That's why all that genre of cases are dealt with by our regular policemen. I shall be both fetched and delivered by them too. I have asked Richard if I may then stay with him. I also had a word with the incomparable little Joanna and she is more than willing.' Suddenly David laughed. 'She said, "Oh goody, then you can baby sit for me while I do my shopping." That shrank me back to normal size all right!'

Later in the day, David slid into a closed car and was subsequently flown to Paris. Here he completed his shopping and was then driven out of Paris to No 4 rue de Champ d'Entraînement. There were bulletins being issued now since the Duke's illness had become critical. The news was very grave. David realised that this would almost certainly be his last visit to a kindly and eminent friend.

As the car weaved through the traffic, his thoughts returned once again to the problem of why such a man had come to mean so much to him, finally acknowledging with a rueful little smile that it had to be his inextinguishable charm because in many ways David did not really approve of him, or indeed what he had done. The car turned in past the opened gates topped by those gilded spikes on the tall iron railings. He glanced up to where *she* had put a small gilded crown upon the lantern which hung above him and wondered again how remarkably she had transformed the two acre estate into a palace in miniature. All done by intent, he decided as Sidney opened the doors to him, greeting him warmly with a welcoming smile lighting up his dark, sombre face. He put out his gloved hands, to take the parcels David was carrying.

'No, I'll keep them, thank you, Sidney,' David told him. 'Is Her Royal Highness at home?'

Sidney hesitated and then replied, 'Her Royal Highness has instructed, "Say yes to Mr Kincale, Sidney, but no to anyone else."'

She was as exquisitely trim as ever. She wore a dark blue suit with her famous pearls and a diamond brooch which David felt he had seen once before on a very orthodox royal shoulder. Her impact was suddenly of a very old woman with a face taut and tightened into a mask. The mask spoke.

'His Royal Highness is awake, David. You had better go up now. He sleeps a lot but knows you are coming and wishes to see you.'

David nodded his acquiesence and said a graceful 'Thank you, madam.' Holding out a small parcel, he then asked, 'May I give you this? I was in Spink the other day . . .'

She brightened instantly. 'My dear, how very thoughtful of you!' She took the parcel from him, while David bowed, turned towards the staircase and went up carrying his flowers and a raft of the day's newspapers. Her voice floated up to him as he hurried up those familiar and impressive stairs. 'You know your way, David . . . my dear, how very charming. Thank you very much.'

The impact was violent. He looked so small propped up by such an immensity of pillows and surrounded, on every piece of furniture, with photographs of his still 'dearest Dolly'. David felt a great weight of pity rise up within him as he came forward and bent his head. The nurse stood up and with a slight but still imperious movement of one hand the Duke dismissed her. Father and son were alone again for the last time.

CHAPTER XX

'Thy seed, my harvest.'

THE NEWSVENDORS WERE out in huge numbers in both Paris and London. The Parisians were avidly reading the story of the great bank raid in Geneva and saying to one another, 'There was no tunnelling, so it must have been an inside job.' Then, accumulating other assumptions, 'Of course it is always possible that the Bank Governor who has vanished was kidnapped; but then if that were so, how did the raiders get in? And what has that dead body in a field outside Geneva have to do with it all? He was shot, you know.' On they went, speculating and fabricating.

The cafés were filled to overflowing. Clusters formed on street corners talking, gesticulating and the air was thick with their improbable conjectures.

Back in London the resignation of the Chancellor of the Exchequer was the main topic to be banner head-lined, first in the *Evening Clarion*, later in all the rest of the evening papers, while frenetic journalists tore about trying to discover the whereabouts of the man who had removed himself altogether from the party political scene. Drawing a blank everywhere, the media be-sieged the Prime Minister who was already in a state verging upon collapse. He had heard from the Bank in Geneva, as had a number of his colleagues.

That this was done with the utmost discretion was of little consolation. All any of them was told was that among many others their strong boxes had been broken into and of course no one at the Bank had the least idea of what the boxes contained, but the police were becoming pressing in their demands for identification. Refusals piled upon silences as the malefactors struggled between the Scylla of their political lives and the Charybdis of their defecting ones.

'No,' the Prime Minister would not be able to appear on television. 'No,' he had no previous knowledge of the Chancellor of the Exchequer's intention to resign. It had shocked him profoundly to receive Mr Kincale's letter of resignation. 'No,' he had no knowledge of Mr Kincale's whereabouts, assuming him to be either at his Westminster house or at one or other of the David Kincale Training Centres which he visited regularly.

Each man concerned was irretrievably locked into reticence and all were too fearful to contact any of their colleagues. Thus each sweated and suffered, writhed and conjectured – but not in solitude. This was denied them. After the riots of the previous night when fourteen policemen were injured, one hundred and four youths had been charged and were currently appearing throughout the day at Great Marlborough Street. The Home Secretary was clamouring for a full cabinet meeting. To pile Pelion upon Ossa for the guilty, the Russian Ambassador had been summonsed to Moscow unexpectedly.

The screw was turning ever faster now and still the dreadful day brought fresh terrors as the hours passed. Confirmation was at hand that in Manchester, Birmingham and ultimately every big city in the country unmanned buses were littering the streets. It was further learned that the women had joined in the fray and were marching with banners declaring 'Enough is Enough' and 'Down with the Government'. The Commissioner of Police was already asking for the army to be brought in.

Meanwhile David's meeting with the *Clarion's* shop stewards had cut the ground from beneath their feet; for the evidence, as Lord Beardmore had said, was incontestable. Anger kept the *Clarion's* presses turning. Blind fury kept the men working as they had never worked before. When the first bundles of newspapers were thrown from the vans, struggling bands of volunteers climbed into the empty buses and drove them away, in an attempt to make the streets passable for the tangle of vehicles which packed bumper to bumper along the roads.

Inside the *Clarion* building the months of work were at long last coming to fruition. The first edition of the *Clarion* blazoned twelve photographs across the front page with the banner headline below:

DO YOU KNOW THESE MEN?

The accompanying text laid all on the line for everyone to read, stating, 'The above photographs were taken from twelve Communist Party Cards which were delivered into our hands yesterday.'

A detailed description of the cards followed with inset reproduction of the fronts, double inside spreads and backs, with an explanation of the significance of the initials from the Russian alphabet. On the inside left hand page every detail of the holder's career was set out and on the facing page was his photograph. The Rules were printed on the back.

The text continued by declaring, 'These are the men who have deceived and cheated YOU.' . . . 'These are the men who have laboured to bring this country down.' . . . 'These are the men who have tried to abolish the monarchy and sell our great country into the bondage and rule of fear of the Communists.'

Then followed the damning details of 'ten men in the Inner Council of the Labour Government and two shadow Cabinet ministers in the Conservative Party' . . . their numbered accounts in Switzerland; the sums stolen; the monies expended on houses, farms, lavish entertainments, bribes and 'official' journeys abroad.

Polishing his copy, Joe Grantley, one time ardent Leftist, was heard to say harshly, 'Those compositors

262

won't be able to work fast enough once they have read this lot. Cuckold must be a word which has many meanings, some of which, in this context, even the basest of us will not tolerate.'

Another banner headline, FOR QUEEN AND COUNTRY, was followed by the plain statement, 'This is the end of parliamentary rule as we have known it for centuries. Tomorrow we will submit for your consideration our proposals for a NEW FORM OF GOVERNMENT BY THE RIGHT MEN FOR THE RIGHT JOBS, ALL CHOSEN FOR YOUR CONSIDERATION REGARDLESS OF CLASS OR CREED. With each name the *Clarion* will publish detailed records so you can judge for yourselves whether they are fit men to govern all of us. This is the end of "jobs for the boys", and an end to figurehead ministers of departments who are passed from post to post irrespective of whether they are trained for their jobs or not. This is the end of power wielding by the "back room boys" who make decisions and shape the policies while the ministers merely act as their mouthpieces.'

Before the news broke, two members of the cabinet had committed suicide and one, slipping through the net, had vanished overseas.

By the time the second edition, long prepared and sweated over, was on the streets, the great mass of the British people were numb. Their incredulity was confounded by the tacit admissions of the 'leaders'' irrefutable guilt and these men's attempts to escape. The bell tolled for those who remained, with the appearance of men in belted raincoats who entered their homes and led them off to their waiting cars.

It was as if the whole nation had drunk of some drug which froze them in overwhelming and icy apathy.

The following day while the telephone, radio and television networks of the world chattered out their startling stories, no disclaimers were forthcoming from Russia where there had been a total clamp down on all news.

By now the entire media had swung to the *Clarion's* support. By unanimous consent a Nelsonian eye was

263

directed towards those smaller traitors who fled the country by any means at their disposal.

Then the next day's issue, snatched at and devoured by the thousands who gathered outside the *Clarion's* London and provincial offices waiting all night, was read and debated. When Lord Beardmore, who, to use his own words, decided, 'It was time to test the temperature of the water,' came out of the *Clarion's* swing doors and walked among them, a cheer went up and he was carried shoulder high to his car. All around him the dense crowd clamoured, 'Where is David Kincale?' and chanted, 'We want David . . . David Kincale.'

'Read your papers first,' bawled 'The Lord', snatching a megaphone. 'Give yourselves time to think.' Then he was driven off to the small Chelsea house where David and Mary waited.

On the third day the *Clarion's* headlines read, WE PROPOSE A RULING COUNCIL OF TWENTY HONEST ABLE MEN TO RUN OUR COUNTRY, LED BY A LORD PRESIDENT OF THE COUNCIL AND COMPOSED OF MEN IN WHOM YOU CAN PLACE YOUR ABSOLUTE CONFIDENCE. The front page continued, 'Study the records, set out in detail herein. If you can recover sufficiently to think clearly at this terrible time, and if you are satisfied that these men will put our country's interests above all other considerations, then vote for them. The facilities have long been prepared. We have already established polling booths up and down the land and in anticipation we have also prepared your voting papers. All you need do, when you have had time to reflect upon what we propose, is to choose twenty names from the forty on your voting papers. Either append your signature or just an X and finally fill in the name you choose to lead your selected twenty in the gap left for your vote after the words "Lord President of the Council".'

David and Mary were sitting on the floor of Joanna's small playroom. The carpet was littered with the components of Leggo, from which Jonathan was making a space station, while Mary and Elizabeth played with the new dolls' house. Joanna was in the kitchen preparing dinner when the front door bell rang. She ran to answer it with flour on her nose; Lord Beardmore stood outside.

'Good evening, my dear,' said he at his most benign. 'Might I come in? I believe both Mary and David are lurking in here somewhere.'

Speechless, Joanna stood back. 'Of course,' she gasped. 'I'm sorry but I'm just in the middle of getting dinner and we're in a bit of a mess. Mary and David are in the playroom with the children.'

Lord Beardmore grinned. 'Then please take me to them for my business is somewhat urgent.' He chatted to Joanna easily as she led him up the staircase, opening the playroom door as Jonathan shouted, 'Here's my space station! Uncle David, look at my space station!'

Then four pairs of eyes swung to the figure in the doorway. David scrambled to his feet first. 'I'm sorry, sir,' he apologised, 'but you didn't warn us and it's playtime for small fry at this hour.'

The old peer's face crinkled. '"The time has come," the walrus said, "to talk of many things,"' he told his audience, vastly amused despite the strain he had endured. 'David, you must return to your house. Have no fear, we'll smuggle you in somehow, and the media won't bother you because they have drawn a blank so far and are reasonably assured you will not return. Mary, we can take you along too if you wish. I can arrange that. Now you must let me have David for a while as he and I have matters of some urgency to discuss.'

'How goes it, sir?' David asked quietly.

'I'll tell you in a minute.'

David led Lord Beardmore back down the stairs and into the small drawing room, saying, 'We can talk in here undisturbed, just give me a moment to warn Mrs Llewellyn.'

'You might tell her for her vanity's sake,' Lord Beardmore added, producing his cigar case, 'that she has a large streak of flour on her very pretty nose while you're about it, and that Llewellyn will be home shortly.'

After 'The Lord' had left, Mary came into the drawing room very quietly. 'Well?' she asked calmly. 'Where do we all stand?'

David told her and finished, 'Six days to go and then Joe Public votes. Tomorrow sees the publication of the first twenty dossiers. The other twenty appear on the following day. This waiting is, I think, the worst part. We dare not show ourselves, yet I want to be out there with them, not skulking in here as if I were indeed one of those unlovely men. But we do return tomorrow by devious routes to Westminster where you will be adequately chaperoned by Mrs Binns and Bronson – if you want to come too.'

When they were safely installed with Bronson fussing over them behind the shutters he had closed four days before and Mrs Binns cooking for them from supplies smuggled in under cover of darkness, David was once again in telephonic communication with the big guns of the *Clarion* and he was able to work at last.

Besides the promised 'dossiers' the *Clarion* now exhorted Joe Public to return to work. To their astonishment he did, and by the end of the week all services were restored and the factories were fully manned.

'Place no great importance on that,' Sven warned in one of his regular talks with David. 'This way they can all discuss and compare, but things do seem favourable at the moment.' He went on to say, 'The voting is scheduled for next Monday and I want your open letter for publication tomorrow, so get cracking – sir.'

He had it and this time the *Clarion* shared its exclusive with every newspaper in the country.

All through the week Sir Frederick Musgrave had divided his time between the telephone in the hotel suite where he had established himself temporarily and the *Clarion* offices. He too talked regularly with David but at the weekend flew off to Paris so that he and the Duke, whose life hung now by such a slender thread, should be together to share the final outcome of what the pair of them had begun all those years ago.

David wrote his open letter, setting out quite simply what he had felt was happening to the country when he first took office under the Liberals. He explained, 'I found nothing to suggest that any of my fears were rooted in this party. I had by that time been fortunate in drawing Labour's attention towards me, so I crossed the floor on their invitation to play my own kind of traitor, either to work for and with them or against them according to what I discovered about them. For all those years I debarred myself contact with any of my friends who might seem suspicious to my new associates. Then, as I began to discover what was afoot, the whole exercise became infinitely worthwhile.

'These discoveries and your tremendous support and friendship to me compensated for all the rest. I came to the conclusion that the atmosphere of fiddling, swindling and general mistrust were all that stood between you and success. We know and have always known that the management gets the staff it deserves and only the wrong management invites slackness and the awful "I'm all right, Jack" attitude which has damaged the country over recent years.

'My conviction grew that given a fair deal you were the same splendid people you were during the last World War; in the factories, in the mines, at sea, in the air and on land. Given the right men to run the country you could and would be so again. My basic thinking has been borne out by events.

'If, I argued, men like those who run that vast chain store enterprise so brilliantly could be empowered to handle the business side of running our country, we could all prosper, secure in the knowledge that any remaining slackers would be dealt with by the overwhelming majority who saw that it was at last in their own interests to give of their best.

267

'That I believe is what we can do now. Of course the moles will begin burrowing once again; but having removed the cankers from Government, we can leave it to you, the workers, to deal with any recurrences before they become sufficiently powerful to damage us again.

'If you study the names and histories of the men the *Clarion* proposes for the new form of government, you will see that some have been Labour, some Liberal and some Conservative, but all have made a success of their chosen careers. All in fact know their jobs inside out and have an enormous talent for organisation. Some of them are indeed totally disinterested in party politics.

'It is my belief that the men we have named for your consideration are clean men, honest men, as their records show. Above all they are men who know that nothing is more important in Great Britain than our Queen and the Royal Family who are without any shadow of doubt our greatest asset and who must at all times be given our unquestioning loyalty and support.'

The *Clarion* published this letter, leading off with their own words. 'We proudly present this remarkable man's record and his ideals for the restoration of greatness to our country. Remember what you are seeking: THE RIGHT MEN FOR THE RIGHT JOBS. Study their profiles once again. Add to your lists the name of David Kincale. You believe in him and equally HE BELIEVES IN YOU. So now MAKE YOUR OWN FREE CHOICE.'

The turn-out was astounding. Huge queues were still standing patiently outside the polling booths for hours after the scheduled closing times. Of course none were turned away.

After the people of Britain had made their choice, the counting began. Richard Llewellyn, moving among them, saw to his astonishment innumerable Union officials counting and stacking as steadfastly as all the others. He telephoned his reports as he moved from one polling station to another.

When at last the tallies were complete and the names

and numbers received at the *Clarion* offices, Lord Beardmore picked up the telephone in his inner office and put a call through to Buckingham Palace. He spoke to an official. Thirty minutes later this man, bowler-hatted and wearing striped trousers with a black jacket and carrying a rolled umbrella, came out of the Palace and set off for Westminster in a small chauffeur-driven car. The driver inched his way through increasing masses of people who overflowed into the road which led to Smith Square and the house where David lived. The crowds streamed down the Mall, thronging into Horse Guards Parade and thence into Parliament Square where the car was reduced to a snail's pace. The Queen's representative abandoned it there and struggled through on foot the rest of the way.

Acting on instructions from Lord Beardmore, Richard headed in the same direction, catching up with the exhausted royal emissary as he reached his objective at the foot of the steps leading up to the door with its bright brass hand doorknocker. His way was barred by two burly policemen. He produced his identification, stood mopping himself while the fatter of the two conferred through an opened crack in the door. The two men were admitted just as David put down the telephone and came out into the hall to greet them.

Richard forced his way forward. 'David,' he shouted, 'you've won! They have voted for you to lead them. It has happened so now I can be the first to have the unofficial honour of telling you that you are now Lord President of the Council, nominated by the people, because they love and trust you.'

David retreated into the ground floor room where Mary was folding back the shutters. Before he could reply, the Palace emissary said, 'Mr Kincale, I am commanded to tell you that Her Majesty the Queen wishes to receive you.'

Mary touched David lightly on one shoulder as he stood in silence. 'David my love,' she said, 'your people are waiting for you too.'

David turned his head away so that only she could hear his reply. 'Forgive me, my darling, but that telephone call – it was from Paris . . . it seems the Duke passed away a few moments ago – peacefully and in his sleep – but Fluff had already told him we had won. The Duke said something strange, when he learned the news. "And so the circle is completed after all." I wonder what he meant by that?'

Mary's eyes were brimming as she urged him once again, saying, 'David, please acknowledge them . . .'

He nodded and turned towards the windows which Richard was even then opening for him. The stiff and exhausted messenger just caught his whispered words as he turned, 'And then, my dear Mary, we shall have to determine your rank and style after we are married.'

David moved to the opened windows alone. To the watchers in the room it seemed as if, quite suddenly, something akin to royal dignity transfigured him. A huge deafening roar rose from the massed men and women outside. He seemed also to lean against the deafening thunder for a moment.

Then he lifted one hand to quell them. 'I am proud to tell you,' he shouted into the sudden silence, 'that I have been summonsed to the Palace by Her Majesty the Queen. Before I go I must say to you all that with God's help I know we can do great things together for this country of ours. *This time I promise you something shall be done.*' He turned away little realising the significance of what he had just said.